THE STORY OF
JOHN DEEGAN
THE CHOSEN ONE

Louis Romano

ISBN: 978-1-944906-54-2

Publisher: Vecchia Publishing
Editing, cover design & formatting: F. Spaaij, Spaaij Design

*Human predators rent a
space in the mind of their prey*

-John Deegan-

LR

PRELUDE

My name is John Deegan, and I have a story to tell.

Monday, September 22, 1958

The weather was still warm. The remnant of a very hot summer. It was a day I will never forget.

I had just turned 8 years old in June and was now in the second grade. I couldn't have been more innocent as to the ways of the world, the desires or men.

I was called from my class to go to the rectory to help Father Edward O'Gorman. As a first grader, I had been in and out of the rectory and convent many times to help the nuns and priests with various tasks. I was the top student in the grade and the most compliant with anything that was asked of me.

This visit to the rectory had a profoundly transformative impact on my life.

Father let me in the front door of the rectory and walked me down a darkened hallway.

He wasted no time explaining that God's love came in many mysterious ways. Father O'Gorman sat on his musty-smelling bed. He had me stand between his open legs while he held my small hands in his large, soft fingers.

Moving me around, my face was pushed onto the rough coverlet on the bed. It smelled funny, like a sort of damp odor.

He pulled my blue uniform pants down to where they covered my polished black shoes. I tried to pull them back up, but the priest pushed my hand away.

The only time I had to lower my pants was to get an injection from the doctor or a thermometer, loaded with Vaseline, which my mother would put in my butt to check if I had a fever. I hated both.

The next thing I remember is the smell of the Vaseline and Father's large hand around my mouth. I was sucking air through my nose and was confused as to why the priest was doing this. After all, he is a priest, the messenger of God, so how could he want to do anything to hurt me?

Suddenly, there was something being shoved up my butt, something way larger than a thermometer. It hurt so bad I tried to yell out and twist myself away. The weight of the priest was too much for me to move even an inch. My scream was stifled. I felt snot running out of my nose and spittle pushing into the priest's hand.

The thing in my butt was going in and out. Every time it did, I felt a burning and exultating pain.

Father O'Gorman was making noises and breathing like a horse.

The next thing I knew, the priest moaned and almost crushed me under his weight. I felt like I was about to suffocate.

When he got off me, I quickly reached to pull up my pants. I passed a lot of gas and felt liquid going down my leg. I looked to see what it was, but the room was too dark. My butt began to throb.

Father took me into his arms and told me we had just done God's love, and it was our secret. If I told anyone, God would be angry with me, and my mother would become ill and die.

I was dazed and went back to school. The nun looked at me, my white shirt was crumpled, and my snap-on tie was askew. She came to me, straightened my tie, and tucked in my shirt.

I saw tears in the sister's eyes. She knew.

This is where it all began, the memory that shaped me and influenced many.

John Deegan

This book is not intended to offend any religion;
it's a work of fiction.
Religion is beautiful, and the fact that we have
freedom in it is a blessing.

CHAPTER 1

How do I get here?

I ask myself that question several times a day of late, now that I'm an old man with not a lot of Saturday nights left.

It's not that I'm asking myself how I got to live in this magnificent villa in Lugano, Switzerland, overlooking the Bay of Lugano. I'm questioning how I became an old man so fast, and, on the way, I somehow became known as a wanted international criminal with the moniker of serial killer attached to my name.

The last time I checked, my wanted photograph had dropped to seventh on the FBI Most Wanted list, after holding first place for nearly six years. The age of the photo and the way I look now, more than a bit stooped over, receding white hair, lots of craggily wrinkles, and limping like a Neapolitan beggar, I'm positive if I walked into FBI Headquarters in Washington, D.C., even the facial recognition computers wouldn't figure me out.

I'm still number three on Interpol's most wanted, but those clowns could be hanging out in the town square of Lugano for the past ten years and wouldn't be able to collar me while I'm having an espresso at the table next to theirs.

So, tonight I'm sitting on the veranda as the sun is setting over the bay with the deep blue and turquoise waters playing tricks on my eyes, glistening beautifully off the glacial lake. I bought my villa on the Swiss side many years ago because I have less of a chance of being extradited than on the other side, where the Italians would arrest and convict their own mothers.

I dislike referring to my house as a villa, so I'll revert to the former. Two-bedroom houses in Tuscany are typically referred to as villas. Such a played-out concept to get tourists to be able to say they rented a villa near Florence, Sienna, or San Gimignano.

We, my wife Gjuliana and I, have way too much space for just the two of us. Eight bedrooms, ten bathrooms, two live-in servants and a driver, plus gardeners who come virtually every day to see the place is manicured and trimmed, and, God forbid, a weed raises its ugly head. They also tend to our beloved Honeysuckle bushes.

I always had this thing for the Honeysuckle fragrance ever since I visited my friend's aunt's house at Long Beach, Long Island, in the mid-1950's. There were only two bushes in the tiny back yard of their bungalow right off Reynolds Channel, which is connected to the Atlantic Ocean. These shrubberies gave off an incredibly strong, sweet, and citrusy floral scent. Sometimes it smells lemony, and other times it gives off notes of jasmine or vanilla. From those two six-foot bushes, I took away a lifetime of aromatic pleasure. Whenever I get a whiff of those incredible bushes, I sigh about the time before I was molested. We have approximately forty Honeysuckle bushes on our seven-acre property in Lugano. The aroma is heavenly.

I'm blessed with a photographic memory. Not only with what I read but also with what I hear. I recall, like it was yesterday, living in the smallish Bronx tenement apartment with my parents and four siblings.

I was the chosen one, being the second born and the first boy. A born showman, I would mimic the movie and television stars to a T. I would dance and act like Jimmy Cagney in Yankee Doodle Dandy or Spencer Tracy in Old Man and the Sea or Boys Town, to the delight of my entire family and friends in the five-story walk-up building. I did voice imitations of Ricky Ricardo, Jackie Gleason, Art Carney, and Andy Devine in his Saturday morning show, Andy's Gang. I even imitated Froggy, his reptilian sidekick puppet. You name the TV show from the 50s, and I would do a thirty-minute standup, contorting my face to look like Ed Sullivan, and several of his guest stars like Signor Wences and the great musical icons Elvis Presley, Johnny Mathis, and even Connie Francis. I would comb my hair and dress up like the performers entering our 12X12 feet living room to raucous applause.

I honed my craft watching the dark brown 12-inch black and white Andrea television, which was so fuzzy at times I had to take the rabbit ear antenna from the top of the TV and walk it over to the nearest window. There were only 7 stations, but we never watched Channel 13, the educational channel. There was no one for me to imitate there.

I was the chosen one, in more ways than just entertainment. My alcoholic father could care less, but my mother was bound and determined for me to be a Catholic priest. In those days, every first- and second-generation Irish family had to have a priest or nun to brag about. Mom would drag me every Sunday to church with her and my father, and even though we were always late for Mass because dad was hungover from a Saturday night binge, she would make sure we would somehow cram ourselves into the first row. We had to be seen, not so much by the congregation, but by the priests who would mill around after Mass on the two steps in front of St. Martin of Tours Church.

The priests were always amazed at my saying the Latin liturgy that altar boys had to memorize to serve Mass. I was four or five years old and recited the Confiteor, the longest of prayers during the Mass, word for word in perfect Latin.

"He's our little priest," Mom would say any chance she had with a knowing nod to anyone within earshot. I knew the correct way to put my hands in prayer, both palms pressed against each other, pointing toward heaven, and the proper way to bless myself and to bow my head each time the name of Jesus was recited. I even knew the proper way to genuflect at the sight of the holy altar. The nuns were astonished at my perfection.

Today, I'm convinced that at least one of the priests and all the nuns were licking their chops at the thought of me starting first grade when I was six in September of 1956. The Dominican nuns, most if not all being of Irish descent, could barely wait to have this blond-haired, blue-eyed Irish boy, who was seemingly as smart as a whip, to mold into someone who would go on to take religious vows. I wasn't much smarter than many of the other kids, but I was obedient and, most of all, I was compliant.

Some of the priests thought the same, to bring me into the vocations and wanting to encourage and bring along another servant of Christ, while others had more nefarious motives.

Mom had me moving from priest to monsignor to bishop to cardinal before she closed her eyes and went to Jesus. Should one of my two sisters have entered the convent, she would have been ecstatic. Her job as an Irish Catholic mother would be totally fulfilled and surely guarantee her a place in heaven.

I was compliant with all her demands, including praying several times a day, reciting countless rosaries with her, and attending Mass at least three times a week.

My dad had poker cards and chips for when his drunken beer-guzzling cronies would come to play cards. During the day, when he was at work, I would line up the blue Tally Ho playing cards on every flat surface in the apartment and pretend they were parishioners while I gave them the poker chips as pretend communion wafers. I wore one of Mom's colorful blouses as a Chasuble and one of her old lace slips as a makeshift priest's Alb, and my grandmother's yellow and black cur chef, which hung around my neck as the celebrant's Stole. I felt like a holy priest doing the Lord's work. To me, the priests were Godlike.

Mimicking what I saw at the altar during Mass, my hapless Italian friend from the second floor would hold a small tea saucer under the poker chips like an altar boy did at Mass as I placed the faux wafer on the playing cards. I recited at each "communicant" in Latin, "*Corpus Domini nostril Jesu Chrisi custodiat animan tuam in vitam aeternam. Amen.*" May the body of our Lord Jesus Christ preserve thy soul to life everlasting.

Looking at what I experienced as the chosen one, seventy years later, it was nothing less than brainwashing and child abuse.

CHAPTER 2

As the summer of 1956 began to turn into fall, I recall the feeling in my stomach, which my mom called "butterflies." The fluttery, tingly feeling would only last a few seconds and come and go as the word school or church or if I saw an ad for Robert Hall back to school clothes or any reference to school on the T.V. Now I know butterflies are a release of hormones like adrenalin and norepinephrine that are associated with anxiety but when I was 6, after being prepared from birth for a Catholic education the fluttery feeling began to come in silent waves the closer I got to the first day of school.

The Sunday before school began, we were in the first row for the twelve o'clock Mass, late as always, and I was absolutely sure Father Edward O'Gorman was looking directly at me from the pulpit. My mom was in all her glory when she chatted with Father after Mass. My dad stayed clear because he still reeked of booze and beer, his eyes red like the priests' vestments.

After Mass, later that afternoon, my mother made a pot roast and wide German noodles with margarine and brown gravy. We never had butter; that was for the lace-curtain Irish who could afford such a luxury. Dad slept most of the afternoon. I could barely eat with the anticipation of my first day at St. Martin of Tours.

Sleep was restless, and I can recall to this day what a horrible dream I had that night before my first day at school. I was running from a large serpent with dagger-like claws. I thought the snake was the devil who wanted to steal my soul and bring me to a fiery hell. I saw a small, dark cave and thought the snake was too big to enter, so I belly-crawled into it. I was wearing the school uniform: navy-blue pants, a lightly starched white cotton-rayon shirt, and a clip-on blue tie with "SMT" embroidered in the center. In the dream, I was upset that my uniform got dirty from crawling in the clay-colored dirt. The snake shrank in size and entered the cave, opening its mouth to reveal two enormous fangs. That's when I woke in a sweat, trembling, nearly in tears. I almost screamed out when I noticed the uniform and my black laced Buster Brown shoes resting neatly on the painted brown chest of drawers next to the statue of St. Michael the Archangel. It was only a dream, and I said a silent Hail Mary, looking up at the crucifix over my bed.

The five-block walk to school with mom holding my clammy hand was a combination of nonstop butterflies and trembling knees. I felt my mom tugging at me as I wanted to pull away from her and run back to the safety of the apartment. I hadn't gone to kindergarten, so this was truly my first day in any school.

We caught up with the other moms and kids on

the way to school; the kids looked like lambs being led to slaughter, and the moms had wet eyes and pursed, red-lipped lips. We all crossed the wide Crotona Avenue and then the smaller E. 182nd Street, arriving at the boys' entrance of the school. There was also a girls' entrance, but I was too focused on the word Boys to notice.

The mother superior awaited us, taking the kids gently from our mothers, lining us up in size order. Sister Elizabeth said, "Hello, John." I was the only kid she called by his first name. I almost genuflected.

The nun addressed the mothers. "That will be all, mothers. Please leave quickly. And one more thing, the Blessed Mother did not wear slacks, so please, when you come to school, the proper attire is skirts."

The look on my mom's face was incredulous, but she bowed her head in quiet obedience.

Now, right there on the street, attendance was taken, and we were put into three different groups. Each group was a classroom assignment. I was in room 101, headed by the kindly-looking Sister Jarlish. The girls were lined up next to the boys, and we were told to hold hands. One of the boys from my block didn't want to hold hands, so Sister Jarlish took his hand, firmly smacking it twice, and he quickly complied. Tears ran down his angelic face, but not a sound came out of him. My eyes were as large as my mom's teacup.

We were given seat assignments. Girls on one side of the room, boys on the other. I was placed in row 1, seat 1. Sister called me by name when she sat me there. She never said another name. I felt special. My mom always told me I was special, chosen by God to be His soldier.

＋

I don't remember what happened that morning. Maybe she started with religion or the alphabet, but we did say three Hail Mary's. Well, the nun and I said the prayer out loud while most of the other students mumbled. In a few days, they would all be saying the prayer from rote repetition.

After lunch, we all brought a brown bag because the cafeteria wasn't yet operating, we got a surprise visit from Father Edward O'Gorman.

The door to the classroom dramatically swung open, and in he walked, this large blond-headed man with a four-cornered black cap with a red bon-bon on top. He wore his priestly vestments to terrify the five- and six-year-old children.

Sister Jarlish was in her glory, looking at the priest with adoration. She told us all to stand and then to kneel. O'Gorman blessed us all in Latin, and we were returned to our seats. I wasn't at all afraid, as I was so familiar with the priests, but rather in awe of this towering representative of God Himself.

The priest slowly looked over the overcrowded class of about fifty students, paying special attention to the boys.

We were told that we, due to the grace of God, were in this school. Other children were not as fortunate and had to attend public schools. We owed it to our Lord Jesus Christ and His Blessed Virgin Mary, and to our families, to do our best within the walls of this school and in the community, making an example of the Holy Catholic Church.

Near the crucifix at the head of the class, over the alphabet, was a large, framed photograph of Pope Pius XII. He was the epitome of Godliness, his hands in prayer while he looked up to heaven.

O'Gorman was looking directly at me again as he had yesterday at Mass. He then looked at Sister Jarlith, and she commanded us to stand and kneel once again. Father blessed us again in a dramatic wide fluoresce of his large thick hand, letting the vestment fall naturally to his elbow. His left hand rested elegantly on the red sash around his ample waist.

We were again told to sit. The priest walked slowly toward the door, but before he left, he patted my left cheek and smiled at me. I was the only one. I was special, I was the chosen one.

CHAPTER 3

Admittedly, I have killed scores of human beings. A good amount in the service of my country and a bunch of men and a few women, for what I believe, until this very day, was a just cause. I will likely have a few more notches on my belt before I leave this life. To me, that is a certainty.

I wasn't born a killer. Certainly not a serial killer who enjoyed what I did. There was no one in my family, ever, who committed a misdemeanor, never mind a murder felony, or in my case, multiple killings. We were a peaceful family with a strong religious background, dating back to Ireland as far as anyone could remember.

Hardworking civil servants, such as police officers and firefighters, bus drivers, accountants, a few farmers who followed their cousins from the Old Sod, and a couple of heavy equipment construction workers who made a substantial amount of money. We were not vengeful nor warlike people like the Albanians or the Sicilians, who seemingly have fighting and killing in their DNA. The worst my entire family ever saw was a good old-fashioned bar fight with fists. The scuffles were soon forgotten after the rift and always ended with drinking and a song to celebrate a bloody lip, a broken nose, or a knot on the head, courtesy of the opponent.

It begs the question to why I, John Deegan, became a menace to society, still sought after on two continents, into my mid-seventies?

Allow me to continue my saga.

†

The first year at St. Martin of Tours was fabulously successful. I was at the top of my class in grades. Not only the best in class, but the best student in the entire first grade. I was second to none. I was in the choir and even had a solo at one of the children's 9 O'clock Masses. The annual school play featured me as a bunny rabbit — the only one with a few lines in the packed gymnasium, bowing to loud applause. I really loved the attention and the limelight.

Because of my grades and the adulation of the sisters, I was chosen to meet Francis Cardinal Spellman with a handful of other students throughout New York City at a Mass at St. Raymond's parish. I was the only first grader given that special honor. My mother called every relative and friend of the family who had a telephone. She was over the moon with pious delight.

Speaking of grades, I recall waiting for my father to get home from work so he could see my first report card. The front of the card listed all subjects, ranging from arithmetic and religion to English and penmanship. The flip side of the card listed things like Completes Tasks. Assigned to Works Well With Others, and similar attributes. I was so proud that there was not a blemish on the report. Straight A's all the way up and down the card. Mom was delirious with joy, kneeling to say an Our Father in her gravy-stained apron on the blue and beige linoleum kitchen floor. Dad walked in, his necktie down below the third button on his shirt, his dark blue suit jacket crumpled from the subway ride home. There was that ever-present odor of beer on him because he had a couple of long glasses of Rheingold at lunch and at least one pop and a shot of Irish whiskey at the Silver Slipper before he came home.

I ran to him at the apartment door and was beaming with accomplishment and pride in my work.

"Look, Dad, my first report card," I announced.

He took the card from my hand. Took his glasses from his jacket pocket and placed them on his nose. He looked at the front, taking his time to see all the grades. His face was serious, and his large brow was furrowed. He flipped the card over and scanned it quickly. He didn't smile.

"Well, Johnny Boy, all you can do now is go down," he mumbled as he flicked the report card back at me.

I was crushed. Maybe crestfallen is a better word. I expected him to lift me up into his arms, maybe hug me, and tell me how proud he was. Who would do that to a kid who did his best to show everyone how smart he was? Now, Jack Deegan was that kind of guy.

* † *

The rest of the year was more of the same. All A's and nothing less. The nuns gave me every chance to be the star pupil. After all, I was one of them. Irish, with perhaps a little German mixed in, and the most compliant student they had likely ever come across. I could see how they treated the Italian kids in the class. Unless their parents owned the pastry shop or the funeral home or the famous restaurant in the neighborhood and gave good donations instead of nickels and dimes in the weekly envelope, the good sisters didn't spare a pointer on the Italians. The sister would roll her eyes and look at me with that "what do you expect from a dago" attitude. One Puerto Rican kid in the class was tossed out for being a poor student and incorrigible. The boy spoke little English and received no help with it, yet he never once caused a problem in class. The nuns were never crazy about his mother, whose clothing was too revealing and too tight. Maybe that was it.

In the meantime, if there was any chore needed in the school, in the convent, or in the rectory during the day or right after school, I was summoned to help. Help to wash the blackboard and clap the erasers to get the chalk powder out, remove a mousetrap with the smashed occupant under the stove in the convent kitchen, or help Father

O'Gorman remove the weeds in the small vegetable garden he had behind the rectory. He would talk to me about my home life, and what I thought of the Yankees? (I didn't. I was just too young, but I knew Mickey Mantle and Yogi Berra were great.) Have I ever considered the priesthood? Mind you, I'm six years old. I wasn't thinking about very much at that point.

Occasionally, after we were finished working on something, Father would take my arm and hold it while he brushed dirt or dust off my back and legs.

There were times during the day I would be summoned by the Sister Superior to run to the rectory to help O'Gorman with this or that task and told to hurry back as soon as I was finished. I clearly remember the facial anxiety Sister Jarlith would express when I got one of those commands. I knew she would cover any topic I missed with me one-on-one so my grade wouldn't be affected, but her concern, in retrospect, had nothing to do with classwork. When I returned to class, often out of breath from running and sometimes sweating, that sweet Sister Jarlith would take me to her desk, take my face into her hands, and ask me if everything was okay. Everything was always great in my life, at least until my second year.

CHAPTER 4

The summer of 1957, between the first and second grade, zipped by in a flash.

I remember the Johnny Pumps (fire hydrants to those not from New York City) were always turned on, blasting cold, refreshing water on us during the dog days of summer. The asphalt in the streets gave off a momentary steam with the aroma of fuel. The police would come by and shut the water off because if there were a fire, there wouldn't be enough water pressure. As soon as the cops were gone, the old lady from the fifth floor would lower a bucket down, which had a wrench in it, and the older kids, or a dad, would turn the water back on again. It was a hysterical cat-and-mouse scenario.

I also remember Dion and the Belmont's who had not yet come to fame singing their songs on the corner of Clinton Avenue and East 180th Street. Belmont Avenue was the next street over.

Once in a while, one of the dads would bring a couple of watermelons at night, and everyone would get a slice. It was great fun and I felt like part of a much bigger family.

The highlight of the summer was when Father Edward O'Gorman came to bless our apartment and stay for supper. Dad made sure he had to work overtime on a project for the company president, but in fact was at the Silver Slipper, tying one on.

Mom spent two days and nights cleaning, vacuuming, scrubbing, and polishing everything in the apartment. The linoleum on the kitchen floor shone like marble in the Vatican.

She spent an entire day making her mother's recipe for Shepard's Pie with real ground lamb, fresh peas, and carrots. The mashed potatoes on top were creamy and without a single lump, all hand-whipped, unlike those made with today's blending machines.

Every wall in the apartment was covered with wooden crucifixes, and the statue of St. Michael the Archangel was brought out from my room and placed on the table. My siblings were sent to our Italian neighbors for fear they would say or do something to screw up the supper.

Father O'Gorman arrived with a ring at the doorbell. Mom had her hair all done up with a dollop of rouge and no lipstick. She borrowed a sincere, floral dress from her best friend, Millie, and paired it with low black kitten heels. Father blessed each room, spending extra time at my bedroom door.

Mom made sure I said grace and drilled me until I could say it backwards. *"Bless us, our Lord, and these thy gifts which we are about to receive from thy bounty, through Christ, our Lord. Amen."*

O'Gorman talked about Cardinal Spellman, Pope Pius XII, the need for young boys to take up the vocations, and how much every penny was needed by the church. I was to speak only if he asked me a question, which he didn't. Children should be seen and not heard was the command of the day.

I remember Father O'Gorman drinking two of my dad's cold Rheingold beers with the Shepherd's pie he said reminded him of his sainted mother, and a shot of Four Roses with coffee.

I felt the presence of God in our crappy Bronx apartment.

* † *

In the neighborhood, the extended family consisted of Irish, Italians, Germans, and Jews. They were mainly reformed Jews, but some were religious. A few of them had the numbers tattooed on their arms, and they had heavy accents. We were taught to be respectful to the Jews, but we were also told not to even look inside the Young Israel of Tremont Synagogue. The temple was directly across the street from our building. I have no idea what would have happened to us if we had looked inside the temple, but whatever it was, I wasn't going to look because it wouldn't have been good. That was all that we were told negatively about Jewish people. This stuff we were supposedly taught about the Jew's killing Jesus was just horseshit. The Jews we knew were decent people and just as poor as we were. But they were different in their beliefs.

I still got those butterflies as school approached in September, but not nearly as often or as intensely. I could hardly wait for school to begin. Mom and I still spent a lot of time at the church, attending Mass or just stopping by for a visit or to light candles for deceased relatives. Occasionally, we would see the nuns or the priests, especially O'Gorman, who always outstretched his arms for a big hug. I remember the same smell on him that my dad had. I think it was Four Roses whiskey and sometimes beer. The hugs were longer than I wanted, and I felt almost suffocated by the embrace. Mom would stand there beaming that the priest was so fond of me. Whenever she was around the priests or nuns, she had this look on her face that could only be described as saintly, her hands always locked in the prayer position. When I got a little older, I realized she was full of shit, going shot for shot with dad. I've never seen another woman with the capacity for booze and beer like Josie Deegan.

* † *

Back to school was not nearly as eventful as first grade had been. We had our cereal breakfast or maybe toast with some margarine, and off we went. The most significant change was that I now had drip-dry white Dacron shirts that mom would rinse out by hand for the next day.

The greeting my new teacher, Sister Margaret Mary, gave me was like Caesar coming back to Rome after a victorious war. The baton of John Deegan, future seminarian and priest, and who knows what after that, was passed onto her by Sister Jarlith and the rest of the Dominicans. Sister Margaret Mary was rue to screw up perfection. It was her job to guide me through the second grade and pass me on to the next good sister, ensuring my path to ordination was unobstructed.

Mom made sure I was always immaculately clean and scrubbed. My hair was perfect thanks to Vitalis hair cream, and my always-smiling face was sparkling, adding to my Irish wholesome look. My baby teeth were still as white as pearls, and my shoes were polished as black as Louis Armstrong's shiny face.

Father O'Gorman wasted no time. I was now 8 years old, and the expert grooming was complete.

After lunch, I was summoned to the rectory to help Father with packing some boxes with canned goods for the poor or some other needed labor.

I rang the doorbell of the rectory, and the door was instantly opened by O'Gorman. It's as if he were waiting by the door for my arrival.

I knew the inside of the rectory pretty good. The kitchen, the living room with the TV, the reading room, and the small bathroom. I never saw the bedrooms or the main bathroom and shower.

Instead of heading toward the kitchen, the priest, who was in mufti, not dressed in his priest habit or Roman collar, told me to follow him. The rectory was dark and a bit musty and much cooler than outside. I had never seen a priest in street clothes, so I was surprised by his attire.

He led me to his darkened room and shut the door behind us. I immediately got those stomach butterflies, but these were different. I had a moment where I wanted to open the door and flee, but why would I with this great priest in the room? After all, he is God's representative on earth.

I could smell the alcohol coming off him.

"Now, John, there is a certain love between men, men who represent our Lord, Jesus Christ, and men who will one day enter the priesthood, which I am certain you will."

The priest sat on his bed. It was a high single bed with the sheets and a rough brown blanket tucked in, like I saw in army movies. Above the bed was a large wooden crucifix. Across, on the opposing wall, was a photo of a smiling Francis Cardinal Spellman and a somber Pope Pius XII looking down on me. The shade on the window was pulled down and the curtain was closed so no outdoor light entered the room.

"Come closer, John, don't be afraid," O'Gorman muttered.

Dutifully, and always compliant, I stepped toward the seated priest. He took me by the shoulders and quickly spun me around, so I was sitting in his lap.

"Not many boys have the honor of being in the rectory, never mind being with a priest in his room in a solemn moment." O'Gorman declared.

"Now, John, I want you to just relax and say a prayer with me."

We recited a Hail Mary together. The pungent aroma of beer and whisky made me lower my head, trying to avoid it.

O'Gorman took my hand and put it on a lump down the leg of his pants. I had no idea what it was.

"Squeeze that, John. Squeeze it like the rubber duck you have in your tub at home."

I complied. He remembered seeing my bathtub duck. The priest's familiarity with my home seemed nice to me.

"Now, John, I'm going to lie you down on my bed and we will say another prayer," the priest said breathlessly.

The next thing I can remember is my face on the musty blanket and Father lowering my pants. I recall trying to lift them back up, but he forced them down to my ankles.

He started to say the Our Father, which I didn't join in on because I was pretty embarrassed. I remember the smell of Petroleum Jelly. The only time I smelled that stuff was when my mom took my temperature putting the slim thermometer in by butt. I hated it, and the smell lingered.

"Just relax, my boy, this is what God's love feels like," O'Gorman panted.

The next thing I remember was excruciating pain. I felt as if my insides were being ripped out. I tried to scream, but O'Gorman put his beefy hand over my mouth. I felt as if I was going to be suffocated with my mouth covered and his massive weight behind me. He suddenly made a groan and I felt something slip out of my butt. The pain was unbearable, and I felt a lot of moisture running out of my butt. I started to cry.

"There now, John Deegan, this is what love is amongst men. This comes from the Lord thy God, Jesus Christ, for only the chosen few. You will become used to it, believe me. But...you cannot tell anyone under the pain of a major sin. Only the two of us will ever know of this, or something evil will happen to your family. Probably first your mom and then your dad. Being an orphan is not a good thing. Just remember this is our Godly secret, John."

CHAPTER 5

Instead of running back to the school as I always did, I walked back slowly. The pain in my butt had turned into a dull throbbing. I felt as if I had to poop but the rest of me was numb.

The door to my classroom was open. I stood in the door for a moment, feeling strange and a bit hesitant to continue that afternoon. The students were busy copying the homework assignments from the blackboard into their black and white composition notebooks. The parents had to sign the assignments and see that their kids did the work. Sister Margaret Mary didn't play any games. She was a real taskmaster.

The nun took one look at me and walked over to the door in a hurry. It's funny what you remember when your head is scrambled eggs. The large bead rosary beads she wore around her waist and the crucifix seemed to be flying behind her, almost in suspended animation.

"John? Are you alright?"

"Yes, sister," I croaked.

"John, you look pale, and your hair is a mess." Sister helped me to tuck the back of my shirt into my blue uniform pants.

Evidently, the Vitalis hair oil rubbed off on the degenerate priest's bed cover.

Right there and then, I should have told her what happened to me. I felt my bottom lip momentarily quiver, but I shook it off. I would have saved myself years of degradation, physical and emotional pain, and anguish. Instead, in fear of terrible things happening to my parents and me and my siblings becoming orphans like in the movie Boys Town, I told Sister Margaret Mary I stumbled running back to school. I was also not sure if this thing this priest said, the love of God wasn't true. I lied to a nun, which had to be some kind of sin, but I saved my family.

I was quiet when I got home and got right to my homework. Mom asked me if I had a good day, and I lied again.

I will spare you the horrible details of the continuation of Father O'Gorman's control of my body. A few weeks went by, and I was called to help out at the rectory again. After that, it became a weekly thing. After a while, I would follow the priest into his room, and I was conditioned to drop my pants and put my face onto the bed. I felt nothing after a while. I would pretend I was in a movie with my favorite stars or TV shows. Cary Grant, Jimmy Stewart, The Dead-End Kids, Ed Sullivan, Leave it to Beaver.

I think Sister Margaret Mary knew what was going on. I could tell by the way she looked at me when I got back to class after being summoned to Father O'Gorman. Well, she may not have known for certain, but I'm convinced today that her suspicions were accurate. I guess you're thinking why she didn't report it. Well, I know she did. She went to her boss for sure. After a while, the Sister Superior would see me in the hallway and give me a knowing, sympathetic look, sometimes taking my face in her hand with watery eyes and a squeeze of my cheeks.

The priest was a protected species. If the nuns were to report him, their days as teachers would be over. They would be sent from the school to a convent somewhere because the bishop would shield the priest. This was the late 1950's and things like this weren't supposed to happen in the church and they circled the wagons to protect clergy.

O'Gorman kept me his sex slave throughout my time at St. Martin of Tours. At the end of my fourth year, I have a vague memory of being in O'Gorman's room, and while he did his thing, another priest was sitting in a chair just watching. I can't recall ever seeing that priest before or since that day.

After three Puerto Rican kids jumped me in front of our building and they robbed me of the 45 cents I got from returning soda and beer bottles to the grocery store (we never had Puerto Ricans in the neighborhood until 1959), we abruptly moved to a nicer apartment near Fordham Road.

* † *

We were now members of St. Nicholas of Tolentine parish under the auspices of the Augustinian order. Of course, I continued at the Catholic school there.

I flourished academically. I was still the chosen one as my mom made sure to let everyone at Tolentine know I was headed to be a priest. That, my Irish Catholic face, and my straight A record put me in a position of clerical success.

No one bothered me at St. Nick's. O'Gorman would occasionally visit my mom and the family to see if there was an opening with me, but I made myself scarce when he was around. After a while, we never saw him again. He likely had another student who helped him at the rectory.

* † *

High school at St. Nicholas was nothing less than triumphant for me.

Mom was still at the school and church on a daily basis and dad found another local watering hole, I still had straight A's, the brothers and priests told my parents I was gifted, I played basketball, served as an altar boy, was in every club they had, I was still compliant with the nuns, priests and brothers, and I met Gjuliana a beautiful girl from an immigrant Albanian family.

Albanians were a rarity in the Bronx at that time, and she was beautiful. They were a mysterious bunch. The older woman wore a kerchief on their head and never made eye contact, and the men were all serious, furrow-browed, and never smiled. I could always tell an Albanian man because their head seemed a bit larger than most. They looked as if they would rip out your throat if you crossed them.

Gjuli could never have a Catholic boyfriend, much less a non-Albanian one, so everyone at school knew we were just friends. She wanted more. I just couldn't make a move to kiss her or anything else.

I was so confused about my life. By that time, I knew what O'Gorman had done to me. Was I a homo because of that? We never used the word gay back then. It was fag or homo and I wondered if I was one of them although I did like Gjuli in her tight shorts. Something was stirring within me, but I couldn't act on it. I did jerk off to the bra and panty models in my mom's Sears and Roebuck catalog, so I was probably not a fag.

Gjuli and I were constantly together, but there was always the fear that her father or one of her many surly cousins would see us together. They would have kicked my ass in, and Gjuli would have been at the very least grounded or sent back to Albania to her many aunts.

We never held hands as we walked in the neighborhood. Never even kissed. When I was playing handball or basketball during the summer months at the Aqueduct, our local park, she was always there watching, rooting for me, and giving me a furtive smile.

At the Tolentine dances, we would have a few dances together, and she always made a point to get very close and sometimes grind on me. She was ready. I was confused.

* † *

Disaster struck the Deegan family in my junior year at Tolentine. My dad, Jack Deegan, who provided for the family the best he could, dropped dead of a heart attack. His sedentary lifestyle and alcoholism killed him. He would go to work and drink. That was him.

The family was left with enough insurance to bury him and a few bucks left for about three months' rent. What do we do with all the catholic school tuition fees and a mom who never worked outside the house her entire life? All the questions that were going through my mind. Answers came from different corners.

* † *

It was Senior year at Tolentine, and it was clear that I would be valedictorian. Every year, I was approached by the monsignor about the vocations. Was I planning to attend the seminary? Did I feel the calling? Was I prepared to give my life to Jesus Christ and His church? The answer was yes to all.

It was a fait accompli that I would attend Villanova under the watchful eyes of the Augustinians, majoring in religious studies, and then proceed to the seminary there.

I can only remember applying to Villanova University and Fordham during my senior year. Fordham University was practically within walking distance from our apartment, and both schools offered me a full ride. No tuition. My family was broke, so that was the luck of the Irish. I knew the Augustinians pulled out all the stops for my entry into Villanova, and I owed them, plus I liked them better than I disliked the Jesuits.

I accepted Villanova's offer, and my mom was beside herself with religious glee.

I was anticipating taking the summer off, hanging out with Gjuli before the first of many farewells, and hopefully convincing her to find a nice Albanian guy. After all, it would be four years at Villanova, followed by a few years at the seminary, and then the vow of chastity, which, frankly, I was looking forward to.

I was summoned to the principal's office around ten o'clock on Friday morning. Commencement was a week away, and I had already memorized my speech.

I entered Father Brendan Ryan's office, and I almost swallowed my tongue. An immediate rush of intense stomach butterflies closed my throat.

Sitting there was Father Edward O'Gorman and another man who I recognized as Bishop Enzo Peroni. O'Gorman looked older, his face redder and he was bloated. I could barely look at him when he rose from the chair in front of Ryan's desk.

Bishop Peroni, who had said Mass at Tolentine Church, offered the ring on his right ring finger, and I dutifully kissed it.

"John, Bishop Peroni asked to see you. He and Father O'Gorman are old friends and went to seminary together at Dunwoody. I thought it appropriate to set the meeting here," Ryan offered.

"I'm delighted to meet you, John. I must tell you I've been hearing your name for years. Edward here has told me what a brilliant student you were at St. Martin's, and Father Ryan confirms he has never had a more gifted student in his years of teaching," Bishop Peroni said.

I was able to croak out an almost whimpering, "Thank you, Your Excellency."

"I must say, the decision to remain under the umbrella of the Augustinians is a good choice," Peroni added.

I could feel O'Gorman's eyes looking me up and down.

Father Ryan had a blank look on his face which I could not read. I would have thought he would be beaming with pride that a Bishop asked to see the class valedictorian, a student he oversaw for four years.

"Anyway, John, I'm sure you are chomping at the bit to get to Villanova and begin your religious studies. I'd like to know more about you. Let's have lunch tomorrow at my residence," Peroni announced.

Instead of making an excuse that my grandmother had died today or that I had to work, the compliant John Deegan accepted the invitation.

CHAPTER 6

Father Ryan gave me the address of Bishop Peroni's residence. I could tell Ryan was giving it to me with a hint of hesitation. But he gave it to me anyway. I was soon to find out why one of my mentors at Tolentine went from friendly to reticent in the blink of an eye.

I walked to Jerome Avenue and took the train into the city. In those days, it was 15 cents in each direction, but to save money, I borrowed a transit pass from a classmate. We had no money to spare.

The bishop's residence was located in a prestigious neighborhood on the Upper East Side of Manhattan, in a mid-block brownstone flanked on either side by identical properties. I felt out of place and small.

I discovered much later that Peroni was from a wealthy Northern Italian family who subsidized his living quarters with the archdiocese. He was very young for a bishop. He was diminutive in stature and wore fancy Italian eyeglasses. I learned while I was in seminary that Peroni's family was among the top seven richest families in Italy. But I'm getting way ahead of myself.

A handsome male servant wearing a gray pinstriped double-breasted designer suit with a scarf around his neck, slicked-back hair, and very pointy brown shoes answered the door of the brownstone. He escorted me up a carved and curved mahogany staircase. He never said a word.

The home was lavish to say the least. Where the flooring wasn't green and white speckled terrazzo marble, there were colorful Persian rugs over long shiny cherry wood boards. Dotting the walls as they ascended the staircase and approached the bishop's personal rooms were oil paintings, each with a lone light shining on it from the ceiling. I was not, then, nor am I now, an art expert, but to me, they looked like original works by the masters. Some of them looked Italian, while others looked Dutch. They were all housed in ornate gold frames. The home was like a museum. That much I knew. There was an aroma of peppermint and incense throughout the house that was both calming and arousing at the same time. I also caught the scent of garlic and basil, as well as the clatter of pots and dishes, coming from what I imagined was the kitchen on the first floor. That was likely an Italian lunch. I was famished.

"John, so good to see you again," Peroni came out of his office to greet me in the darkened hallway. The servant seemed to vanish into the walls.

He offered his ring, but this time it was with an almost feminine flourish. The bishop wore a sweet-smelling cologne that was more like perfume.

He walked me into his study, where there was a bottle of expensive-looking Scotch on a silver tray. There again, I was out of my element. I knew of Four Roses whiskey and one of my uncles worked for Cutty Sark. That was the extent of my knowledge of spirits.

Even though I was underage, Peroni poured some of the Scotch into an ornately carved crystal glass for me. There was no ice, and he didn't offer any. It seemed very sophisticated to me.

We chatted about Tolentine at first, for a short time, and my nervousness seemed to dissipate. The bishop encouraged me to sip the drink slowly, and I followed his example.

"John, are you excited about the prospect of going to Villanova after your senior year?" he asked.

"Yes, Excellency. This is a wonderful opportunity for me. I'm grateful for your help in allowing me to complete my time at Tolentine without incurring tuition costs. And for my brothers and sisters as well," I replied. I almost started to cry thinking of my siblings and the generosity we were getting.

"Looking at your grades since elementary school, you earned it. I suppose you will miss your family when you enter college?"

"I'm sure I will."

Peroni took a long sip of the Scotch. I copied him again.

The bishop paused. "Are you leaving a girlfriend behind, John?"

"No bishop. That is not of interest to me," I pronounced. I thought of Gjuli.

"Good. The fewer the distractions at school, the better. Father O'Gorman has shared with me the special relationship you and he had."

Peroni was staring at my eyes, waiting for my reaction.

I nearly shit myself. Without a doubt, the leering bishop picked up on my adrenaline surge. Those dammed butterflies!

I tried to recover.

"I'm not sure it was a relationship. It was a long time ago," I said in a near whisper. My eyes were looking at the drink I held in my hands.

"John, you will see that in this life you are about to join, cooperation, or shall I say compliance, will help you rise quickly. The church is like any other organization or corporation. Only richer. It's being smart, of course, and that you clearly are, but it's also who you know and who you become close to. I am willing to show you the ways of the church from the Bronx to the Vatican," Peroni offered. He poured another Scotch for both of us. Not being accustomed to drinking anything but warm beer, leftover in Rheingold cans the morning after my father had a few too many, I was feeling the first one.

I didn't reply.

"John, I have helped several young men to move up the ladder from high school to schools like Villanova, Fordham, Georgetown, practically all the Catholic universities. I am very happy to say that I helped them when they started their undergraduate studies, and I am still guiding them in the priesthood. They have shown great gratitude for my consideration toward their careers. I have great relationships in many of the seminaries as well.

"For example. You can spend the summers in Rome at my family's home in Trastevere, very near the Vatican. By the way, have you been to Rome?"

"No, bishop, I've never been out of New York City," I replied feebly.

"You will love it, my dear friend. I think we can arrange a trip this summer, or at a time that suits you. Fully paid for, of course. My father will arrange for you to meet His Holiness. You will be in awe of what we can expose to you. For example, I can arrange for you to have your own room at Villanova. Privacy is a wonderful thing, especially when you need to study. And, I can come visit and stay with you," Peroni hinted.

"That's okay, excellency. I don't need any special handling," I blurted. The word handling came out wrong.

"Nonsense. You will have special benefits from today going forward. But John...we must consummate our relationship. Sort of what you and Father O'Gorman had once in a while, but much...much more."

For all I know, Peroni was the priest who watched...

CHAPTER 7

It was Senior year at Tolentine, and it was clear that I would be valedictorian. Gifted, brilliant, remarkable, smart as a whip, funny, handsome are the words I kept hearing all my life. Every year of high school, I was approached by the monsignor and my homeroom teacher about the vocations. Was I planning to go on to the seminary? Did I feel the calling? Was I prepared to give my life to Jesus Christ and His church? The answer was yes to all.

It was a fait accompli that I would be going to Villanova under the watchful eyes of the Augustinians, majoring in religious studies, and going on to the seminary there.

I can only remember applying to Villanova University and Fordham. Fordham University was my unnecessary backup school, which was practically within walking distance from our apartment. Both schools offered me a full ride. No tuition. My family was broke, so that was the luck of the Irish. Mom would call it the hand of God. I knew the Augustinians and Bishop Peroni pulled out all the stops for my early entry into Villanova, and I owed them, plus I liked them better than I disliked the Jesuits.

I accepted Villanova's offer, and my mom was beside herself with religious glee. Dad smiled down from heaven, with a boilermaker in his hands.

I was anticipating taking the summer off, hanging out with Gjuli before the first of many farewells, and hopefully convincing her to find a nice Albanian guy. After all, it would be four years at Villanova, followed by a few years at the seminary, and then the vow of chastity, which, frankly, I was looking forward to.

Instead of a relaxing summer, I was enrolled in summer classes at Villanova. Peroni had his hand in that and in getting me my own, large dorm room. I wanted to be at the Aqueduct shooting hoops and playing handball, but the bishop had other plans for me.

You would think that I would have rebelled against the church due to the abuse I encountered from Father O'Gorman and Bishop Peroni. Peroni visited me at Villanova on a regular basis. Instead, I delved deeper into my religion, and at the same time, found comedy was my best outlet to push the deviant sex I was having with Bishop Peroni out of my mind.

Instead, I created a mask for myself and developed various personalities to deal with my trauma. I knew what was happening to me was wrong. In my mind, how can a priest and a bishop be evil or do any harm? Outside of my studies, I fell into a world of make-believe. I mastered accents, mimicking movie stars and politicians, telling funny jokes and stories, and making various disguises to enhance the comedy. My quick wit, comic impressions, and voices put me further under the spotlight. Someone said I was the biggest thing at Villanova after the basketball team.

* † *

I was now in the seminary. I had taken my first vows. I had successfully repressed the years of buggery, oral sex, and fondling into a tiny compartment in my mind. I had to ward off a dozen fellow novitiates who wanted to have a "personal relationship" with me. I didn't think I was a homosexual. In fact, I would detach myself, physically and emotionally, from the sex acts. I had no enjoyment, no sexual release, and no attachment to Peroni at all. As a matter of fact, I would be looking at myself from above during the encounters, like when people say they have died and re-entered their bodies.

I had loved everything about being Catholic. I was looking forward to being ordained and sent to a parish to be the best priest I could, for the love of Jesus Christ, His Blessed Mother, and all the saints. Then, one night, something snapped inside me.

I was in the Bellesini Friary at Villanova. Another seminarian came to visit me in my room to study. He had more than studying on his mind. I noticed he had a bulge in his pants, and he was tugging on it. He asked me if he could suck my dick. Years of this deprivation surrounding a beautiful religion and soiling the name of Jesus Christ ran through me like a sword. Those recurring stomach butterflies returned, but this time with a vengeance. This time, they put an electric shock throughout my entire body. I felt as if I could kill this future priest. I felt as if I should kill him to make an example out of him. I was looking around the room for something to bash his skull. I saw myself choking the life out of this guy. Instead, I grabbed him by his shirt collar and threw him out of my room.

The next morning, I was on a bus back to the Port Authority Bus Terminal of 42nd Street in Manhattan.

CHAPTER 8

Mom was in a fit of depression. The Kleenex box was always next to her, and the waterworks never stopped. Her drab housecoat hung from her frail frame. She was drinking Rheingold beer with a rosary in her hand and kept asking the question, "Jesus, Mary, and Joseph, why John...why? You were so close." If it weren't so sad, it would have been hysterically funny.

My only answer that made sense to everyone was that I didn't think I had found my true calling. I could not reveal the debauchery I went through and the rampant gay activity in the seminary.

Mom called her closest friends and relatives with the unthinkable bad news and sobbed into the telephone. Like a wake in those days, this went on for three days. The only difference was that there was no body to bury.

I saw Gjuli two days into my mom's grief-stricken opera. Gjuli was trying to mask her joy at having me back in the Bronx. She had matured and looked more beautiful than ever. Her high cheekbones and cascading brown hair made her simply breathtaking. I knew with my next planned move, I was going to break hearts again. Mom and Gjuli's.

A day after spending time with Gjuli, I walked down Fordham Road to the Grand Concourse promptly at 8:00 A.M. and entered the United States Army recruiting station. In two weeks, I was sworn in and headed for basic training. Gjuli and my mother were in mourning.

I felt free for the first time in my life.

* † *

During and after basic training, I took a bevy of tests. When the test results came in, I was told by a lifer colonel that I had genius-level aptitude and was needed by my country. Once again, I was the chosen one. I was treated like royalty and immediately sent into officers' training. The Vietnam War was winding down, but there were plenty of places the United States government needed a genius.

More special combat and special operations training was thrown at me. Instead of sending me to the Pentagon for intelligence work, the army, in its infinite wisdom, taught me for months how to be a covert killer. After my extensive field training, I was able to kill someone with my bare hands or a teaspoon.

I found I enjoyed this more than I enjoyed being a devout Catholic. Seamlessly, I went from saying daily vespers to learning how to eviscerate a person or the technique of ripping out a man's larynx with a twist of my wrist.

My first assignment was at Fort Gulick in the Panama Canal Zone. I was immersed in the Spanish language as much of the action I eventually saw was in Nicaragua. I had a keen ear for Spanish and was able to speak in several dialects without an accent. I could mimic any dialect to perfection.

I was eventually transferred to the 3rd Battalion, 8th Special Forces Group, which primarily operated in Central and South America for covert military operations.

The CIA monitored me for 18 months. The operative at Fort Gulick introduced me to a lot of bad guys who worked for the CIA in the drug and corrupted region. One guy in particular was insanely brutal. Manuel Antonio Noriega Morena was my instructor who taught me the finer points of clandestine torture and murder. Snuffing out the lives of drug cartel members was easy and most times enjoyable.

I am convinced the sexual brutality I suffered at a very young age built up an anger in me that made killing someone routine. I had no remorse whatsoever. The rationalization that I was doing heinous torture for information and snuffing out a human being's life once I obtained what we needed, I did it for national security and the love of my country was total bullshit. I liked doing it.

Just like when O'Gorman and Peroni were doing their perverted thing, I detached myself mentally, and with deadly accuracy, I was able to infiltrate, disguise, interrogate, and eliminate my targets with aplomb.

I had a six-year commitment to the United States Army, and I thoroughly enjoyed my time there. Catholicism and the priesthood were not even in my memory. The harder the job, the more dangerous the assignment, the more I planned and prepared.

Close to the end of my time in special ops, my body count was in the hundreds. Maybe there was someone, some bean counter in Army Intelligence or at CIA headquarters in D.C., who kept better records of my kills than I did. I could care less.

Throughout the time I was doing whatever the brass and suits instructed me to do, letters from Gjuli were delivered to me monthly. The letters were funneled to me through a cryptic Washington, D.C., address. I sometimes replied, but only with vague answers to her undying commitment and love for me. Some of her letters were graphically sexual. I felt nothing.

None of the many victims of my work were murdered. They were eliminated for cause.

I committed only one murder while in Central America.

I was in Nicaragua, in a pretty posh hotel hand-picked by Noriega. I was thinking about what my next step in life would be.

I was being debriefed. That's a fancy term for the Army and CIA to determine if an expertly trained, almost mad-dog killer should be let back out into society. There were two ways out. One was that they forced me to stay where they could keep a close eye on me. The other was for them to kill me if it was determined I was too far gone mentally or emotionally.

At the risk of self-aggrandizement, this is where the word genius comes in. I was able to fake my way through the many psychological tests and interviews with the best and brightest doctors and agents the CIA and the army had. There was no way they could beat me in this game of chess.

I did my duty for my country, and that is where I compartmentalized it. I convinced everyone who was probing me that I was devoid of anger and never wanted to even kill a fly.

I planned to turn my energy into the world of finance because I was good with numbers, and I was excited by the next step in life. I convinced them that I wanted to return home, to my loving girlfriend (I knew they read her letters), get married, have three or four children, and a house in the suburbs, where I would run for town council and coach kids' sports.

They bought it.

And I had almost convinced myself this would be the life ahead of me.

In my mind, I was able to turn off the killing machine by force of will. Or so I thought.

There must be a sign on my back that reads hit me if you're gay or some other nonsense. I met this Catholic priest while I was staying at the hotel in Nicaragua. Seemed like a nice enough guy who was, like me, taking a break from the action. I was winding down the maiming and killing machine, and he was taking a time out from passing the word of Jesus to the outer jungle villages.

We had had a few drinks, he a bit more than a few, and had dinner together once or twice. I bullshitted him that I was with army intelligence, and I couldn't discuss what I was working on. He bullshitted me by never letting on he was gay.

After dinner and drinks, it was about three o'clock in the morning, the priest, I think he said he was a Marist, made his move on me. He plain out asked to have sex with me. The butterflies came in one huge wave, and along with them came a torrent of obscene memories from when I was in second grade, right through seminary.

The hotel staff had all retired for the night. A dense forest surrounded the property. Not a jungle, but thick trees and bushes, with a horse-bridle path that ran off a clay dirt road. I said something to the effect that it would be fun to do it in the jungle. My heart was beating so fast that I needed to control my respiration.

He followed me into the woods. I stopped walking about 100 yards from the dirt road. The moon had cast enough light to see more than just darkened shadows. I kept my back to him, which he took as a suggestion. He put his hands around my waist and nestled his head into my neck. Soft kisses on my shoulder and a grab of my butt were his idea of foreplay. The reach around would be next.

I looked to my left and saw a tall lemonwood tree.

The lower branches had their leaves nibbled off by the white tail deer, which are common in Nicaragua.

In one quick motion, I snapped off about 15 inches of the brushwood, turned, and jammed it under his chin through his mouth and into his brain. The poor bastard never knew what happened. His warm blood seeped down from my hands onto the forest floor. I could feel the last twitching of his nervous system and watched as his eyes rolled back into his head.

I made quick work of dragging the body into the thick underbrush. I smoothed over the bloody leaves and soil and left the wooden murder weapon where I put it.

The next day I rose at 10:00 A.M., had a fruit and coffee breakfast, and lounged around the pool reading a ten-day-old Wall Street Journal, shooing away chichas and their mothers. An American military man, alone in this hotel, was worth a month's salary in Nicaragua given the right talents.

I left the next morning to return to base and attend to my business before departing the army. It wasn't until the next day that the stench of the priest's decomposing body began to bring attention to his demise.

A few days after that, I was questioned about the murder by local and military investigators. All they could prove was my being at the hotel when the homicide occurred. I was free to go.

And go I did.

CHAPTER 9

There was no going back home to the Bronx for me. It was impossible on many levels.

Even after my six-year stint in the military, which none of my family had the slightest clue about, my mom was still forlorn and depressed about me leaving the seminary. You have no idea how many times she asked me if I was thinking about going back to the priesthood. I wanted to tell her many times that I would rather be dead than rejoin that life of depravity and impiety.

A few of my siblings were drinking heavily, following in my dad's footsteps. I adored all of them; however, I needed to maintain my distance to avoid slipping into the same alcoholic pit and to move forward into the next chapter of my life.

Gjuli was ready to move in with me. I wanted no part of that for several reasons, but on top of the list was the sexual part of a relationship. The abuse and licentiousness I experienced had me confused and afraid when it came to intimacy with any human being.

Gjuli earned her PhD in child psychology from Fordham University and held a prominent position at

Columbia Presbyterian Hospital in Manhattan. She was waiting for me and still lived at home with her stifling, old-country Albanian family.

I had saved some money from my time in the army, even though I sent funds to my mother every month. She never asked for anything, but I had a sense of obligation toward her. I rented a studio apartment in a walk-up on the West Side of Manhattan. With the guidance of some contacts from my time at Villanova as an undergraduate, I landed a decent position at one of the major Wall Street investment firms.

Eighty-hour work weeks for a solid two years was my training ground in the finance world. When I wasn't working at the office, I spent my time reading anything I could get my hands on about the financial world. I became immersed in that world. I was killing it. I never imagined I could earn as much as I did, rapidly advancing within the firm and building amazing connections.

The terms "genius" and "gifted" were frequently used to describe me within the company and the industry.

I had no social life and saved more money than my father ever made in his entire life. I would occasionally visit my family and made sure my mom was more comfortable financially. I would go out with Gjuli, but stopped doing that after a while because she was determined for us to have a relationship and move in together. She constantly professed her love for me, which chased me further and further away from her.

I will admit now that I always loved Gjuli. She was perfect for me. I was so damaged by what I went through in school all I wanted to do is work and make a shit load of money.

The financial world came easily to me. It was as if I were born for this world. Banking, stocks, bonds, risk management, insurance, trading, puts, calls, hedging, derivatives, arbitrage, leveraging, swaps, and other financial instruments fed my desire to be rich and powerful. And I was on my way.

An article in a major business magazine referred to me as John Deegan, the "boy genius," the "whiz kid," the "prodigy from the Bronx," and other accolades. It fed my ego. Once again, I kept thinking of the words, 'the chosen one.'

After that fateful article was circulated, I was offered a partnership in the firm I was with. Staggering sums of money were on the table. Practically every major Wall Street investment house threw signing bonuses and guaranteed income that were like telephone numbers at me. My phone never stopped ringing with opportunities for partnerships and appearances on television shows. I accepted none of them.

I thought to myself, if I'm as good as they say I am, I don't want to work for anyone but myself. I'll make myself rich and compete with all the big boys.

I started my own company, and over time, I attracted the best and the brightest people from my contact list. My firm grew exponentially.

Within ten years, millions quickly became billions. Within twenty years, billions became tens of billions. I had hundreds of people relying on my methods to make their living and their fortunes.

Money became my god. It was the end-all and be-all of my existence.

* † *

Gjuli kept in touch, usually at Christmas time, with a religious card, simply signed "LOVE Gjuli," with a broken heart she had drawn. She seemed to have given up on us ever being together, and that was fine by me. I still loved her, but I was in a dark place when it came to intimacy. Love and affection were something I could not buy. I became asexual.

I was actually in that place when I joined the army.

I was generous with my siblings and their children, wanting them to forge their own paths in life. I made it a point not to allow any relatives to work at the firm. I established the Deegan Family Trust, which provided full college tuition or funds for a business upon turning twenty-five.

I covered the costs of alcohol rehabilitation for two of my brothers and one sister, as they were struggling with the same curse that plagued our father. It was heartbreaking to see them battle their demons, and I felt a deep sense of responsibility to help them break free from the cycle of addiction that had affected our family for so long. I hoped that by supporting their recovery, they could find a healthier path and reclaim their lives.

Even when I was rising with my firm, and I visited my mother in the Bronx, I could still see the disappointment on her face that I was not a priest or bishop, or God knows what else within the Roman Catholic Church. I ruined her dream of having a priest in the family, and my sisters were never going to wear a religious habit. Mom never had to want for money, although she still insisted on living in her apartment to be near the few family members and friends she had left. A big house up in Westchester County wasn't for her. She still walked to St. Nicholas of Tolentine Church every day for Mass and to receive Holy Communion.

✝

Mom passed in a nursing home with her rosary beads in her hands, her room surrounded by the crucifix that hung over her bed in her Bronx apartment, and the St. Michael the Archangel statue from my bedroom on her nightstand. My father's funeral card from Walter B. Cooke funeral home on Jerome Avenue was pinned to her pillow. She went to heaven, never knowing of the abuse her son had suffered at the hands of her beloved clergy.

CHAPTER 10

Nothing in my life had prepared me for the world of finance. I had no idea this life existed.

Not my education, which I must admit was excellent, but rather my experiences prepared me. Aside from all he negatives attached to the church, the education is superlative. The military didn't teach me anything about the business world. They taught me how to kill human beings with precision and devoid of emotion.

I can't even tell you why I selected the financial markets as my career. There were numerous job opportunities selling life insurance for Prudential and Wausau. I didn't see myself in sales of anything.

I devoured the New York Times because they had a better jobs section that the rag New York Daily News and the crappy New York Post. I had no idea what I wanted to do, nor where I wanted to work. I soon became fascinated by the financial section, with all the stock market prices, options, and the numerous indices reported daily. I seemed to be comfortable with numbers and would remember the prices of stocks for many companies.

I started tracking some stocks, not on a computer, but on a yellow legal pad with a #2 pencil. I had reams of those pads.

The Wall Street Journal was another newspaper I studied almost from the front to the last page. I followed many companies' news and trends, looking for opportunities to make a buck.

I applied for a junior analyst position at a major investment banking firm. My veteran status, perfect grades, and a high score on an aptitude test they administered got me in the door. The Personnel Director was also a Villanova alum, so that helped.

Following the rules and protocols of the company was not my strong suit. I did enough of that with being compliant at school and in Special Ops in the United States Army.

I had an uncanny ability, through my analysis of traded companies, to make money. I avoided those that were overvalued, high-risk, poorly managed, and in many cases had bloated and misleading financial statements. I taught myself how to dissect a financial statement and could smell the fake ones.

Focusing on firms that I believed were undervalued and under the radar of the pundits and the media big mouths, I made some moves that came to the attention of the middle managers of the firm. As time went on, I made some bigger and bolder plays using options and futures to play both sides of various markets.

I pissed some people off at the company when I started to short individual stock which is selling stocks that we didn't own. I would then buy them back later at a lower price, pocketing the profits. What upset many of my superiors was that I wanted to short stocks that my own investment bank was promoting as winners to our clients. That's a no-no, and I heard about it.

I was targeted as a cowboy and ostracized by many of the firm's partners.

So, here I was, John Deegan, a nobody wet behind the ears and not part of the good ole boys drinking club. Although they knew I was smart, I was not being compliant.

I was lined up to be summarily canned, except I had developed a rabbi. Stuart Goldberg was the senior partner of the company and for whatever reason, believed in me. That pissed off a lot more high-level people, but I was shielded by the old man. I was living in a snake pit, and I was never frightened. I didn't have one sleepless night about what was going on at the company. My past had continued to give me more sleepless nights that you can ever imagine. This was child's play in comparison.

Goldberg and I had a special relationship that saved my ass on many occasions. The old man and I would spend hours and hours analyzing and debating on which stocks to buy and which to sell. It was challenging and fun.

Stuart was brilliant and his experience taught me how to navigate the markets and keep risk to a minimum.

Goldberg, while I didn't want to consider him a

father figure, was the closest thing to a best friend that I had since I was seven years old on Clinton Avenue in the Bronx.

Because of Stuart Goldberg and my ability to be on the right side of the trades I was making a ton of money for the firm and for myself. I had little use for the money with my hermit-like lifestyle and saved an incredible percentage of my income. I kept my head down and worked my ass off not paying much attention to my personal worth.

Stuie, as he wanted me to call him in private decided at 86 years old to call it a day and retire. He was a multi-millionaire and deserved every penny. My mentor, my rabbi was suddenly gone leaving me exposed to the jealous wolves in the pack. I saw the handwriting on the wall and kept doing my thing, assessing risk and getting the rewards.

Without Goldberg around me daily, I began to lose interest as the fun and the challenge was waning. It was like I had lost my best friend.

Then one day, when I was feeling empty and about to throw in the towel, Stuie called me to have lunch. For him, I broke my rule of not eating and just plowing through the workday.

I felt my heart race in Goldberg's presence. He still had an amazing brain. There was a magic in our relationship like no other in my life.

Over the hours long lunch we discussed the markets, the lack of deep value buys at that time, and the risks we both saw. One major play was a preposterous idea of portfolio insurance and how it was being pitched to the largest pension funds. We agreed, based on the fragile market at the time and the portfolio insurance concept that we should short the market.

We agreed that the best play in the business was to short the market and the perfect way to achieve our theory was to short the S&P 500. The big question we had to be concerned about was when. When should we pull the trigger?

The perfect moment for our strategy came the week before, black Monday, the crash of 1987. Weeks before that momentous day we couldn't find any stocks to buy. There was no inventory of undervalued stocks and we only saw speculative bubbles in our research.

I could now only continue to raise cash. Shorting the stock indices was a gamble and I added to it by using margin. Buying big money on credit. My neck and my balls were on the line, but I was convinced beyond any doubt our theory was correct.

I was betting against the entire financial system. I had to put up cash to use the leverage. I knew the margin interest alone could bankrupt me.

What I figured in my mind was 'no guts no glory.' I came from nothing and if we were wrong in our assessment of the market, I would be dead broke and drummed out of the industry for good. I'd be back to looking in the papers for another opportunity.

The Friday before black Monday, I went all in on

the theory of shorting the S&P 500 index. I also targeted those companies that were the most fragile, poorly managed, and the most susceptible.

The result was an epic move. Our theory made over 28% in one trading session. All in all, we made a 50% return on the money in just 8 hours by covering and closing on our short position. Our bottom line realized a massive 56% gain.

* † *

Soon after, with all of Wall Street acknowledging I was the young genius of the business, I went on my own. I was no longer in the back-biting environment of the partners who wanted to cut my balls off when Goldberg was no longer there to protect me.

They, among many others, had made me all kind of promises and rewards to stay. I wasn't smug, I didn't say go fuck yourselves as I really wanted to. I moved on to make myself a wealthy man.

Was it luck? Was it true genius? Was it balls as big as cantaloupes? When I look back on that fateful day, I am convinced it was all of that plus maybe my success was pre-ordained.

My mother always said I was special. The chosen one. To this day I don't think that highly of myself.

CHAPTER 11

I had already made my first billion. The company was flourishing beyond my wildest dreams, and there was no end in sight.

It was midday, I was in my office in Manhattan scanning the majesty of Central Park from the forty-fourth floor. It was fall, and the trees were starting to turn colors. Light and dark green, yellow, orange, and red, in a fabulous palette of splendor. The large gray, red, and brown towering apartment buildings surrounding the park were glistening in the sunlight.

I impulsively decided to leave the office to take a walk in the iconic park and be part of the scenery. Maybe I would even get one of those dirty-water hot dogs from a street vendor for lunch. I never took lunch; I thought of it as an interruption of my valuable time. Time I could use to build my fortune. If I got hungry, I'd grab a handful of almonds or a Snickers bar. I drank gallons of coffee.

There were throngs of people on the streets this crisp sunny day. I crossed Fifth Avenue and headed to the park entrance. The first vendor I saw had a large red umbrella over the stand. The aroma of the food made my stomach growl. I stepped up and ordered one dog with mustard and sauerkraut. I dropped a ten-dollar bill on the aluminum counter and walked away. The vendor didn't offer me the $8.50 change, and I didn't ask for it.

I walked a bit into the park and opened the napkin. I took a bite of the frankfurter. It snapped in my mouth in an explosion of garlic, a dash of salt, and a bit of vinegar from the sauerkraut. It was awesome. I had forgotten how great the taste was.

Just then, I spotted a young boy and his father walking toward me. The boy was holding his dad's hand, looking up at him with a cute smile. The child was young. Maybe four or five years old.

Suddenly, I was overcome with panic. Was the man really the kid's father? Was the man a pedophile who just snapped the boy up in the park? Would the man do what O'Gorman did to me? Did my father ever hold my hand in a park? The panic turned into grief and into a full-blown flashback.

I dropped the rest of the hot dog onto my shoes and stood there paralyzed. I had no idea how long I had stood there. When I snapped out of the trance, the boy and his dad were gone. A fitly homeless guy with a shopping carriage full of clothes, cans, and bottles was about ten yards to my right. He stood there staring at me. I took two twenties from my pants pocket and handed the cash to the poor thing. He just kept staring at me. He reminded me of one of my disguises. I suppressed another flashback.

I felt a trickle of perspiration running down my back under my suit jacket. It took me a few seconds to get my bearings. The sound of the buses going by, the honking of car horns, and a police siren a few blocks away started yet another panic attack. I took a few deep breaths and cleared my mind, fighting off the attack.

I got back to my office, closed my door, and sat on a divan. I was completely spent. I breathed in deeply and let the air escape slowly from my nostrils.

When I felt relieved and safe again, I realized how truly damaged I am. I couldn't even enjoy a beautiful day outside of my office and have a damn hot dog. The slightest thing could trigger me. A little boy and his dad holding hands, walking together in a park, turned into something nefarious. Something evil.

My mind and my soul were taken from me by two men who had represented God.

The Central Park incident was not an isolated incident. Whenever I wasn't immersed in my business, I felt like a hamster on a running wheel. It was as if my past was chasing me, and I could never get away from my memories. The faster and longer I ran, the memories were right on my heels, waiting to overtake me.

The recurring recalls of being sodomized became almost as terrifying as the act itself. The pain, the embarrassment, the questioning of my sexuality, the numbness, and the lack of feelings toward people were getting worse as time went on.

It had gotten to the point where nothing was holding my attention.

I had all the money I needed to have anything any normal person wanted and then some. All I wanted was peace of mind, and I came to realize that was too elusive for me. I needed to do something to eliminate or at least reduce the haunting recalls.

Why didn't I enjoy watching sports, racing cars, shooting guns, flying planes, hanging at the bar drinking or having cigars and talking, chasing women? There was a simple answer. Virtually everything involved interacting on a personal level with people. Weather it was men or women I could not bring myself to trust anyone.

* † *

I had been led to believe for as long as I can remember that the church was my only means to a fulfilling life and eternal reward. My mother wanted me to be a priest so badly; there was only one thing I had to do, and that was to fulfill her dreams. Margaret Deegan bet her son's life on a dream and lost.

My life no longer had meaning; nothing to strive for. I realized my piles of money were meaningless. What was I to do as an old man? No family, I abandoned them, except for giving them money. No wife, no friends, no hobbies, and certainly no faith. I knew I needed closure on what was done to destroy my life. It wasn't going to go for mental treatment or prescription drugs. How could I trust doctors if I couldn't trust a priest?

I had one thing left to do with whatever time I had left. No one, five generations from now, was going to give a rat's ass how many deals I had made, how many times I was on the right side of the markets, or how much money I made.

I knew there would be one way for me to become immortal.

I reverted to my backup behavior. The skills I had learned in the military would help me rise above the muck of guilt and shame. I would get off my spinning hamster wheel, let my demons catch up to me, square off, and eliminate them.

I had to go back and settle the score, not just for me, but for any child who was violated.

I would soon join a long list of immortals.

CHAPTER 12

I was worth billions of dollars and had moved to various apartments several times along the way. I was never big on cars, boats, vacations, or dining at fancy restaurants around the world.

I bought a fabulous apartment in the newly gentrified DUMBO neighborhood in Brooklyn, offering the most amazing view of the Brooklyn and Williamsburg bridges, as well as the lower Manhattan skyline. My plan was to make this my forever home. I spared no expense in making it the coolest and most comfortable place for me to rest my head and relax. No one, not even my family members, would ever be invited. I wanted to be a recluse. I had no need for companionship.

I would often cook for myself, making simple meals, and on occasion, I would make a Sunday sauce that my mother had learned from her Italian friend, whom I called Aunt Millie. Meatballs, hot and sweet Italian sausages, beef braciola, and a fat piece of pork made the canned tomatoes and tomato paste one of the best things I've ever eaten in my entire life. I remembered the recipe by heart as nothing was ever written down. I would freeze most of the sauce in small Tupperware containers and serve myself while looking over the fabulous view from my living room. I even remembered putting a dollop of fresh ricotta cheese on the macaroni and sauce that I learned as a child. I don't think any Irishman could duplicate Aunt Millie's sauce, but I did.

* † *

But there was a problem brewing inside me. After a while, I grew tired of the business and sold my company for more money than I had ever dreamed of. Suddenly, the work I emersed myself into no longer mattered. The nuns always said, "An idle mind is the devil's workshop." In my case, it was a truism. I had no challenge anymore. There was nothing I was interested in. I had no hobbies. Never played one hole of golf, had no interest in traveling the world, I didn't want to be around people, and I had no interest in buying a football, baseball, or basketball team like so many old rich guys did for ego, profit, or entertainment.

I had repressed the molestation I suffered as a child for all those many years. I took long walks around the neighborhood to keep trim, and my lunch was usually a slice of pizza or two, a few blocks away from my apartment at Grimaldi's. Even though I didn't have to wait on the hours-long lines, I did it to hear the conversations of the mostly young people. I would wear different disguises to overhear what was being said about me. That was fun, but it became unrewarding after a while.

I began having dreams that turned into nightmares that turned me into an incurable insomniac. I didn't want to sleep, fearing I would have these very realistic, detailed dreams. They usually began with me being summoned to Father O'Gorman, and what happened to me every time I got to the rectory. The memory of the pain returned as if I were there today. The nightmares included washing blood and semen off my underwear in the bathroom sink were disturbing to say the least. In the dream, I could never get the stains to wash out. Even if I tried to nap during the day, the repressed reality would come to me with a vengeance.

I was beside myself. My innocent 8-year-old self had come back to haunt me.

One morning, after being up all night and in a daze, I was reading the newspaper over coffee and came across the obituary of Bishop Enzo Peroni. There was his photograph of when he was young, staring right up at me with what I thought to be a smug grin. He succumbed at his residence in Manhattan after a long illness, the article stated. I knew in my heart the fucker had died of AIDS. I hoped he had suffered immensely.

The obituary went on to report that his funeral Mass was concelebrated by New York's Eminence Francis Cardinal Galvin, a lifelong friend, and Father Edward O'Gorman.

I read the obit about 5 times. Each time, I became more infuriated. O'Gorman was still alive! The bastard who stole my young soul lived to a ripe old age. That evil bastard was still breathing and likely was buggering some young kids.

I stared at the death notice for what felt like an eternity. The name Edward O'Gorman seemed to turn into capital letters and jump off the page.

The butterflies returned with a retribution that called for action. What was I to do? Let the pedophile live to keep doing his sinful acts, or take my revenge?

* † *

It wasn't hard to find out where Father O'Gorman was living. One call to 1011 First Avenue, the Archdiocese headquarters, answered my query. He was in residence at St. Martin of Tours Rectory in the Bronx. He was still there! God only knows how many children he molested. How many lives and families did he ruin? How many suicides followed his shamelessness?

Using the church as a shield and the name of Jesus Christ as his weapon, his self-indulgence had carried on for decades.

I knew at that moment, I was going to snuff out his useless life...

CHAPTER 13

I walked up and down 182nd Street and Crotona Avenue for nearly two weeks casing the church and the rectory of St. Martin of Tours. I never went without disguising myself in some fashion.

I had a few flashbacks. One recurrence was on the first day my mother walked me to school, and the nuns taking me inside for the first time. I remembered those first day butterflies and felt them again. Another recollection of walking back from the rectory to the school after Father O'Gorman had his way with me. I recalled the feeling of confusion and guilt. I knew something wasn't right with what he did to me. Still another memory of my family and me taking photos after my first Holy Communion in the grotto of Our Lady, located on the side of the church. I remember the cool water running down into the tiny stone basin and wanting to put my hand inside.

Every day during my surveillance, I would get to the parish grounds early, around dawn. There is something about the Bronx in the early morning that still gives me solace, even though the area is no longer safe. My neighborhood was great in the 1950s. I miss the extended families, the clean streets, the friendly storekeepers who didn't have to turn their shops into fortresses with steel pull-down grates. During my diligence in casing the area, I stayed late to see if and when Father O'Connor left the residence to walk around or go into the church. I wanted to know the foot traffic around the rectory and the church, especially late at night.

I alternated my disguises. I transformed myself into a very old Italian man (yes, there were still a few holdouts left who would never leave) with a crumpled suit and too-short tie, a cane, and a Di Nobili cigar hanging from my mouth. I became a Con Edison electric meter reader one day and a plumber carrying a tool bag the next.

Walking past the rectory on Degroat Street many times each day to see if the priest was out and about, I would sometimes stop at the blue, white, and gold statue of the Sacred Heart and feign a prayer to our Lord. All the while I was looking in the windows for any chance to spot my target. One day I saw O'Gorman, in mufti, sitting down for breakfast at 7 A.M. I had all to do to keep myself from breaking inside and garroting the evil bastard. The one thing I learned in covert operations was to be patient.

My time was coming...

CHAPTER 14

I knew when the nuns from Aquinas High School, across from the rectory, went to early morning Mass. I saw their bedroom windows that overlooked the rectory. This could be a problem if any of the sisters heard too much noise and peered out their windows.

I saw Father O'Gorman several times outside the rectory and followed him as he walked down the block to a local bodega to purchase a newspaper or whatever else he was there for. Each time I saw him, the memories launched in my mind like missiles. The sickening feeling in my stomach made me nearly puke each time I followed him.

Inside the church, one Saturday afternoon, I sat in a pew not far from the confessional with his name on it. O'Gorman was hearing confessions for about an hour, and I watched the parishioners, mostly older Spanish ladies, go in and out of the wooden confessional. I would get close enough to hear the murmuring of the parishioner and O'Gorman. The woman spoke Puerto Rican Spanish, and he responded with a poor imitation of the accent. My intense stare followed him after he was finished. He walked toward the altar, genuflected, and then disappeared through a door at the side of the altar. He moved slowly and was a bit stooped over due to his age. O'Gorman had a hard time standing after he knelt using a pew to rise and balance himself. He was no match for me.

At night, when I drove back to my apartment in Brooklyn, I made detailed notes of the church and drew a diagram of the entire interior and exterior, including the rectory and convent, studying it until I could close my eyes and visualize the surroundings.

I was making plans to get O'Gorman into the confessional box after hours, deciding which door to use to enter the church at night, and my escape route after I was finished with him. The planning was similar to what I would do in special operations in the army. Leave nothing to chance, be prepared for any eventuality, and have contingency plans as backup.

I was ready with my disguise and an outdated Fairlane Ford, which I had purchased for cash from a used car lot in Brooklyn. I wanted the vehicle not to stand out in the poor neighborhood. The car was perfect, and I parked it in the middle of the block, a few streets away from the rectory. The license plates were taken one late night off a random car in the lot where I had bought the Fairlane.

I disguised myself as a ragged old man with dirty clothing, scraggly beard, dirty hands, and matted hair as if I hadn't bathed in a while.

I knew the front doors of the church were locked after 3 p.m. This prevented anyone from entering the church to pray or light candles. I made my plan around getting Father O'Gorman to take me into the church to hear my emergency confession.

I rang the doorbell and lightly knocked on the door of the rectory, and as luck would have it, O'Gorman answered the door.

I begged him in the raspy, desperate voice of an old man to hear my confession, telling him I had to cleanse my soul of murders I had committed. I insisted on being heard in a proper confession. Reluctantly, O'Gorman agreed, taking pity on my fake sobbing.

I carved the bottom of a wooden crucifix I had purchased online and had sent to a fake post office box. The crucifix was shaved into a pointed tip. I also made a wood jam for the bottom of the confessional door to prevent the evil priest from escaping. I kept both the door jam and the crucifix in my greasy, dirty jacket pocket.

I verbally toyed with O'Gorman for a few minutes while he was trapped inside his confessional, telling him of the killings I had committed.

I changed my voice from that of an old man to an Irish lad and then to a young second-grader. I think I used a few other impersonations to strike more fear into the doomed priest.

When I reminded him what he had done to young John Deegan, many years ago, in my child's voice, and then let him know I was John Deegan. That's when he completely panicked. O'Gorman tried to leave the confessional to no avail. The door jam worked perfectly.

The ill-fated priest knew he was in a perilous situation. He screamed out for help, but there was no one around who could hear him. He begged and pleaded. I could smell his adrenaline and the foul gas that had exploded from his bowels. The foul smell of the alcohol and nicotine on his breath was a nasty combination.

I then encouraged him to pray. I was about to take out my revenge from many years ago. I clearly recalled the first and last time he had molested me.

The panicked look on his face when I removed the jam from the door was priceless. There was just enough light for me to see that his mouth was agape, and his eyes were widened to the size of small apples.

I moved with cat-like speed and dug the sharpened crucifix into his neck and twisted it several times, severing his carotid artery. Dark red, almost black blood was spraying everywhere. He kicked his legs and flailed his arms trying to breathe. With each movement, with each attempted breath, the blood spray from his neck shot higher.

I used his purple confessional stole and his cassock to cover his neck and keep the blood from squirting on me. O'Gorman was moaning. I heard his death rattle. I brought my face close to his so the last thing he would see in this life were my cold blue eyes and my wide smile.

When he slumped to his side with his head resting on the inside of the confessional wall, I waited until he bled out. I took a moment to enjoy the work I had just done. Looking at my rapist and tormentor in this state was justice served for Father O'Gorman's stealing my innocence and my young soul.

As a final insult for a message and my first clue to the police, I pulled down the priest's pants and desecrated his private parts. I shoved his shrived up wrinkled penis into his wide-open mouth.

I stood there for a minute or two looking over O'Gorman's corpse, enjoying my work. I felt great relief from the years of bottled-up hatred I had inside of me.

It was drizzling a bit when I left the side door of the church. As I strolled to the car, content with my covert operation, I almost started to whistle "Singin' in the Rain," clicking my heels like Gene Kelly did in the movie. I thought better of it so as not to bring any unwanted attention.

When I arrived back in my apartment, I looked at myself in the bathroom mirror. I was proud of myself for avenging the abuse I suffered under this miserable, hideous priest. I enjoyed killing him. I smiled at myself.

✝

The next day, I was using the remote control on my television like piano keys. I searched and searched until I found a report about a murder in a church in the Bronx. The news was sketchy, and the report had a video of the outside of St. Martin of

Tours church. I have never been more delighted about a news report in my life.

CHAPTER 15

The reports of the murder of a priest inside a Catholic church were all over the place. The entire city was shocked, unless you were one of the unlucky ones to have been sexually abused by a clergy member. Then you would have had your own personal parade.

I stayed in my apartment in Brooklyn for two days, watching the reports on a dozen media outlets, including the BBC and RAI Italia. The Daily News and the New York Post, piecing together information outside the crime scene, did a fairly good job. Their headlines were tabloid masterpieces. FIND THIS CREEP! The Post shouted. The Daily News plastered BELOVED PRIEST SLAUGHTERED IN CONFESSIONAL.

I wanted to go up to the Bronx to watch the police and media circus. We've all heard many times on television crime shows that the murderer always returns to the scene of the crime. Knowing that police would be watching the area for that reason, I decided to stay put and enjoy the show from the comfort of my apartment. I was elated just watching the parade of cops, clergy, politicians, and sobbing

Latinos being interviewed behind the yellow crime scene tape.

It was the first time I saw Vic Gonnella. A reporter from Channel 5 News interviewed him. Gonnella was the lead detective on the case, so I went online to get to know everything I could about him. He would lead the manhunt for the killer. That would be me. It would take weeks, if ever, for him and the rest of the police department to begin putting the pieces together. I had to assume they would eventually lead to my apartment at 1 Main Street in Brooklyn.

The New York City mayor, the cardinal, and the police commissioner conducted their dog-and-pony show interviews, with the cardinal calling for a time of peace and prayer. They all swore to bring the murderer to justice. That would be enough pressure to light a fire under Gonnella's ass.

The message of sexual mutilation on Father O'Gorman's corpse would send law enforcement delving into his carnal habits. If Gonnella and his platoon of detectives were any good, they would track down some of O'Gorman's victims. Hopefully, there were more recent objects of the priest's debauchery.

I knew I had to make solid contingency plans in the event that Gonnella et al found I was the killer. I took a private jet to Switzerland and purchased a property in Lugano to use as my safe haven. I returned to Brooklyn in three days as the owner of this lovely house overlooking the lake.

The reports were fewer and less intense when I

returned to New York, except for covering O'Gorman's funeral Mass at St. Patrick's Cathedral. Pomp and circumstance for a serial pedophile.

I had started my chess game with Vic Gonnella and the NYPD. What I had thought was justice, the world thought was a heinous act of a madman. So be it. They say the line between genius and insanity is the size of a hair.

✝

A much bigger problem was brewing.

As soon as I saw O'Gorman's dead body, after all the twitching and gasping, I had this feeling of enjoyment. I never had such a feeling like this before. I liked my job in the army. What I was doing in the service for my country, I thought, was for a noble cause, but I never enjoyed the killing. Killing were just the ends justifying the means. Anyway, that was business. Killing, or let's call it murdering Father Edward O'Gorman was necessary.

So many people in authority had abused children and vulnerable adults for so long that someone had to at least try to stem it. Draw attention to the horror and see if society at large even gave a shit. The Catholic church wasn't going to do it. Mostly, from all the reports I read and from what I knew on the inside of the church, these pedophiles were simply moved around to protect them, not the potential victims. Nothing was being done to protect little children and other weak individuals. The church would make a few payments to families, prolonging the process for as long as possible. The rapists were being sent into a different venue and being prayed for. The victims were left to fend for themselves, except for the church's most generous offer of some psychiatric counseling.

I could have been sent to the Freud Institute in Vienna, Austria for a decade and still would have been as fucked up as I am today.

After slaughtering O'Gorman like the pig he was, I decided to continue to seek out revenge for people who were harmed by degenerates, not only within the Catholic church, which is an easy mark because so many pedophiles flock there, but in all walks of life. I would turn my so-called genius into a crusade. I have the money, I have the time, I have the skills, and most of all, the chase will be fun.

I decided to pick and choose my victims and make it a global search for these degenerates.

I ordered eleven more wooden crucifixes, which I would carve down to a pointy weapon, from a company I knew could be tracked. After all, I had to give the cops some sort of chance to catch me, or there would be no fun in the chase. I needed the pressure of being caught to stay sharp and one or two steps ahead of the law. They were playing checkers, and I was playing chess.

Why 11 more crucifixes, you might ask? I had already used one. I left it sticking out of O'Gorman's fat neck. That would be my calling card. Twelve is an important number, and I thought it would take me

some time to do my research, planning, and killing.
There were twelve apostles, twelve tribes of Israel,
the Chinese calendar has twelve terrestrial branches,
twelve apostles of Christ, the Mayan calendar ended
in 2012, and there were twelve Knights of the Round
Table. Oh, and there are the twelve days of
Christmas.

So why not twelve in my crusade?

CHAPTER 16

Grinding. That's exactly what Vic Gonnella and his army of detectives were doing.

Chasing down every lead, every possible crumb of information on Father O'Gorman and any forensic information they could find. I left them nothing except the wooden crucifix I carved into a deadly weapon. Not a fingerprint, I used gloves, not a bit of hair, I wore a tight cap, and I certainly didn't leave a footprint in the pool of blood which leaked out of the confessional.

There were no eyewitnesses. There was no video camera evidence, nor was there any license plate recognition, as is the case today. They would eventually get some leads on O'Gorman's pedophilia, and that could possibly lead to me if they went back to the student records from 1956-1960. If they were that good, which I doubted, the odds of them capturing me were minuscule.

I have a master of the universe computer information at my disposal, and I'm very good at it to my advantage. I learned a lot from the CIA operatives and army intelligence personnel I worked with, and was able to hack into almost any mainframe I needed.

In a couple of days, I received the eleven wooden crosses, which were mailed to a fictitious identity post office box on the Queens border of Brooklyn. I may have been a little sloppy on this one because there are cameras in that post office, and I went in a few times without a disguise. This would make the odds of them finding me a bit better.

Now I started my search for my next victim. I spent a few twelve-hour days in the selection process. Not wanting to do another piece of work right away in New York City, I narrowed the search down to six potential abusers. I had an excellent candidate in Brooklyn, but pursuing an interstate crime brings a greater audience to my crusade. Of the six current candidates, there were a couple of Boy Scout leaders, a couple of priests, and a couple of individuals with questionable backgrounds who made the cut.

I had heard of the case of Father James Herman at the parish of Sacred Heart of Jesus Catholic Church and Interparochial School in Parsippany, New Jersey.

His name came up as one of the six finalists to be dealt with. I decided to make him my second case of retribution. I went from a poor parish in a bad neighborhood to a wealthy parish in a boom town area.

I had not been in New Jersey more than two times in my entire life. I know nothing about anything in that state, so my research was from the ground up. I quickly discovered that Parsippany fell under the auspices of the Archdiocese of Newark.

I did as much research on Father Hermann as I could online. Hermann was 47, handsome, a graduate of Dunwoody Seminary, with eighteen years of experience as pastor of a highly successful church. Success in Catholic terms was largely about financial gain. While other parishes were experiencing a decline in parishioner attendance and weekly revenue, Hermann not only saw a significant increase in weekly attendees but also experienced tremendous growth in charitable donations. The Sacred Heart of Jesus was a model for every parish to strive for. More importantly for me, I discovered through newspaper articles that Hermann had a huge ego. There was a YouTube video showing the priest's swagger and evidence of his thirst for publicity. I squeezed as much as I could out of the internet, getting a clear picture of Father James Hermann. I knew I had to appeal to his ego.

I hacked into the mainframe of the Newark Archdiocese. The personnel file on Father Hermann further convinced me he was an absolutely disgusting human being. A predator in priestly vestments.

His career started at a parish in the Bronx where he was accused of raping a young girl. He was quickly moved to New Jersey. His charm and intelligence moved him quickly up the ladder, and he was eventually sent to Parsippany. There were several allegations against Father Hermann, including his connection with a young man who took his own life. None of the accusations could be proven. I knew in my gut that Hermann was a slimeball and had to go.

My research on Hermann took a solid month. I laid the groundwork on how to con this priest into being alone with me. I went out to see the church a couple of times and knew immediately that I could not deal with him anywhere on the grounds of the church. This was a vibrant church in an exclusive community. Too much foot traffic, too many students, too many after-school activities with clubs and sports, and parents' organizations meeting at all hours. This wasn't like St. Martin of Tours, where everything was buttoned up at three in the afternoon.

I appealed to this priest's ego. I became Todd Cymbol, a successful movie producer who had heard about the epic Father James Hermann's great work, and I wanted to make a documentary about him. It would be great for the parish and certainly get attention from the Vatican through my many contacts in the Rome movie industry.

I disguised myself with a dark suntan, makeup, expensive suits, and designer sunglasses. I rented a Maserati under a fake name and using a stolen credit card. I was the epitome of a La La Land movie producer.

I created a fictitious company, Aqueduct Productions, named after the Bronx public park where I used to play basketball, handball, and hang out with Gjuli. I designed a website that had dozens of bogus productions, many of which were pro Catholic. That was painstaking work, but I needed it to show Father Hermann to build credibility.

In summary, I was able to massage this guy's ego effectively, and after a few visits, I had him completely in my grasp.

All it took was for me to get him to my hotel suite at the Hilton Hotel in Parsippany to enable me to cut his meteoric career short. I manipulated him beautifully, if I say so myself.

Once in the fancy rooms, befitting a well-to-do producer, I slipped him a micky, a date drug, in a glass of good scotch, knocking him out cold.

When he awoke, he found himself naked and tied down on a portable table I had brought along, another piece of evidence to give to law enforcement. The only obstacle for the cops was that I paid cash for the table and purchased it with my Todd Cymbol disguise. My own mother wouldn't have been able to recognize me.

When Father Hermann came to, he was tightly bound and gagged. I spent some time with him until he could clear out the brain fog and truly enjoy the procedure.

I was now appropriately dressed as an altar boy. His suicide victim was one of his mass servers. A good boy, from all indications. I used my young boy voice and alternated between that one and several others. I had no lights on in the suite. Instead, the room was illuminated by a few stand up votive candles. The room had eerie shadows enhanced by the flickering of the flames.

Needless to say, the handsome, swaggering child rapist priest was terrified. He peed and shit himself, making the hotel suite smell like a men's toilet at Yankee Stadium. The stink of his fear reminded me of the tortured drug dealers I had dealt with in Central America.

I ceremoniously prayed over him in both Latin and English. For that, I used my James Stewart impersonation, which I perfected. I loved that halting voice Stewart had in his movies.

Father Hermann was mumbling through his tight mouth gag. He was probably begging for his life or some other nonsense. Maybe he just didn't care for my improvised voices. The good father should have vomited, swallowed it, and choked to death if he knew what was good for him.

One thing was very satisfying. I got him to admit by nodding his sweaty head that he had indeed raped the little girl in his first assigned parish in the Bronx. He also admitted having sodomized on several occasions the altar boy who killed himself. He nodded that there were others he had molested, and he was grooming a couple of 1st graders. He nodded to every question I asked, including being a bedmate of the archbishop in Newark. There were rumors of that guy in Newark for years.

When I showed Father Hermann the sharpened wooden crucifix, he made a noise through his gag that didn't sound human. He expelled some more gas, and some more shit came out of him, which was all liquid. It was gross.

I used the cross to open him up like a fish. Slowly, I ran the crucifix down his body so he could feel the tearing of every inch. I think he died of a heart attack when I was halfway done with the procedure. His eyes bulged, and his body lifted off the table. His sphincter muscle let loose, removing whatever was left in his bowels. The smell was horrific.

To let the cops know it was me again, I removed some of his insides, a few feet of intestines, and his liver, and piled them on his pubic area. Of course, I left the crucifix in his heart.

Todd Cymbol vanished forever. Except for one more appearance where I needed him...

CHAPTER 17

PRIEST KILLER STRIKES AGAIN, the New York Daily News headlined the next day. The New York Post had PRIEST KILLED IN NEW JERSEY. The subtitle was, Do we have a serial killer?

This was exactly the kind of publicity I was looking for. My crusade against pedophiles would be national and global. Every news outlet ran the story. Some had interviews with former FBI profilers who insisted they didn't consider a case to be a serial killer situation until three people were killed with the same MO and evidence. They wouldn't have to wait too long for the third.

I loved it. I was already launching research for my next victim.

Vic Gonnella and his team, including a lady cop, raced to the scene in Parsippany. When I saw her on a televised news report, I hacked into the NYPD mainframe and discovered her name. Raquel Ruiz. Not a detective, but she was involved with the O'Gorman case. I discovered she was Puerto Rican, a divorcee, no kids, and quite the looker. Gonnella was also divorced with two kids. Both boys.

My mind went four steps ahead. Two divorced cops, a good-looking guy and a hot Latina, on the same case. There was always the possibility of a relationship. In time, I would discover that my thought process would naturally be correct.

I was able to obtain their home addresses, as well as their cell and home telephone numbers. They both lived near each other in the Bronx. Very convenient, don't you think?

From my apartment with a bowl of Aunt Milles' sauce and some nice rigatoni, I watched as the mayor and police chief of Parsippany, the governor, the head of the New Jersey State Troopers, and the limp wristed Archbishop of Newark do a dog and pony show news conference in front of the cathedral in Newark. It looked like a small army of news trucks, cameramen, sound people, and reporters all vying for the same story, and all hoping to get an exclusive.

The governor declared there was a serial killer out and about. The silly Archbishop said a prayer for Father James Hermann and warned his parishes to double down on their security. The head of the New Jersey cops swore to apprehend the beast who killed the much-loved priest. Great sound bite for the Deegan crusade.

I was giddy with excitement. I also enjoyed flaying this menace, Father Hermann. It felt every bit as good as killing my own abuser.

* † *

My next victim, who wasn't a priest, was back in the Borough of Brooklyn. A much easier commute for me and a much more challenging piece of work. I could literally walk to the Hasidic Jewish neighborhood in Williamsburg.

I had read about the allegations made by a young man by the name of Yiddy Rosenberg. He had gone to the Brooklyn District Attorney and filed a complaint against his rabbi for molesting him many times while he was in school and studying for his Bar Mitzvah.

This was unheard of in the Satmar Hasidic community. If you were in the community, and there was a problem, the Rebbe, the head Rabbi, was the arbitrator and judge with the final word on any matter.

The accused was Rabbi Tzvi H. Gottlieb, the descendant of a prominent family of Rabbis from Europe.

I dove into this man's past. I discovered from the D.A.'s office where I broke into the computer system that Rabbi Gottlieb had had several complaints about molesting his young male students. He was also accused of raping a 12-year-old girl. None of the families whose children were sexually assaulted by Gottlieb would press charges.

The community would likely shun the families at large due to such a scandal.

Yiddi Rosenberg waited until he was of age to press charges. His family had begged him not to do it. A firestorm of Satmar unity destroyed his family. Yiddi's mother was spat upon as she walked on the streets of Williamsburg, and the family could no longer go to shul. Yiddi's siblings were thrown out of the Yeshiva school they attended, and his father's business was destroyed. No one in the Satmar community entered his store. They couldn't even return to Antwerp, their hometown, as they would be ostracized there as well.

I neglected to tell an important part of this story. When the Rosenbergs went to the Rebbe, which is what they should have done in their culture, the Rebbe found in Rabbi Gottlieb's favor. He determined that Yiddi Rosenberg, at 12 years old, seduced Rabbi Gottlieb. Clearly a biased ruling on the Rebbe's part.

* † *

Now, Todd Cymbol, we redeployed. As part of my disguise, I had to dress as a proper Hasid. I entered the famous G and G Clothing on Flushing Avenue in Williamsburg disguised as the movie maven Todd Cymbol. What a job Todd did.

The store manager, a Satmar named Klein, loved the idea of a feature film being made about a Satmar Hasid. All the clothing needed for the disguise was bought and fitted in an hour, including the yarmulka and the fur hat.

Now I had a few significant hurdles to jump before I made my final visit to the Hopper Steet Synagogue to dispatch this slimy rabbi Gottlieb.

I had to get Gottlieb alone, preferably in his office at the Synagogue. More difficult, I had to find a way to communicate with the rabbi. I could mimic an English Yiddish accent perfectly, but I couldn't speak the language.

I devised a genius plan, if I may be allowed to brag.

When I met the Rabbi Slimeball I handed him a note in Yiddish. Around my neck, I wore white surgical bandages. The rest of me was full-blown Satmar Hasid, from the hat to the shoes.

The note read, "I have that thing, and cannot speak, but pray, I can, blessed be His Name."

That thing is cancer in Yiddish vernacular.

I was in. The next moment, I was embraced by the Rabbi and invited to pray, and then we met in his office. I mimicked the rocking Hasids around me and pulled it off like I was one of them. The praying went on for quite some time. Once the crucifix I had carved to a lethal point, which I kept hidden up my jacket sleeve, almost fell to the ground. That would have been a disaster. Was I slipping, or was I just careless? I made a mental note of this error. I cannot make mistakes like that again.

I found myself alone with Gottlieb inside his office. He was jovial and animated. I just kept smiling and nodding my head at the unknown Yiddish, all the while waiting for the right time to strike.

After a few minutes, I stood up and smiled broadly. I went to the door and locked it. Gottlieb was perplexed and put his arms in a what's going on position.

I sat back in the chair across from his desk. I kept smiling. Finally, I spoke in English.

"So, Rabbi Gottlieb, I have come to bring the wrath of the Lord upon you. The young boys who you molested, the little girl who you raped, I am here to see that justice is done for them, you bastard. You thought you were protected by your rules. How many rules do you have, Rabbi? I understand there are six hundred and thirteen, is that correct?"

Gottlieb was dumbfounded. He didn't know if he should shit or wind his watch.

I jumped around and behind the hapless and doomed Rabbi. I exposed the wooden crucifix so he could see it and quickly used it to put it on his throat so he couldn't call for help.

"Your community protected you because of your lofty position. You have had your way with these innocent children for far too long. You destroyed their souls, Gottlieb. For those who spoke up, you destroyed their lives. I seem to recall a few of those rules I asked you about. Not to commit sodomy with a man. Did you forget that rule, Rabbi, or was that not meant for little boys? Do you just pick and choose from God's commandments and your so-called rules?

Gottlieb was gasping for air. The crucifix was crushing his throat. I was really enjoying this, but I had to get going. The last thing he heard in this life was:

"Leviticus tells us not to take revenge. That's another one of your rules, isn't it? But guess what, Rabbi Tzvi H. Gottlieb? I'm not Jewish. I have my own set of rules that I believe in. 'And whosoever shall offend one of these little ones that believe in me, it is better for him that a millstone were hanged about his neck, and he were cast into the sea.' I don't see a millstone handy, so I guess I will have to improvise."

I released the pressure on Gottlieb throat and, in one motion, plunged it into his carotid artery and ripped it across his wrinkled neck. He tried to rise from his chair. I pushed him down with ease. His blood sprayed all over his desk and onto his library of Hebrew books. He died within seconds. I left the crucifix sticking from his throat. I wanted to open his pants and mutilate him, but I wanted to get going. In retrospect I should have cut his dick off as another message to the world.

* † *

By the time Vic Gonnella and Raquel Ruiz were summoned to the Synagogue, I was in my apartment having lunch. I picked up a nice corned beef on rye with a pickle and a homemade round potato knish at a Glatt Kosher deli a few blocks from the Hooper Street Synagogue.

CHAPTER 18

After Rabbi Gottlieb was taken out, the search for the murderer, me, was ratcheted up a notch.

The FBI, which was watching the murder of the two priests closely, now decided there was a serial killer on the loose. They needed three. They got three.

Another dramatic press conference was called, and there were as many bodies behind the microphone as possible, more than news reporters and camera people. The circus continued without the big top.

Behind the makeshift podium stood the NYPD police commissioner, his chief of detectives, the department's chief, the mayor of New York City, the Brooklyn district attorney, the lieutenant governor of New York State, his Eminence the cardinal, the main Rebbe from upstate New York with two of his curly haired assistants, Vic Gonnella and Raquel Ruiz, and Sean something or other from the FBI and another FBI guy in charge of the New York office. I suppose the commissioner of the parks department was busy.

Most everyone wanted the mic. Every law enforcement official who spoke to the public said they had leads and would soon apprehend the perpetrator…lies. The religious all said prayers for the dead…lies. The politicians all said the public had nothing to fear, and they were confident the killer would soon be caught…even more lies.

The truth was, they had no clue who was committing these killings, and they were not anywhere near finding me.

In typical FBI fashion, they wanted to take full control of the investigation. However, it was decided that the NYPD and the FBI would do a coordinated effort to find me. They formed a few joint task forces. They had no shot, as we used to say in the Bronx.

Little did they know I was reading both NYPD DD5s, their daily reports, and the FBI 302 reports. My CIA hacker guys taught me well.

They were correct in thinking O'Gorman's murderer was sexually motivated. With the sexual mutilation of the body, what else would it be? They went down that avenue and started from when O'Gorman was a young priest.

The alumni list at St. Martin of Tours, which fit a partial profile developed by NYPD intelligence personnel, showed 420 potential suspects. That would take a battalion of detectives to follow up on, but with the help of the FBI, some bright individuals over there, specifically a genius profiler by the name of Gail Gain, also known as G.G., it was determined that the list would be far less.

She theorized the killer would likely be an altar boy...correct on that...and had to be left-handed. She could tell that from the way the victims were stabbed...correct again.

I was still over a hundred men who needed to be interviewed. Good luck finding half of them.

Vic and Raquel were spinning their wheels tracking down some of O'Gorman's recent abuse victims. I guess they were trying to prove O'Gorman was a pedophile, and his recent victim was the killer. I get it. They were in the right church but the wrong pew.

I immediately started my search for the use of the 4th crucifix. This time, however, it would be a layperson pedophile. That would shut down anyone who says the general public has nothing to fear. Fear is a wonderful thing. I had a certain expertise in fear from my covert interrogation work in Central America. I would go so far as to say I was an expert in understanding what fear could do to the human psyche.

* † *

There was a sudden breakthrough in the investigation. That's what was being reported to the muckety mucks in NYPD police headquarters. The reports read "EYES ONLY." Yea. My eyes.

The crucifixes were all purchased from Sheehan's Religious Articles of Boston, Massachusetts. They were mailed to a post office box in Queens, owned by one Todd Cymbol. They were paid for with a money order purchased at a CVS store in Teaneck, New Jersey. All very correct.

NYPD and the FBI were on it like they could taste the collar.

Here is what they discovered.

They studied videotapes from the Father Hermann case. The Todd Cymbol in Parsippany, New Jersey, was a man in his early fifties. Tanned and dressed to kill. Constantly on his cell phone. Drove a Maserati sports car. The Todd Cymbol, who owned the P.O. Box, was a man with a Dominican accent, dressed in a loud Tommy Bahamas type shirt, balding and chomping on a wet cigar. The money order was purchased by a weird older black woman who talked out loud to herself and smelled really bad, according to an eyewitness cashier and an in-store videotape. Dead ends all around.

Didn't I tell you I was a genius? And a master of disguise...

* † *

The day after Rabbi Gottlieb was killed was the day he was buried. There was this whole thing about the Medical Examiner wanting to keep the body and look for more evidence and a full autopsy. The Rebbe wouldn't hear of it. Gottlieb had to be buried before sundown the next day by Jewish law. That's that, no wiggle room. The local rules in New York City bound the coroner. The city lawyers got involved.

The Rebbe, who told the entire Hasidic world in New York state how to vote, and vote as a block, didn't get excited. He made one call to the governor, who was trying to be reelected, and Gottlieb's body was immediately released. How's that for power?

When you stop to think about it, the man's throat was cut. An autopsy? C'mon now.

I wanted so badly to walk over from my apartment and watch the ceremony at the Hooper Street Synagogue. I would dress up in something other than my Hasidic outfit, but I may have been recognized, so I just watched the doings on my television at home with some nice Nova lox and fresh bagels with a smear of cream cheese. All in Rabbi Gottlieb's memory.

Throngs of Hasidic Jews in their solid black coated garb with a variety of black and brown hats, men only, clogged the streets around the shul. They carried the plain wooden coffin on their shoulders in and out of the temple. Loudspeakers were used to amplify the Rebbe's voice as he officiated at the funeral.

The news media were there in force. Trucks with their rooftop electronic dishes broadcast the afternoon funeral worldwide.

The Deegan crusade was gaining much wanted exposure.

CHAPTER 19

I was half thinking about taking a flight to Lugano to spend a few days at my house. I kept the housekeeper and the gardener from the previous owner, and knew the place would be kept pristine. However, my crusade needed me to take relatively quick action. I wanted to do a non-clerical hit.

My father gave me a knife that belonged to his grandfather on my quarter-German side. The knife had an eight-inch blade and a metal handle that was worn and beat up. The blade was dark and dull with age. A few years ago, well before I started my crusade against pedophiles, I took it to a local shoemaker and had the blade sharpened and polished. I bought a sharpening stone and kept the only heirloom I had from my family, like a razor. There was no intention for me to slit anyone's throat with this knife. I kept that idea in the back of my head. I used this dagger to sharpen the crucifixes I bought one by one while I made plans to dispatch my next victim.

* † *

Who would have imagined the Boy Scouts of America would turn out to be a pedophile's playground?

The organization was aware of the perverted things that went on among their goody two shoes' troops. They knew about the pedophilia in their midst and did little to stop it. They were forced by the courts to expose over 1,200 cases of scouts being molested. This was discovered among 15,000 pages of internal documents on men who were accused or suspected of abuse.

The whole "Scout's honor" thing was only good for the boys. The organization had no honor all the way to the top of the organization.

All that stuff about trustworthy, brave, helpful, kind, courteous, and clean was great on paper.

I already had my fifth and sixth targets on the table. That would be in Boston, Massachusetts. Right now, I was returning to New Jersey to meet up with a disgusting pervert, an assistant Scout leader by the name of Ralph Mineo.

One of the great things about being super wealthy was that money was no object. I never had to even think about what things cost or hesitate to do anything I wanted.

I hired a jet to take me from Teterboro Airport in New Jersey to Boston in a few days.

This Mineo character was a troop leader in Rutherford, New Jersey, which was a few minutes from the airport. Perfect location for me to send Mineo to hell and hop on the plane to the next leg of the crusade.

The back story on Ralph Mineo was, for lack of a better word, deplorable. Mineo targeted a 9-year-old, Scott Becker. Soon after the boy's father passed suddenly, Scott naturally became depressed, and his mom thought it was a good idea to get him into the Boy Scouts. Meet some other nice boys and perhaps pick up a father figure.

Mineo started grooming the boy from day one. Within a few months, Scott was performing sex acts with Mineo, who led the helpless boy into engaging in sex with two older Scouts. Mineo filmed and photographed the boys, sending the videos and stills to a pervert friend who distributed child pornography.

Mineo made a ton of money from the global distribution of his work. He was able to start a photography business in the Garden State Plaza in Paramus, New Jersey, near his home. Try to guess what his specialty was? Yup, photographing kids and young adults. And... he made house calls.

Fast forward to when Scott Becker had grown up. He was tortured by the years at the hands of Mineo. He came forward about the abuse and hired a lawyer to go after Mineo and the Boy Scouts. To put it simply, Scott lost the case. The statute of limitations on the crime had passed. The Boy Scouts disavowed any knowledge of the alleged abuse.

I did all the background research on Mineo that was needed. I checked into a hotel nearby, paying cash. My English was so bad that it was almost funny dealing with the receptionist. I registered as Raul Espinosa, a flamboyantly gay man. Back at my apartment, I had forged a Dominican Republic passport. Yes, I learned how to do all that from my CIA counterparts in Central America. I learned well. It was, after all, the cap to my years of disguise and imitations.

I studied the layout of the Garden State Plaza mall. I went to the mall not as Raul Espinosa but disguised as a mall walker complete with a Yankee cap, a gray wig, sunglasses, sneakers, cargo shorts, and a Walkman. I learned the angle of every security camera.

I sat across from Images by Mineo at a Starbucks and watched the parade of parents taking their kids to be photographed. I saw Mineo and his staff fussing over the kids and parents. I walked around and drank coffee until 9:30 P.M., when the mall closed. I knew exactly what I was going to do the next day.

The next evening, at 8:30 P.M., I returned as Raul Espinosa with spiked blond hair, wraparound sunglasses, tight jeans, a purple linen shirt, and lavender ankle boots with ostrich feathers on top. I got a few nasty looks and a smile or two from some light in the loafers' guys.

I waited until 9:20 P.M.

When Mineo's staff had left, there were three of them: one a photographer and two young women. Mineo had halfway lowered the security gate at the front of the store. He was busy fussing around when

I called to him through the gate. He raised the gate a bit for me to enter.

I told him, in a better, more understandable Spanish accent than I used at the hotel, that I was very impressed with his work, and I owned a young boy's boarding school in the Dominican Republic. I went on saying I was searching for a gifted photographer to work with our students. I let him know it was a school for wealthy students, and he would be well-paid. Mineo's eyes lit up. I'm not entirely sure, but I think, by his wry grin, he saw himself frolicking on the beach with tanned, tight-bodied Dominican boys.

We chatted for a few minutes. I asked to see some of his past work other than what was in the store's window. That led us to the back workroom through a wooden door.

He led the way, and I quickly kicked the door shut behind us and grabbed the unsuspecting Mineo from behind, covering his mouth with my hand, which I had draped in a dishtowel. I pulled his neck back until I heard some cracking.

I told him, now in perfect English using my own voice, that if he struggled, I would make his pain excruciating.

I said something to the effect, "Where is your stash of the pictures you've taken that the mommies and daddies never see?"

He pretended not to know what I was referring to.

I stretched his neck back further, making the pain soar to a level nine.

"I'm losing patience. Where the fuck are the pictures, Ralph? I can give you enough pain that you will beg to die."

Tears flowed down the creep's face. He flashed his eyes to a four-drawer tan metal cabinet. I dragged Mineo across the room, and muffled noises came out of him. He let out a large fear fart that filled the air of the office with an unpleasant smell.

He looked at the bottom draw of the cabinet, his hands were trying to pull my arm away. I smacked him hard in the head with my free hand. He stopped.

The cabinet contained manila folders filled with black and white, as well as color, photos. I grabbed one of the folders and dragged the sicko across the room to a table with files underneath. One of his loafers fell from his foot.

I dropped the photographs on the table.

Then I started really fucking with him.

Mineo was a peculiar-looking man. He reminded me of an opossum. His face was pointy, and his head had strands of hair that were now sticking up in several directions. His ears protruded like Dumbo the Elephant. Mineo was short. Maybe 5'5" at most. His arms and legs were skinny. He had a protruding, low pot belly. He was easy for me to manipulate.

I said something like, "Ah, I see now. This is what Scott was trying to tell everyone. You are a freak and a pedophile. Luckily for you, your lawyers were better than his, and you skated away. Money talks and bullshit walks as the old saying goes."

"Look down Ralphie boy. Look at your work. Can

you imagine what these poor kids were going through? Can you imagine the damage you caused them for the rest of their lives? I can tell you, Ralph. It was done to me. It ain't too much fun, Mineo."

I forced his head down on the table within inches of the photos.

I think I heard him shit his pants, but I had already made my move.

With my left hand, the pointed crucifix, which I had tucked in the back of my jeans, flew into Ralph Mineo's neck. I twisted the weapon around a bit, feeling the bones in his neck. He writhed in pain, moaning and trying to free himself from my vise-like grip. The last thing he saw in this life was his blood pooling onto his disgusting photographs. I dropped him onto the table with his mouth open and blood pouring from it. His eyes were at the back of his head.

Unhappily for me, he didn't suffer too much.

CHAPTER 20

The flight from Teterboro to Boston's Logan airport was a quick up-and-down ride. Another great aspect of being rich and flying private is not having to wait in long lines to go through TSA security checks and having to deal with miserable, uniformed employees shouting instructions at you.

Anyway, or like we used to say in the Bronx, anyways, I checked into this fancy hotel in Boston to continue my crusade. I was having the time of my life; I was relaxed, happy, and determined for the world to understand just what a pedophile did to their victims' physical and emotional well-being.

After each killing, I felt the same tingle of satisfaction I did when I murdered my own abuser, Father Edward O'Gorman. If there is a hell, I will meet him and the rest of the disgusting bastards whom I send to the devil.

In the morning, the televised news reports of the Paramus, New Jersey, mall murder were the lead story, even in Boston.

I went online to read the New York newspapers. The Daily News sensational headline blared, IS ANYONE SAFE? They had a photograph of families entering the Garden State Plaza. The New York Post headline was a bit more intense. CRUCIFIX KILLER STRIKES AGAIN. The captioned photo had a replica of one of the murder weapons. Nice touch.

How is that for selling fear, to sell newspapers?

Later that morning, yet another full-blown news conference was called. The usual suspects were all in attendance, and the same blabber was spewed over the airwaves. Prayers, warnings, threats, and promises abound. Frankly, I was hardly interested in the soundbites. What caught my eye was how tired Vic Gonnella and Raquel Ruiz looked at the last presser. It was clear that the bosses at 1 Police Plaza and their bosses wanted them to stick with the case no matter how far it took them. I needed to become much more familiar with these two officers. I made a mental note to call Vic. I would first send him a few messages. Through my eavesdropping on the NYPD reports, I discovered that another detective was now assisting with the case. A veteran by the name of Joe Flores. So, these three cops, with the help of the FBI, and their lead dog Sean Lewandowski, I could feel their breath on me for the first time.

Just before I left for Teterboro airport, I was interviewed at my building in Brooklyn by a couple of drunken Irish detectives who could care less about what they were doing. They were marking time, counting the months on their fingers until their retirement. My name was on a list of students from St. Martin of Tours. The two numbskulls were just checking in to find out if any alumni knew why someone would kill the legendary Father O'Gorman.

Using the chess game in my head, and thinking four moves ahead, it was just a matter of time before the SWAT team and the whole NYPD converged on 1 Main Street in Brooklyn.

I was a bit surprised, Vic Gonnella and company figured out the alum thing. I figured it would take them longer, but no harm, no foul.

Honestly, the two mick cops that came to interview me were the best warning I could have had.

When I left for New Jersey, I knew it was the last time I would be at my lovely and expensive apartment. And when I departed from New Jersey, I knew I'd never see the Garden State again.

I destroyed any evidence on my master of the universe computer and made several copies of what I needed to keep and reset. If they found out I was an expert hacker, it would cramp my style. I packed some much-needed disguises and makeup, along with my family's heirloom dagger. Anything else I could replace.

I also took what I needed the most — my remaining crucifixes.

* † *

So now I was in Boston. I took a beautiful suite at the Ritz-Carlton hotel overlooking the Boston Commons. I checked in as Dr. Alfredo Ledon of Costa

Rica with all the necessary documents in order.

My disguise was brilliant, if I may say so myself. I made myself look years younger with a wig of thick wavy hair, a killer goatee, black horn-rimmed glasses, and expensive clothing. I paid in cash for three nights. This gave me more than enough time to take out my two targets.

It's a very nice city as cities go, but I truly hated Boston, not because of the Red Sox or the Celtics or the Bruins. I could care less about sports rivalries. I detested Boston because of the Catholic church there and in the Vatican. One hundred and twenty-five priests were implicated in a massive abuse of young children not so long ago.

The clergy sex scandal in Boston was second to none. The archdiocese was forced to close sixty-five parishes and pay out 95 million dollars in settlements for the abused boys and girls. The stupid-looking skinny cardinal resigned in disgrace, and the Vatican welcomed him with open arms. They put this creepy cardinal in charge of so many departments in the Vatican, it was as if they had promoted him for bad behavior.

I remember watching the funeral Mass of Pope John Paul II. Guess who officiated at the ceremony. Yup! That damned Cardinal. When I saw him on the altar at St Peter's Basilica, this putrid pedophile protector, I threw a glass paperweight, smashing my plasma television.

Now I was in Boston to take some much-needed revenge against the church.

* † *

My targets were two filthy priests for whom the church had settled sexual molestation cases.

These two mutts were now living in a rectory together. Do you think they would stop their pedophilia? Nope. They were still doing their thing at the Arnold Arboretum, trying to meet young boys. They would groom the kids by playing with remote control cars and hooking them. By and by, they would buy a remote car for a boy and work their magic from there.

The afternoon I arrived in Boston, I walked around the Arnold watching them. Now it was time to do my magic.

Making a long story short, I made my way to meet with the priests under the guise that I was a wealthy sugar magnet who wanted to start a scholarship program for Hispanic boys. Wealth always appealed to the Catholic church. When I dangled $25 million to start my program, they were hooked.

We had a delightful lunch in my well-appointed suite. I told them about my wealthy family and how I wanted to share my good fortune with less fortunate children. They were chomping at the bit. And these two priests knew how to down the McCallan 15.

I told my two target priests I wanted to tour the city a bit to learn about the poorer sections. Fathers Rosado and Burns offered to chauffeur me around in their car. I sat in the back seat, waiting patiently to pounce.

I asked to see the Arnold Arboretum. The car came to a stop on a road near the park. I didn't pay much attention to the name, but we were parked under a big, beautiful oak tree.

I said, now in my own unaccented voice, "This is perfect, quiet just like I wanted it." Or something to that effect.

The two hapless priests looked at one another in surprise. "Dr. Ledon, I don't understand," Rosado said.

I took the crucifix I had hidden in my suit pocket and slammed it into Rosado's neck. Blood erupted like a volcano. I moved Rosado so his blood sprayed all over Burns, covering his shocked face. I pulled Father Burns by his blood-soaked hair, exposing his neck. I slowly put the point of the crucifix into his neck and pulled it across his throat. Dark blood covered the entire front interior of the car. Those miserable bastards died without even knowing what hit them. I wish I could do that one over again.

I had planned to use two crucifixes. I used only one.

I decided to leave a message on the inside window.

V. G. VI quod requiētum

That's the message I left, and I'll explain that later. I was now off to my next planned execution.

Long Island, New York.

CHAPTER 21

While I was in Boston, as I expected, the NYPD and the FBI finally discovered that I, Mr. John Deegan, was the serial killer at large.

The news went around the world in minutes. Billionaire, former seminarian, ex-special ops assassin, and all-around nice guy was the biggest villain since the Lindberg baby killer.

I'm sure Gjuli passed out at the news, but I couldn't or wouldn't contact her. My siblings and other relatives were no doubt dumbfounded. Some of the Deegans would be raising a glass in my honor. There was no love lost toward the church. The folks in the company I founded, who adored me to my face while I was lining their pockets, were probably tarnishing my name.

I don't know what went on when the NYPD and the feds raided apartment 11 K but I can tell you one thing, the doormen were pissed off because I tipped them very well.

My first communication with Vic Gonnella was left in an envelope addressed to him that I left on the dining room table.

It's worth repeating my whole note.

Hello Mr. Gonnella.
Glad to make your acquaintance.
Pay attention, please.

Matthew 18: 1-6
At the same time came the disciples unto
Jesus, saying, "Who is the greatest in the
kingdom of heaven?"
And Jesus called a little child unto him, and set
him during them,
And said,
"Verily I say unto you, except ye be converted,
and become
as little children, ye shall not enter the
kingdom of heaven.
Whosoever therefore shall humble himself as
this little child, the same is greatest in the
kingdom of heaven.
And whoso shall receive one such little child in
my name receiveth me.
But whoso shall offend one of these little ones
which believe in me, it were better for him
that a millstone were hanged about his neck,
and that he were drowned in the depth of the
sea.
Woe unto the world because of offences! For
it must needs be that offences come; but woe
to that man by whom the offence cometh!
Wherefore if thy hand or thy foot offend thee,
cut them off, and cast them from thee: it is

*better for thee to enter life halt or maimed,
rather than having two hands or two feet to
be cast into everlasting fire.
And if thine eye offend thee, pluck it out, and
cast it from thee: it is better for thee to enter
life with one eye, rather than having two eyes
to be cast into hell fire.
Take heed that ye despise not one of these
little ones; for I say unto you, That in heaven
their angels do always behold the face of my
Father which is in heaven."*

I was going to write, say hello to Raquel, but I
thought that would be taken the wrong way.

* † *

Back to Boston. I promised to tell you about the
message I wrote in Rosado and Bruns' blood on the
inside of their death car. It was not such a cryptic
message, but I wasn't dealing with too many
geniuses on the Boston PD.

V. G. VI quod requiētum.

The message was addressed to V.G., Vic Gonnella.
VI was 6. The Latin is ... and rest. Six more crucifixes
and I would rest.

I was telling Gonnella et al that I was only halfway
through my goal. They discovered I was the crucifix
killer quicker than anticipated. From that point
forward I tried hard not to think they were total
buffoons. There were some brains in that outfit, and

I had to work hard to keep these cops a full step behind me.

CHAPTER 22

The jet circled around MacArthur Airport in Islip, Long Island. For some reason, I hadn't seen this part of the shore from the air before. I was enjoying the view and at the same time remembering my time as a boy in Long Beach. I couldn't remember if it was before or after O'Gorman first molested me at St. Martin. I'm pretty sure it was the summer just before my life changed for the worse.

I rented a car from one of the sleezy, off-brand rental places outside the airport. I paid for the bullshit insurance scam so the guy could make a few bucks. The owner copied the information off my fake driver's license and showed me there was no damage on the car, and the tank was full.

I took my time during the hour-long drive to take in all the sights I hadn't seen in a long time. I have always loved Long Beach and have returned there every now and then.

This time, I made a point of stopping at my friend's aunt's bungalow on Pennsylvania Avenue. The aunt was long gone.

I pulled the car next to the high curb, beside the tiny house. It was about midday, the sun blanching the street and bouncing off the blue water of Reynolds Channel about 50 yards away.

The house had new maroon awnings, probably a new roof, but otherwise looked the same. An attractive young woman in a two-piece bathing suit was sunning herself on a chaise lounge in the small front yard. Next to her were two little kids, playing in a once-beautiful flower garden. It was only dirt now.

The woman could have been the babysitter, or the mom, and I couldn't tell you if the kids were boys or girls. I said hello and told the young lady my friend's aunt owned the place back in the day, and I was wondering if the honeysuckle bushes were still in the rear yard. I didn't have to ask because the perfume of the bushes surrounded me. It was pure bliss.

She invited me to go back and look at the Honeysuckle. The two kids followed me, scampering ahead and making a lot of noise. Here I was, an international serial killer, my body count was rising quickly, and I was in this familiar backyard, with the two kids, and a woman sunning herself was watching. The children were never safer in their lives than at that moment with me, but just think about the idea of it for a second. I could hear my mother saying, "John, never trust strangers." Sure, Mom, isn't a priest a stranger when you come to think about it?

So, I enjoyed seeing the bushes again after so many years. They were clipped back poorly, but the leaves were still full, and the aroma was magnificent.

I stood there for a few minutes, closed my eyes, and took the biggest breath in trying to capture my youth even for a moment.

I had rented a room at a bed and breakfast spot right on the beach on Oceanview and New York Avenue. I think it was New York Avenue anyway. Aside from the honeysuckle, I loved the sound and smell of the ocean in Long Beach. I hoped to have the same experience when I would soon be exiled in Lugano, Switzerland. I would sacrifice the sea for a lake, but I would still have my perfumed bushes. That's if Vic Gonnella and his lady friend Raquel didn't catch up to me. I knew I had to be on my game to avoid the long arm of the law.

* † *

My target was a basketball coach. See, even you thought it was going to be another priest.

His name was Tony Oatley. He was a decent ball player in his day, but didn't have what it takes. He was, however, an incredible coach. He was the winningest coach on Long Island out of Christ High School. Forty-five years of God knows how many kids, athletes, no less, he had abused. And from what I could gather, he was still at it. There were a few legal actions taken against Tony Oatley, and the Archdiocese protected him. Look to the money. Tony raised lots of it with his sports program.

For a few nights, Kenny Walsh, also known as John Deegan, drank at a bar on New York Avenue. Tony

Oatley now owned the spot. I don't remember now, but I think he had stopped coaching. He was just a legend and a pervert.

The word on Tony was he likes to not only bugger the players, but he loves to watch. He would watch porn with the kids when he was grooming them and feed them beer and booze. He liked to watch the players have sex with one another and would, on occasion watch them cavort with a hooker or two. The real deal voyeur.

Now, I made Kenny Walsh into a craggily old Irishman from the other side. I wore a tight, brown sailor's cap; my brogue was so thick you had to listen carefully and slow me down if you wanted to pick out the English. My eyebrows were white, bushy, and one. There was more hair coming out of my ears and nose than under my cap. My fingernails were untrimmed and dirty. I tried to look as if I smelled badly, and if you got too close, it wasn't pleasant. My brown corduroys could stand up by themselves, and the blue and white check flannel shirt I wore needed to be burned. It was warm out, but I still wore fall clothing.

I made sure Tony Oatey took a liking to Kenny Walsh. We would drink until closing time and then stay an extra hour. Oatley would laugh at everything I would say, especially if he didn't understand me. A few times, I really laughed instead of faking it.

One night, after legal hours, I feigned that I had fallen and hit my head inside the bar. Tony was all concerned. He walked me out, and I staggered under the boardwalk. He walked with me as I feigned puking. When he turned his back, I bashed his head with something, I don't recall with what now. When coach Tony Oatley came to, he was bound at the wrists and ankles and gagged with some heavy-duty tape I had hidden under the boardwalk.

I gave him this long speech about how bad he was, and that I was here to take retribution, all in my original Bronx accent. Oatley realized I had set him up and that pissed him off.

The coach was gasping for air through his nostrils, his eyes bulging as if they were about to pop out of their sockets. He had sobered up quickly. That happens with drunks. Adrenalin can do that, you know. The rest is pretty much the same with the crucifix, I slapped him multiple times in his neck, twisting my homemade weapon up, down, and sideways. But this time, I did something different for yet another message to Gonnella and his friends. I discovered that I really enjoyed the chase and sending these messages. I planned to step that up a bit.

After my speech and just before I dispatched Tony Oatley, I had a tablespoon I had taken from the bar and kept in my pant pocket. I got close to the fear-ensured sex degenerate, showing him the spoon just before I scooped out each eyeball. The eyeball can be removed quite easily, as I learned from my CIA friends while serving in the army in Nicaragua. I left both coach's eyeballs hanging by their white and red gooey veins on his cheek as he writhed in pain and shock on the damp sand under the boardwalk.

I let him deal with that for a few minutes. He, knowing his eyes were ripped from their sockets, made him squirm in surprise and pain.

Then I slowly finished him off. I cut him up like a fish pulling and poking his flesh until my hands hurt. His body went into a convulsion just before he took his last miserable breath.

CHAPTER 23

I was determined to go to Ireland and make my crusade international. There was no going back to Brooklyn, or probably the United States, at least for a while. My new residence would be in Switzerland, but I had a few things to attend to on the continent before settling in.

When my ancestors went to America fleeing famine and the fucking genocidal British, they had no intention of returning. I would be the first to go back to Ireland in generations. I planned to make my visit unforgettable.

I'll get to my next targets on the Emerald Isle in a wee bit.

We were in the air somewhere over Greenland when I decided to make a call back to the States.

I was the only passenger aboard a 12-seat Hawker jet that had been leased. I made sure, when I leased this baby, there would be no way for the law to track me. I was, for the moment, Kiernan Dolan. There wasn't an Irishman on the planet who could tell my brogue was fake.

I had Vic Gonnella's cell phone, which I had hacked from the NYPD computers, but I wanted to have some more fun with it. I called the squad where he worked and told them I was John Deegan and wanted to talk with Vic. Mind you, there had to be more than a few pranks and imposters calling the police. Mind you, again I'm calling from a scrabbled, untraceable apparatus from 30,000 feet in the sky.

It was ten minutes before I could give a hint that I was really John Deegan. Some dope of a cop believed me and passed me on to the lovely Raquel Ruiz. I discovered her to be bright. I told her I would give her some evidence that I was the real deal. Nowhere in the media had it been printed where I got the crucifixes from. I told her the name of the purveyor. Then, to verify, she asked me to tell her what was left behind under the boardwalk in Long Beach. That was easy. I drew a Jesus fish in the sand. The next thing I knew, I was talking to the man himself.

Vic the Slick got on the phone and started playing a game with me, which I loved. He asked me what the fish was about. I told him it was a clue. Over water, on the water, in the water. He had to figure it out. I loved toying with him.

He told me it was time to stop the killing and offered to get me some help if I turned myself in. I roared with laughter. Get me some help indeed.

I asked him if he knew what Sigmund Freud said about the Irish, and he didn't even get a chuckle out of it.

"This is one race of people for whom psychoanalysis is of no use whatsoever."

We went back and forth for a bit. I was playing

chess again.

He finally asked the right question. Why was I doing this?

I told him he already knew the answer; I was molested by those creeps, O'Gorman and Peroni.

I went on to tell him about my mission for all the other kids that were raped and sodomized. At that moment, when Vic went silent, he was taken aback and couldn't respond quickly, which is when I suspected that he was among those molested kids.

After a pause, he asked me about the priest I had taken out in Guatemala. Was he the catalyst? For the first time, I admitted I did that killing.

Gonnella asked me if the priest sparked my need for justice.

My answer was dramatic and clear, and Vic fell quiet again. His voice changed after I told him why.

I explained that my little brother Jimmy, the sweetest man who ever lived, told me O'Gorman molested him. Something painful that I only learned later in life, when it was too late for him. Two weeks after he told me this, Jimmy hung himself in the basement of a building where he was superintendent.

Gonnella didn't recover well from this information. He could barely speak.

I asked him what he would do if he or a loved one were molested. He became angry. Gonnella dropped his guard.

He asked me why the hell I called him or something like that. I still remember my response.

"To let you know that this too shall pass. I'll be done in a short time, and then I will fade away into the nightmares of people who choose to hurt children."

His voice was dry. He needed a sip of water. He brought up Gjuli to try to rattle me. It didn't work.

He asked me where I would strike next, as if I would tell him.

I simply told him… 'on familiar ground'.

That was my first of many calls to Detective Vic Gonnella.

I had a few crucifixes left. I planned to use two in Dublin.

* † *

Now I knew a lot more about my adversary than he knew about me.

If my thinking was right, and it usually was spot on, Gonnella was damaged goods, and what I was doing, deep down in his psyche, was justified.

* † *

I conducted extensive research on my targets in Ireland. I think even more than the other work I had done.

I learned how to work with precision in special ops, and I was certainly going to use my skills to the utmost in Ireland. One of the things I learned was never to underestimate my opponent. Gonnella and company were certainly proven worthy adversaries.

Instead of flying directly into Dublin, where my targets were located, I flew into Belfast and took a train to my real destination. In the unlikely event that my plan was discovered, I wanted to throw the bloodhounds off the scent.

The two-hour train ride was great. I got to see the lush green countryside and practice my fake accent with a few passengers and crew.

My Kiernan Dolan disguise was lovely, as they say over there. Salt and pepper beard, a short fisherman's cap, glasses, blue jeans, and a golf jacket made me fit right in.

I checked into a quaint B&B hotel a few blocks from my first stop.

My research was impeccable. I surveyed the closed-down Magdalene Asylum and the Monastery of Our Lady of Charity of Refuge.

This horrid place was where fallen young girls were sent to change their evil ways with the nuns. Back in the day, the young girls were sent to places like this, all over Ireland. These girls could have been mentally retarded, promiscuous, flirtatious, or just very pretty or pregnant.

They took in laundry to make money for the convents and learn discipline.

The nuns were brutal to these poor children. And what else did the girls have to face? Some of the priests who came by had their way with them. Had their way is a polite way to say raped and sodomized. Over the decades, many of the babies the girls gave birth to did not survive. Those who survived were sold to families that wanted to adopt a child. The dead ones were buried in the courtyard of the convent with no grave markings.

One of the nuns, according to my research, was among the most vicious, Sister Marie Anthony, who was still living in the convent with a few other nuns, even after the laundry had closed. She was now known as Sister Katherine Foy. They changed the names to protect the guilty. She was in her early twenties when she dehumanized the girls. She was sixty-four when I visited her.

I enjoyed tracking her down. I felt like a detective. It took me a couple of days of following Sister Foy to and from Mass at the nearby chapel.

Mass was at 6 a.m., and the streets around the abandoned laundry were empty, except for one old man who had provided me with more information on the nuns. He was a young boy who had lived across the street and hated the nuns as if they were the devil. He remembers seeing the babies unceremoniously buried. He still lived in the same flat that his parents had left him. My research, combined with the old man's testimony about the comings and goings of the laundry, put all the pieces together.

One misty morning, I met Sister Foy at Mass. I was wearing a backpack with my necessary tools. I approached the wicked sister and gave her some bullshit about my coming to give the convent a donation. Nothing piques the interest of people like this more than money.

I walked with her back to the convent, where I smashed her in the neck, rendering her unconscious. I pulled her into the front yard and quickly hog-tied and gagged her.

"Wake up, Sister Marie Anthony, torturer of young girls and women," I commanded.

She rolled around like the worm she was. She was terrified. I had to work quickly, fearing that another elderly nun might come out of the convent.

I knelt next to Sister Foy or whatever her name was and said an act of contrition for her. I told her it was only fitting that her blood would run over the graves of the babies who were buried underneath the ground where she was.

I took the sharpened crucifix and sent her to the devil. The crucifix was left protruding from her wrinkled neck. I left the high gate of the convent and walked away. Something caught my eye, which could have been a disaster for me. Something I didn't plan on.

There, from the apartment window across the street, was that old man whom I had met. He saw the whole thing. He smiled and waved at me.

I tipped my cap to him. If I could have gotten away with it, I would have taken him to the nearest pub for a pint.

CHAPTER 24

I made my way to the suburban town of Cabra, fifteen minutes outside of Dublin. Lovely little town. Except for one major problem it would have been an ideal place to live and raise a family.

For my crusade, this one was easy and would be quick work. Then I would leave for my next venue and be out of Ireland forever.

At St. Joseph's School for Deaf Boys in Cabra there was a Christian Brother by the name of Jack McCue. He was a good teacher and a devoted Catholic who was also being watched for higher positions in his order. One problem came to the surface, however, he molested boys at the school for years.

It's difficult to imagine that anyone, let alone a clergyman, would harm these deaf kids.

One of the boys he attacked for years went to the Garda Siochana, the Guardians of the Peace, the cops in Ireland.

When he reached 30 years old, the victim, at the insistence of his wife came forward about the abuse he suffered under Brother McCue. Other deaf boys from St. Joseph's, seeing his bravery also came forward. The stories these men told made even the most veteran Garda sick to their stomachs.

What happened to these men, many of them since pre puberty became a national scandal in Ireland.

Jack McCue was found guilty on 9 counts of indecent assault. He was awaiting sentencing in Dublin.

McCue worked in a hardware store in Cabra. I suppose it was a relative who had owned the shop. I surveilled the store the first time and purchased a nine-volt battery. I immediately knew what I had to do.

Still in my Kiernan Dolan disguise I entered the store again and looked around a bit. McCue approached me and politely asked if he could help. I knew it was him from photographs on the web. I needed some penny nails I told the rapist. The wretched, ill-fated Brother brought me to the nails. They were in the back of the store.

I took the nails and punched McCue in the solarplexius taking him breathless to his knees.

I quietly asked McCue a pointed question as he tried to breath.

"Have you ever thought about what it would be like to be deaf, stone deaf?"

McCue looked up at my smiling face with a baffled stare.

"Well, I will show you what it's like even for a moment," I said.

I rammed a couple of nails into each of his ears. He couldn't even scream. He had no breath from the punch. Blood ran out from his punctured ear drums.

He brought his head up; I took the pointed crucifix from my back belt and buried it in his neck. I ran it across his neck. His mouth opened wide as if he wanted to say something; his eyes bulged in terror. Easy work.

Of course, I left my weapon on the floor next to McCue's body.

He was going to miss his court date.

✝

News of the two murders spread like wildfire around the world. Two more victims, both of the cloth.

Now I would have INTERPOL on my ass. I had already hacked into their system when I was back in Brooklyn. I knew my itinerary and I was fully prepared.

Articles began popping up about the dreaded Magdalene Sisters and what they do to the girls and the Christian Brother who dared to molest deaf kids. I had this wish that many people, under their breaths, would think the John Deegan mission was a good thing for society.

One of the things that transcends different cultures is politics. When I was on the jet heading for my next target, I was able to catch the televised news in Dublin. Just like in the states, there were the classic politicians promising a quick capture and justice to the killer, the clergy praying for the repose of two the murdered souls and the cops not wanting to speak too much of an ongoing investigation. All that was different were their accents and clothing.

I glanced in on a few the NYPD and FBI reports on their mainframes.

The FBI and INTERPOL were in contact with the Corpo della Gendarmeria dello Stato della Città del Vaticano. Both agencies were convinced the notorious John Deegan, now being in Europe was heading to kill the pope. They recommended additional security. That woman G.G., the serial killer profiler in Washington, D.C. concurred with their assumptions.

Vic Gonnella was dispatched immediately to Dublin with his entourage of 2. Joe Flores and the prettier by the day Raquel Ruiz. I had guessed right, or so I believed. Just by the way Raquel and Vic looked at one another on the interviews and how they comported themselves I could tell they were now more than just fellow cops working on a case. Watching people closely will tell their story.

I had left another message for Gonnella. By the time I landed at my destination, after the two-hour train ride back to Belfast and the flight, the NYPD contingency would soon be in the Old Sod.

I assumed between the Garda and Gonnella they would have traced me to where I was staying. My assumption, as usual was correct. Remember I am a genius after all. Or so they say.

With a lovely red-headed lass at the B&B a few blocks from the Magdalene Laundry, I left a sealed envelope addressed to Vic Gonnella.

The Guardia, I'm sure they took fingerprints off the envelope. I made sure I left my prints. There was no secret that I was the fiend at large.

Vic would read the following missive.

> *Hiya, Vic.*
>
> *Welcome to the beautiful Emerald Isle. My ancestors should have stayed in this beautiful place, but they were starving to death. Anyway, it's a beautiful place, only surpassed by the beauty of its people. By the time you read this, I will be well on my way to my next mission. I will give you one clue: Europe. I don't want you guys to have to fly back and forth. Actually, my work in the good old U.S.A. is finished. Three more crosses to bear. In just a few hours, there will be only two. All the best to you and yours. JD*
>
> *P.S. Not to steal the FBI's thunder, but I came to Dublin from Belfast airport. Pretty countryside. Like a patchwork of greens. Try it one day.*

* † *

I landed in Munich. Nice city. I wish I had visited it as a tourist before.

Anyway, I dressed like a priest. Made up as an older bald priest with a black fedora, at that. I was in

Germany to make the acquaintance of the Right Reverend August Hoffmann, professor of theology at the University of Munich. He wasn't young, so I imagine he was in the Hitler Youth.

Father Hoffmann was a renowned, internationally recognized scholar in the Old Aramaic and ancient Greek languages. Hoffman had published several notable books; I had read two of them. He was also a known pedophile.

During my research, I discovered that Hoffmann was working at the Vatican Museum, working on ancient scriptures for nearly twenty years. This brilliant man had been accused of molesting boys at an orphanage near Rome. He wasn't the only one doing this at the orphanage.

The clergy sex scandals were beginning to catch a lot of heat back then, and Pope Benedict XVI, a fellow German and a known Hitler Youth, decided to hide Hoffmann. Don't punish him, Your Holiness... just hide him.

The best place to secrete a pedophile was under the shroud of academia at a university.

It wasn't easy for me to get close to August Hoffman. He had students and seminarians around him all the time, and I had discreetly followed him. It took me a few days to get familiar with Hoffmann's schedule.

Finally, I caught up to him just outside his office. He was alone. My heart was racing like the first time I took out a drug dealer in Central America.

I introduced myself and spoke Aramaic, the language of Jesus Christ. I was fluent since my days at the seminary.

"Father Hoffmann, I'm Francis Foster from Cleveland, Ohio. Shlomo."

"Kmijgolit," Father Hoffmann said. "Yalifonomzawno."

I asked if we could say the Lord's Prayer in Aramaic. After we prayed together, Hoffmann complimented me, saying I said the prayer like a true Galilean.

I won him over, and we chatted about my studies with the Augustinians. My heart rate slowed, but it was still elevated. Frankly, I was feeling a bit lightheaded.

I told him I was visiting Munich just to meet him on my way to Rome. Hoffmann was flattered and invited me into his office.

I feigned a limp and said my legs were weak and that I would love to sit with him. I was playing the old priest to the hilt.

Father Hoffmann's office had a small window overlooking a quiet courtyard.

Hoffman asked me if my career was fruitful. My answer was a segue to my actions.

"Well, Father, my career took some turns that I was not equipped to handle frankly. You see, my Church was not everything that I wished it would be."

"You see. I was born into the Church. Some might say I was born for it. Everything about me, about my soul, wanted to work for the glory of our Lord. And then my soul was ripped into shreds."

I took my hat off, and my face was reddening with anticipation.

"Father, you seem upset. Your... your face is getting red. Let me get some water for you."

When this pedophile priest slowly got up from his chair, that's when I hit him hard on the side of his head. In my portfolio, I had the same tape I used on that coach Tony Oatley. I gagged and wrapped the stunned Father Hoffmann to his chair. I locked the door just in case. Hoffmann looked at me with terror in his eyes. I remember what I said to him almost word for word.

"So, are you back with me, Father? Good. Let me continue with our discussion. The Church was to be my life. Then along came a priest; you know how we felt about priests, Father. Priests were just like gods. Everything they said and did was a message from our Lord. Priests were the end-all and be-all of our lives. They had total control of us, of our souls, if you will. My priest, my very first priest, decided that he needed to control my soul and my body. I was a small boy. What could I do? Tell my mommy and daddy? They would have thought I was crazy. Tell the sisters? C'mon, now. I did whatever he wanted, and I put myself, my mind, in a safe place, hoping one day to get even. Are you with me so far, Father August Hoffmann, you rat bastard?"

The old pedophile just mumbled under the tight gag.

"So now, as I finish my intercessory work for our Lord on behalf of all the children who were molested and abused, I have only two more stops to make after I leave you, one in France and one in Rome. I can honestly say that my career has now been fruitful and fulfilling. Thank you for asking."

I told him I regretted not stopping him from ruining children's souls and lives or something of that nature.

Hoffmann tried to break out of the tape as I rose from the chair. I pulled his head back and used the tenth crucifix with precise perfection.

I thought he was going to suck the tape into his mouth.

I avoided the spray of blood and leaned in next to him. I spoke in Aramaic because I love the drama.

"Eloi, Eloi, lama sabachthani?" meaning, "My God, my God, why have You forsaken me?"

Next stop... France

CHAPTER 25

Jacques Russet was a freak. Not that every pedophile wasn't a freak, but this guy wrote the book on child sexual exploitation.

Politically connected due to his wealth from managing a hedge fund, Russet had a Rolodex of pedophiles throughout the world. He made frequent trips to Thailand to satisfy his proclivity for very young children. The younger the better. Babies and toddlers from 18 months to 5 years old were his target. He found Thailand to be fertile ground to invest in poor and indigent families, quenching his thirst for his predilection.

Russet was the go-to for child pornography in the whole of Europe and likely the world. He was known for distributing snuff films. Short movies of men having sex with kidnapped children in their preferred age group, and then killing them in the process. These babies were usually suffocated while being raped.

I had special plans to introduce Jacques Russet to my 11th crucifix.

Unlike the others in his club, Russet had escaped the wrath of the people in Lyon by using his power, money, and expert planning. Missing for years, Jacques was living on the outskirts of Lyon under the very noses of the local police and INTERPOL. Massive plastic surgery allowed him to walk around the community without being detected.

He didn't plan on John Deegan catching up with him. I, too, can spread money around like strawberry jam. And my planning was a hell of a lot better than his.

When I caught up to him, at about 9 p.m. in a not-so-nice motel where he awaited a made-up family that was bringing a three-year-old for his pedophilic penchant, it was nothing less than euphoric for me.

I gently tapped on the motel room door. Russet answered in a white linen shirt with the sleeves turned up past his elbows. Tight black leather pants and no shoes finished his kinky look.

I was disguised as a salt-and-pepper-haired country farmer in denim coveralls and a plaid, blue-and-white checkered work shirt.

I held a cap in my hands with my eyes cast down in a humble fashion.

"Where is the child?" Russet inquired as he looked over my shoulder.

"Please, may I see the money?" I replied, never looking up into his eyes.

He let me in and closed the rickety wood door behind me. Russet pointed to a brown envelope that was on the single bed.

"It's all there, five thousand euros. Now bring the child and pick him up in the morning as agreed.

Now, I looked into his eyes. My glare was intense. He backed up a few feet, his face filled with confusion.

"Those Euros will help at the orphanage in Lyon," I blurted.

Russet instantly realized it was a sting.

I lunged at his diminutive stature, smashing my left elbow into his jaw. He fell onto the bed like a sack of shit.

When he came to, I had him gagged and hogtied.

"Monsieur Jacques Russet, I have a question. Approximately how many children did you molest in your life? A thousand? Twelve hundred?"

Russet mumbled through his gag. His eyes were bulging from his head.

"I'm going with the over. Twelve hundred. And how many did you snuff out for the movies you made? Fifty-sixty?"

The room was filled with the smell of his fear, adrenaline, and gas.

"Now, I will dispatch you to hell where the devil will have his way with you."

I stood over the bed, hanging the cross over him so he could see it. I twirled it for a good 2 minutes. Russet was trying to scream for help to no avail.

I lowered the cross to just below his Adam's apple and inserted it slowly. A puff of air burst from the incision.

Slowly, I tore straight down to below his rising abdomen as his moans became louder.

"Stay quiet, Jacques. It will be over soon," I said.

I took a handful of his intestines and ripped them out, throwing the entrails onto his face. He tried weakly to shake the viscera off. No luck.

"For the sin of watching those poor kids being molested and some of them killed, I will now remove your eyes."

I poked the crucifix under his left eye. It popped out like opening a button. I went for his right eye, but his body began to convulse; in a minute, he was dead.

I was disappointed. I wanted to carve him some more.

CHAPTER 26

I discovered through my diligent computer hacking that Vic Gonnella and company were being deployed to Rome, Italy. Specifically, The Vatican. Deployed is a word we used back from my long-ago life in the military. Let's just say they were sent. Everyone and their brother, including that G.G. woman in the FBI. They were all under the impression I was going to try to assassinate the Pope.

Let me tell you why that was the furthest thing from my mind. There were several reasons. Firstly, to my knowledge, this pope never molested or had even been accused of molesting a child. It wasn't his fault that his predecessors allowed these pedophiles into the church, nor could he do very much about the current scandal.

Pope Benedict XVI sought to halt the decline of the church, largely due to the actions of deviant priests. He also wanted to make other significant changes, which the Curia opposed. Sure, he hid Father Hoffmann, and I'm sure many others, but that is what they all did and for a long time. I took care of that, Hoffmann, anyway.

Lastly, he was the leader of 1.2 billion Catholics

around the world. I wanted to gain the sympathy of the followers of Catholicism, not be the hated one for killing a beloved man. That realistically would never bring empathy to my crusade. I would be considered the scourge of humanity and be hated for eternity.

I had this sense that many people, when they found out the reasons why these pedophiles were dispatched, would understand why I did what I did. I could have eliminated only Catholic clergy; Christ knows there are plenty of them who stole the souls of the innocent. This is why I killed a rabbi, a coach, and the world would soon know of my 11th victim. A layperson.

The pope wasn't even on my radar. I had someone else in mind. Rome just happened to be the final destination of my mission.

✝

I always liked toying with people. I guess it was a result of being toyed with as a child. In the Bronx, we called messing with people's minds, breaking balls.

To break Vic Gonnella's chops (we called it that, too), I called him again after he arrived in Rome.

I was on my way to Rome when I made the call.

I welcomed Vic to the Eternal City. He wanted to know how I knew he was there. I skirted around Vic's question with a glib answer.

Vic told me they knew I would be in Rome to kill the Pope.

He said something to the effect that I had two crucifixes left.

I corrected his assumption, telling him I only had one crucifix left. I could hear his wheels turning after a silence.

I replied that the 11th crucifix was not used on a clergy member. All I knew was that my last 'target' was a pedophile.

Vic snapped at me, "So are you going to tell me, or do we play the 'Where in the world is John Deegan game?"

My reply was simple. The 11th crucifix was left in Lyon, France. I had stopped there after Munich.

Vic was taken aback.

Here is the rest of my conversation with Vic, to the best of my recollection.

"Why in Lyon?

"Very simple. There were a bunch of child molesters who were tried for doing all sorts of nasty things to kids here. Even little babies. There were sixty-two men and women pedophiles who raped, sodomized, and sold kids into prostitution. The people of France were outraged, as they well should be. The courts handed down a significant amount of jail time. However, one disgusting guy got away. Well, at least he thought he did anyway. He was one of the worst of the bunch, but played the hiding game well. Vic, sadly for him, he couldn't hide from me. God would never allow that to happen."

Vic asked. "You killed him and carved him up like some of the others?"

"No, not this time. The body of Jacques Russet is wrapped up nicely in brown and beige comforter along the Promenade du Bas Rhône. It's about two hundred and fifty yards away from INTERPOL headquarters. You would think they would have better security over there. I love breaking balls Vic."

"The eleventh cross?"

"Vic, I don't mean to correct you; it's a crucifix, and yes, it was my eleventh. Just one more to go."

Vic tried me. "I suppose you are after the pope. I also suppose you figured out that security will be tough to penetrate. You may get to him, but forfeit your life."

"My life was lost when I was a small boy, Vic. I think you know exactly what I mean."

"What do you mean by that?"

"C'mon, Vic. I figured you out a while ago."

Here's where I really hit a nerve. "You were also molested as a boy. We are in the same club. We wear the same badge of damaged emotions. Yours is larger than life."

Vic screamed at me, "Just cut that out, okay? My business has nothing to do with you and your killing spree."

I replied in a quiet, unemotional voice, "But it does, Vic. I read somewhere that one in five boys is sexually molested by the time they are eighteen. It's one in three for the girls. You are just not ready to admit what happened to you. I understand, and I feel sorry for you. Your life will not be right until you come to grips with what happened and work this out. Already one failed marriage, your kids have suffered, you are alone and unable to...”

“Shut the fuck up, Deegan. What should I do? Get some more crosses and start killing people like you? I may be damaged, but at least I’m not a madman,” Vic exploded.

“You’ve taken the first step to recovery, Vic. At least you haven’t denied that it happened. Well, at least not to me anyway. How about your wife? Did she know? What about that pretty cop lady?”

“None of your business. Are you?... how did you know about the?... You are very slick, Deegan.”

“No, just a genius. Pedophiles are slick. They know how to groom kids and take them from right under their parents’ noses.”

“John, stop this. You are wasting yourself. Surrender to me. You have already made your statement. There is much you can do to bring the awareness of...”

“Listen to me. One more and I’m done. I will go away, and you will never hear from me again. Then the legend of John Deegan will live on with anyone who thinks about sexually abusing kids. Maybe my church will figure out how to punish these people and work toward their own recovery. After all, who has died? Pieces of garbage, that’s who. I will be finished soon.”

“When?” Vic queried.

“I can’t say that just yet. I will let you know. But don’t assume it’s His Holiness. That’ll keep you very busy.

"I have to try to stop you."

"I know, but you can't. However, I shall give you a hint, because you are one of us. I'm not saying the pope is safe. You need to keep everyone on their toes. Now, the day after tomorrow is a consistory. There are just about two hundred and thirteen cardinals in their distinctive, red capes and hats. You guys can't protect all of them, so I will pick one to be my final intercession. Then I'm off to try to find some peace in my life."

I proceeded to tell Vic my mother had always dreamed of my being a cardinal. I wanted to finish my crusade with a man who wore a red hat. A hat that perhaps would have been mine.

CHAPTER 27

In my conversation with Vic Gonnella, the last thing I said to him was that he should take his pretty girlfriend outside his fancy hotel and show her the Bernini fountain. I wanted him to know I knew exactly where he was and that I was a step ahead of him.

Strangely, I had become very fond of Vic Gonnella. I felt like a father to him in a sense.

I knew Vic was vulnerable. Everything I learned about him, from our brief talks, from his slightly awkward, halting speech in news interviews, and especially from his personnel records, I copied from the NYPD files. Vic was damaged goods. Perhaps not as damaged as me or some other victims, but damaged, nonetheless.

Thinking many steps ahead, I knew that when I finished with my 12th crucifix and got away to Lugano, I would somehow form a relationship with Vic.

Vic contacted the lackeys at INTERPOL after our phone conversation and reported what I had told him. Sure enough, the local cops found the body of my 11th crucifix victim, Jacques Russet, pedophile extraordinaire, on the Promenade next to the river. The INTERPOLE clowns did not miss my insult to them with Russet's body found within a few hundred yards of their headquarters. Maybe I should refer to it as assquarters because they couldn't find Russet if he were in their cafeteria having café au lait and a croissant. He was in hiding for years. I found him in a matter of hours. Like they say, it's all in the knowing.

There was something I did to Jacques Russet's body that was different. I sliced off all his fingers just before I sent him to hell. The fish had a special snack, and my symbolism about not touching kids was not lost on G.G. at the FBI. I know Vic Gonnella figured that out as well.

CHAPTER 28

I was screwing with Vic Gonnella's head. Yeah, breaking his balls to the nth degree and enjoying it.

When I told him to take Raquel to see the fountain, Bernini's Tritone, next to the hotel where he was staying, the Bernini Bristol in downtown Rome, Vic did just that. I think he thought he would learn something, perhaps some clue I was giving. I was about to give him more than just a clue.

Vic and Raquel circled the Tritone. They were studying it closely, looking for any clues, maybe some Latin or Italian carved into the statue, I suppose.

After a while, I suppose they were tired or bored, so Raquel embraced Vic, giving him a long, lingering kiss. I suppose she found the setting romantic.

Suddenly, Vic looked around the square like he sensed something. All good police officers should possess those instincts.

There I was, standing to the left of the entrance to the Bristol hotel. I was disguised in the black priest garb and collar. Vic's eyes met mine. I smiled and waved at him. That kind of wave when you haven't seen an old friend. Vic hesitated for a few seconds, not believing his own eyes, before he started running toward me. Raquel followed. He yelled something at her that I couldn't hear from the noise in the Piazza Barberini.

I took off down the alley and quickly turned right at the next street, Salita di San Nicola da Tolentino. There must be agony somewhere in this as St. Nicholas of Tolentine Street, the high school I had attended in the Bronx and where that bastard Bishop Peroni and fucking Father Edward O'Gorman met with me. Ironic...

Was it planned, or simply a coincidence that this would be the street where Vic and Raquel would try to apprehend me? That will remain my secret.

I vanished into an apartment I had taken. I could peek from the window without being seen. Vic and Raquel ran up and down the street a few times. I heard Vic say, "Fuck" and "Son of a Bitch" and a few other choice expletives in sheer frustration. It was like the games of tag and ring-o-levio or manhunt we all played in the Bronx as kids, except I wasn't going to get caught.

I assumed Vic would have called the army of law enforcement, the Vatican police, the carabinieri, the Guardia di Finanza, or the Italian army that was behind him to do a block-by-block, building-by-building search to catch me.

He didn't. That has always perplexed me. Was it his ego that wanted to capture me himself? Did he want all the glory? Was it his distrust of the Italians? I think a combination of those, plus, and it's only conjecture, he wanted to beat me one-on-one, like a real man.

* † *

I'm certain, knowing that all knew that John Deegan, the international serial killer, was now in Rome with one more symbolic weapon to use, the Vatican police and the Swiss Guard were placing a blanket over His Holiness, the Pope. I laughably envisioned the pope hiding under his bed in the Apostolic Palace with ten nuns surrounding him. I had toyed with the idea of waiting in the long lines, taking a tour of St. Peter's Basilica and the Sistine Chapel disguised as an old man from Spain, but I had some plans to fulfill. Besides, too many ball-breaking moves could lead to disaster for me.

* † *

As I had planned with geometric precision, His Eminence, Francis Cardinal Galvin, would be in Rome. I had a date with him that he wasn't aware of.

Galvin and another Cardinal, Armando Silvestri, who just happened to be the papal nuncio to the United States, were to have dinner at one of the best spots in Rome, Santo Padre. Aptly named for the Holy Father.

Cardinal Galvin wore a St. Louis Cardinals windbreaker and a New York Rangers hat to disguise himself. The fat, red-faced fuck needed more than that.

The dinner was not to be. I waylaid Galvin. I'm good at stuff like that from the army.

I called the restaurant, telling the owner, in perfect Italian, that the Cardinal had been rushed to Gemelli Hospital with chest pains and that a driver would arrive to take Cardinal Galvin to his bedside.

The only thing I didn't say was that I, John Joseph Deegan, was the driver.

✝

I cannot remember having this much fun in my entire life. I could just imagine the pandemonium going on in the Vatican and within all the Italian law enforcement agencies. The local carabinieri, the Vatican police, the Swiss Guard, the Guardia di Finanza, and the rest. The FBI and INTERPOL were busy ordering cappuccinos. They were all shitting themselves that Galvin would be the next victim of the notorious serial killer John Deegan.

I had the good Cardinal Galvin tucked away nicely in my rented place around the corner from the Bernini Bristol, you know, the Tolentine Street, where Vic and company were staying.

I planned to have the cardinal in a somber ceremony to prepare for my discussion with him.

Now, I must give credit to Vic Gonnella. This is what he was taught in the streets of the Bronx and as a narcotics detective. Look where others aren't.

He painstakingly looked for a way to find where I was staying, around the corner from the Bristol, where I had let him see me the day before.

Vic was walking up and down the neighborhood looking for my hideout. Smartly, he felt the hood of the cars to see if any were still warm.

If it weren't for my ceremonious use of incense, Vic would have never found me. Vic simply followed the smell of incense. Brilliant if I may be allowed to say so myself.

I was getting ready to have a nice discussion with Cardinal Galvin. I bound and gagged his eminence, or should I say the pedophile protector.

Gonnella was like a wolf finding its prey.

The NYPD detective followed the aroma of incense to the apartment and picked the lock nicely. Every good detective carries a set of picking tools wherever they go.

I stood in the darkness, ready to pounce on the intruder. I saw it was Vic Gonnella. I couldn't think of anything better to say, so I offered:

"Nice to meet you in person, Vic."

The sound of my voice coming out of the darkened room made him jump just a bit. He had his gun drawn. I'm surprised he didn't fire at me in the dark.

Here is the rest of what happened:

"Deegan, listen to me carefully. Put your hands over your head. I will shoot you if you make any move that makes me nervous. Understand?"

"I'm not armed, Vic."

"Just do what I said, and you will see the morning."

I thought that was a very good New York City cop line.

I went out on a limb.

"Vic, now you listen to me. The cardinal isn't dead. He is drugged up a bit. When he comes to, he will likely start thrashing around like crazy. Don't let that trigger finger react and start pumping bullets around this small room."

"You just do what I said, or I will drop you now, Deegan."

"You will never shoot me, Vic. Put the gun down, and let's talk."

I turned the light on like a bold asshole.

Vic gloated, like a fool, "Don't kid yourself, Deegan. If I walk out of here with the cardinal and you are dead, I'm set for life, and you know it."

"You are much better off facing the demons that your abuser gave you and making a better life for yourself? That lady cop is very special, Vic." I blurted out.

"Leave my demons alone, Deegan. I will work that out another time."

"You mean work on them, Vic. You have many demons. Let's talk for a minute, then you can do what you want with me."

"I would rather you just shut up and walk toward me with both hands on your head."

"Don't tell me you weren't happy to see my work at St. Martin's. A priest killed like that in a confessional of all places. There had to be a part of you that felt vengeance, Vic."

"How did you figure that out?"

"Because you are a man, a human being who was attacked by a creep like that, as so many of us were. I know you stayed up nights, just thinking about how you could kill him if you could only get away with it."

"Mind reader? Magician? Genius? Or all the above?"

"No, just a victim. Just like you, pal. We are both victims. You chased me halfway around the world, but something deep inside you, something you can't even describe, is rooting for me. Correct?"

"Supposition."

"No, Vic, fact. You knew these people harmed kids, and you thought of how helpless you were. You got some satisfaction from what you saw, didn't you?"

"Why didn't you kill Galvin yet? You had enough time. Why is he still breathing?"

"I never planned on killing him. I got what I wanted already. He will now be more understanding of the feelings of people like us. He will listen more and remember that my mercy saved him. God's work has truly been done. You can arrest me now and be a hero and never tell anyone you were abused. You will continue to battle your demons and have a miserable, lonely life. I will do what I can from prison for the victims of sexual abuse, and then I will hang myself like my poor brother did."

Vic lowered his gun.

"I did tell someone. That pretty cop, like you call her and talk so much about, Raquel. I told her last night."

"On the road to recovery, Vic. You are on your way, kiddo. Life will be better, my friend. See, I'm already helping others overcome their terrors. Who said that God is not part of this?"

"Actually, I did. I abandoned God years ago. I thought God couldn't possibly exist if he could allow a person to be treated like that. And you're right, John; I was rooting for you deep down. I wanted you to do your twelfth cross and disappear just as you said you would."

Vic was almost crying.

"The cardinal is starting to stir. The drug has worn off. You still have time to be a hero, Vic. Arrest me, shoot me, or let me go. Whichever way, I am free."

"And if you go, what then?"

"I will live a life of ease in a faraway place. I plan to ask Gjuli, I know you remember her, I plan to ask her to come with me and be my wife. Now, I can finally be a man. A husband, a real husband."

Vic holstered his gun.

"John, get the hell out of here. Move; vanish. I found the cardinal, and you got away. Go fast." Vic wiped away his tears.

"Vic, I will always be there for you."

"No. You vanish. If I hear you have hurt anyone else, anyone at all, I will come and kill you myself. Got it?"

"Yes, I got it. Just one more piece of advice?"

"Yeah, c'mon, he's waking up."

"Marry Raquel. Have more children. Watch them closely."

I handed Vic the 12th crucifix and left.

CHAPTER 29

So now you know the true story of how I got away from a lifetime in prison. I killed eleven people on my crusade, was in the mouth of the lion, and the lion dropped me sort of like that Daniel and the Lion story in the bible.

Vic Gonnella had sympathy for me. He suffered immensely from being the victim of a pedophile, just as I had. It's a sort of club for the profoundly disturbed. A person who hasn't experienced that kind of abuse, feeling guilty, hopeless, where there is nowhere to turn, cannot even begin to understand how a victim feels. That's what makes these pedophiles so despicable. They feed off their victims' desperation.

* † *

Here I am, in Lugano, Switzerland, living in a gorgeous home with all kinds of servants, alongside Gjuli, the true love of my life, albeit delayed, and enjoying a luxurious, extraordinary life.

We named the house Villa Cielo. Cielo means heaven, and this place truly is that. I love the gardens. We have sub-tropical plants, purple rocket, Rose Salvia, and all the honeysuckle I ever wanted. Plus, dwarfed palm trees that I can look at for hours. We have two fountains, one located in the front and the other in the backyard. Most of all, I love the red slated tiled roof.

The interior has the best of modern Italian-designed furniture, which Gjuli wanted.

I spent a fortune on artwork from some of the best artists of our generation. Nowhere in the house are there any religious crosses, paintings, or statues. I just wouldn't have it.

* † *

Every day, I gaze at the magnificent, shimmering lake water and the breathtakingly stunning tree-covered mountains. One mountain in particular, Monte Bre, is my favorite. To Gjuli's dismay, and to her laughs, I called it Monte Tit because it reminded me of a big breast.

Life was splendid. Gjuli and I have the absolute best food you can imagine. Italian food has always been my favorite since being around Aunt Millie as a boy. In Lugano, we also had the availability of fine Swiss cuisine and hearty German fare. We have a great Italian chef, plus I cook from time to time, and Gjuli knows the Albanian recipes passed down from generation to generation without one written word.

Gjuli often makes great homemade pita and fabulous tasting burek. Burek is similar to pizza, with a variety of fillings. When I told her the Albanians learned to make Burek from the Turks, I thought she was going to get a pointed crucifix and stick it in my neck. Her roast lamb was sublime, but I couldn't eat the head or the eyes.

I still liked the big American breakfast with bacon, eggs, and home fries, or pancakes with tiny sausages, but Gjuli wanted me to stay healthy. Most days we have a cappuccino and some homemade baked sweet pastry or croissant. Boring but much better for me.

I wasn't a big drinker like my dad and my siblings. I don't think we ever had beer in the house, but Gjuli and I put together a great wine collection. Lunch and dinner, we always share a wonderful bottle.

Our driver brings us newspapers every morning. I still enjoy reading The New York Daily News and The New York Post, but since we couldn't obtain the actual newspapers, we have to settle for The New York Times and some Italian and British papers. I love doing the Jumble in the Daily News, but have to settle for the online version. There is something magical about folding a real newspaper in your hands.

Every now and then, I would come across an article about Vic Gonnella and Raquel Ruiz. I don't think he listened to my advice. I don't think he married her. These days, marriage is not a requirement for a couple. It's probably for the best in most cases, but who am I to say anything?

Vic is on a lot of TV interview shows talking about

pursuing one of the most prolific serial killers in history and getting to within an inch of capturing him. He is interviewing much better than when he was chasing me. No longer does Vic have that halting speech pattern and wide-eyed look while he is in front of the camera.

Occasionally, Raquel is on camera with Vic. She is stunning, dressed in figure-flattering designer clothing with elegant shoes.

After a short time, I read where they left the NYPD and started their own detective agency.

As the days turned into a couple of years, I found myself missing Vic and Raquel, as well as the chase. The rush I had knowing I was a half-step ahead of being caught was incredible.

There are times I wish I had decided to have 24 crucifixes instead of just 12. I don't have the urge or the itch to go kill pedophiles anymore. Been there, done that. My mission or crusade was satisfied, and I felt I had left at the top of my game like Ted Williams of the Boston Red Sox. He hit a home run in his final at-bat.

I was still being sought after by a lot of people, so I needed to be cautious. I always disguise myself when Gjuli and I go into town or across into Italy. Our brief weekend vacations to nearby Lake Garda, Lake Maggiore, and Lake Como were fun, and my disguises are bold, creative, and hysterical.

Once, a few people thought I was the British actor Sir Michael Caine. I was flattered beyond words. Gjuli thought I looked cute.

But after a while, I became bored. Gjuli sensed it, but she never said a word to me. She tried to fill our days with cultural activities, such as museums and movies. She invited some of her family to visit a few times, which was hysterical. I knew Gjuli was worried that I would take off again and probably be caught and sent to prison for life.

I passed time tracking what the Roman Catholic Church was doing about the pedophiles in their midst. Even though most people who followed my case started rooting for me, some people interviewed after I had disappeared into anonymity said they were glad I had gotten away, some hoped I would pop up again and kill their evil neighbor or boss. If a criminal or anyone else, for that matter, went missing, they were said to have John Deeganed. I was a cult figure to some and a thorn in the side of law enforcement.

Sadly, the Catholic church did little to nothing to curtail the pedophile activity among their priests. That burned me up like you can't believe, but I had hung up the sharpened crucifixes for good.

Some networks, like the History Channel and a few others, show documentaries about the infamous serial killer John Deegan. When I watched them, it was like they were talking about someone else. They showed the apartment building where we lived on Grand Avenue in the Bronx and the outside of St. Nicholas of Tolentine church, St. Martin of Tours, and stuff like that.

One of the broadcasts featured a few of my teachers from high school. They said how brilliant I was and how wonderful it was for them to have me in their class. None of them could even fathom the things that I had done. Vic and Raquel, of course, were interviewed. That G.G. of the FBI would not appear on camera, or if the truth be told, the agency would not let her. She is one strange puppy, that one.

So, now that I'm bored out of my mind, what am I going to do in the twilight of my life? Take up a hobby like golf? Start a stamp collection? Follow all the international soccer teams? None of this ever appealed to me, so I didn't think I would be fulfilled now.

Greater challenges would soon knock loudly on my door.

CHAPTER 30

Ever since I was a boy, I have enjoyed mimicking accents and refining the inflections of people I copied. I am pleased to say that I have perfected impersonations, transforming them into an art form. This goes along nicely with my various forms of disguise. I wanted to conceal my identity. Is there any wonder why?

I love languages and am proficient in six of them, especially Spanish. I often think in the languages I speak to keep my proficiency at a high level. I needed to practice being perfect.

I'm telling you this because I will be using my masquerades and language skills in the latter part of my life as I move outside my safety bubble in Lugano, Switzerland.

†

So, I made the first move and called Vic Gonnella on his cell phone.

Needless to say, he was shocked, but he masked his surprise with a smooth demeanor.

"I just wanted to check in and catch up a bit," I offered a bit awkwardly.

Vic's reply was curt, "That's what friends do, John. I hardly think we are friends."

I reminded Vic we had an incredible history together. He wasn't buying it at all.

Vic asked me what I was up to.

What the hell was I going to say to that question? I'm an old man living in the lap of luxury and in hiding from every law enforcement agency in the world.

I told him I was not happy seeing that even after my crusade, kids were still being abused and molested by clergy and others around the world. The Vatican, in my mind, was a criminal organization using secrecy, guile, and deception not unlike the mafia.

Vic's reply was direct and concise. "It's a cold, hard, harsh world, John. You did your thing. Now, it's time to move forward, don't you think?"

I told him I was getting bored and wanted to get back into the action. Vic reminded me of our deal. If I did any killings again, he would hunt me down, and this time, he would kill me.

Vic sounded annoyed.

"John, why the call after all this time?"

"I owe you my life, Vic. Well, my freedom anyway. I just wanted to say thank you for not killing or arresting me. Is there anything I can do for you in return?"

Vic asked me to be specific. I asked if he needed any funding to grow his company. Naturally, he declined. Vic and Raquel weren't looking for a partner. Especially the serial killer they had hunted over half the world.

I told Vic I had put aside trust funds for his two sons. His answer was very Bronxy, and he sounded pissed off.

"John, I'm not your friend. If I needed a friend, I would get a dog." I felt the pang of rejection.

That was me, breaking the ice call. I had other motivations in mind.

†

Sometime later, when my boredom had gotten the best of me, and at the risk of having Vic scream at me, I called him again.

Gonnella told me my calls were not welcomed. Can you believe that? He made millions on me, and he was now an international celebrity, and he didn't want to hear my voice. But, after all, I am a serial killer.

Making the conversation shorter, I told Vic I was feeling critically bored and needed a diversion. I basically asked him if I could be of service on any of his cases.

Vic said they were on a cold case. A cold case of an abused little boy. The hair on the back of my neck rose, right up my alley.

I said something like, "Vic, I want in. I can help you from here."

We went back and forth, and I could glean from the conversation that the cold case Vic and Raquel were working on was a very cold case, back to the late 1950s in Philadelphia.

I was off to the races. In my mind, I had a job!

I did a deep dive into the Boy in the Box case. I learned as much as I could about one of the coldest cases in American history. The Philadelphia Police Department, to me, clearly did the worst job of finding the killer of this young, nameless boy.

The PPD mainframe showed me how inept they were, back in 1958 when the murder occurred, as well as now. They are unorganized and amateur for a major city law enforcement agency.

After analyzing this case for a few days, I presented my findings to Vic and Raquel.

And I did this in person.

* † *

It was the first time I ventured out of the safety of my home. Gjuli was furious with me, but she knew there was no stopping me. No amount of yelling, crying, reasoning, or demanding would work for my dear wife. She felt, and naturally so, that I would be killed or, even worse, captured and imprisoned for the rest of my life in a Supermax prison.

Now, I must be totally honest with you and myself. I do love Gjuliana. I said it long before now. I always loved her, even when we were teenagers.

Perhaps my feelings of love have been affected by my abusers. No perhaps God dammit, they were.

My love for mental stimulation and action was stronger than my love for Gjuli. In a sense, my love for myself was greater than anything in this world. Tough thing to admit, don't you think?

I always felt an emptiness inside me. I loved the Catholic Church from the time I was a small boy. Or did I? Was I so programmed by my neurotic mother to adore Jesus, Mary, and the saints, and the priests and nuns? I think the answer to that is yes.

Father O'Gorman ripped that affection from me. Without a doubt, he stole my soul.

How else can it be explained that I entered the military and became an expert assassin and killer? And how else did I become the vengeful serial killer wanted all over the world?

I digress again.

I arrived at Teterboro Airport by chartered jet, carrying a bag of disguises, makeup, and phony voices to meet Vic and Raquel.

They knew I wanted to be involved with the Philadelphia cold case. But I felt they were humoring me and wanted to pick my genius brain to help solve this case. That was fair to me, but I needed to get my hands dirty. Not to kill anyone, mind you, but to be back in the trenches, to be back in the chase and break my boredom.

When I showed up as a street bum and approached this now-famous couple, Vic Gonnella and Raquel Ruiz, detectives extraordinaire, they had no idea it was me. Not at first, but they figured me out.

I was back in New York and felt the beat of the city again. My senses were once again alive.

Giving Vic and Raquel, on a silver platter, what they needed to solve this case was part of the challenge I gave myself. I used my brain and geometric logic to help solve the Boy in the Box case.

Later, in Pennsylvania, when I disguised myself as a bishop, I felt as if I were in a Broadway play, looking down on the activity and action.

Vic and Raquel solved the case. They knew they couldn't do that without my help, and the world would never get a whiff that John Deegan had a hand in solving the mystery of a child who was abused and murdered at the hands of his stepmother. There was no retribution here. The killer was long dead and buried. The satisfaction was seeing the poor child's name on his gravestone. I got plenty of satisfaction watching Gonnella and Ruiz and their detective agency getting all the glory and becoming even more famous.

Before it hit the media, I had returned to Gjuli in Lugano.

CHAPTER 31

A good amount of time passed. Maybe a year, perhaps a bit more.

I was back in the bosom of my wife, enjoying the peace and serenity of my lovely home in Lugano. For some reason, I wasn't at all bored like I was in the past. Perhaps returning to the United States and avoiding capture was enough stimulation for me.

I felt I still had my fastball. I was wrong. I could still play in the younger world. Wrong again. I felt age creeping up on me. I wasn't feeling well and hid it from Gjuli, although she would ask me if I was okay on a regular basis.

I blamed it on my past. There wasn't a day that I didn't ruminate over the heinous murders I committed for the sake of justice...and vengeance.

* † *

I went to see my doctor. They knew me by my new identity and new disguise. I was Giovanni DeLuca.

A few days later, I heard from my doctor. I asked our houseman to make coffee and serve biscotti on the veranda to Gjuli and me. It was the hardest thing I've ever faced in my life.

I told her I was sorry I took so many years away from her and sorry her childbearing years were behind her when we finally got together. I was not leaving an heir behind, but I never really wanted children anyway.

Stoically, Gjuli replied, "Tell me what you need to say, John. I know the news is not good. I am not without eyes and ears."

Then I dropped the news. The doctors had confirmed that I had pancreatic cancer. A death sentence.

The doctors informed me there were new treatments in Zurich. I was convinced my end was near.

Gjuli, in her loyal fashion, said she would be with me for every precious moment. She was strong. No wailing, no tears, just regrets.

"John Deegan, don't worry. We will face this demon together, and I will be with you every step of the way," Gjuli blurted.

Gjuli said she would pray, and I should pray too. My answer was almost comical, like gallows humor.

"Pray? Me? After what I did in my life? I'm positive God would laugh his ass off."

I lied again to Gjuli. I told her I needed to visit the pharmacy in Lugano for some prescribed medication and had some business to attend to while I was there.

I disguised myself as an Italian farmer and went to town. I did get the necessary drugs, but there was something else.

A week before, through an encrypted message, just like when I was in the military, through my banker, I received the following:

MUST MEET WITH YOU URGENTLY... IN LUGANO ON 22. NO DANGER TO YOU. 3 P.M. BLUE UMBRELLA PARCO CIVICO, ON LAKE. CONFIRM VIA THIS CHANNEL.

* † *

There was a calculated risk on my part. There was always the likely chance I was being set up. Maybe INTERPOL, perhaps the Americans, I thought. The person who wanted to meet with me went through great pains to do so.

Even though I was in neutral Switzerland and couldn't be extradited, there was the possibility I would be kidnapped and taken to Italy or elsewhere. Maybe I would be killed right here.

My papers showed me to be Giovanni Deluca, but I was John Deegan in the flesh. In my disguise, I didn't carry a firearm or my credentials with me anyway.

Sitting on a table, looking out at the lake, was a man I had recognized from photos and news interviews.

It was none other than Colonel Adrien Zellweger, the commander of the Pontifical Swiss Guard of the Holy See, the supreme protector of the pope.

He didn't recognize me at all. I was an elderly Contadina, a farmer, wearing the ragged clothing of a peasant worker, walking with a limp. I walked by without a second glance from the commander. I walked around for a few minutes looking to see if he had any backup. There wasn't any. I walked by again, this time changing my limp to the other leg. Only a trained man like Zellweger would pick that up. And he did.

He caught my attention and said he just wanted a simple chat with me. He said something to the effect that he had a big reach in Switzerland and knew I was in Lugano. I found that shocking.

"So why not just call me commander?" I asked.

His answer was startling, but I had a stone face. He said what he had to say was private between two men with a common goal. Common goal? My curiosity piqued.

The only goal I had at the moment was to go to Zurich for cancer treatment. I didn't know what he meant.

The colonel shocked me again by telling me he knew of my illness and my new identity. How in hell? This guy was good at what he did, excellent even. He informed me he had a plan. What the hell plan did he have that would involve a dying old man?

He continued. Zellweger said, "What you did to awaken the world during your murderous spree only worked for a short time. I'm afraid things have gotten worse," or something to that effect.

The commander went on to paint a bleak picture of the Catholic church. Pope Francis was doing nothing to stop what Zellweger called the pedophile playground. He said the homosexual priests were running the entirety of Catholicism, plus Pope Francis is ill and about to retire.

I wasn't at all surprised by this information, as I had been following the comings and goings at the Vatican. It was more of a mess than ever before in the church's long history.

I asked him a point-blank question,

"Do you expect me to sharpen more crucifixes and start slaughtering some priests again?"

The colonel had a plan to rebuild the Catholic Church, and he wanted me to be part of it. Zellweger wanted me to use my genius to make my mark in history for all the Catholics around the world. At this point in my life, I could care less.

Here I was, a sick old man with, what I thought at the time, not many months to live. How could this man have found me? I was very disturbed, but didn't show my concern to the colonel. Who else besides this religious zealot knew where I was? I thought my cover was impeccable. I did everything possible to avoid detection. I dotted every 'i' and crossed every 't'. There was no way now that I could disappear and start hiding in another place. I needed to try the so-called new treatment and extend my life. I was trapped. Now I knew for once, there were people smarter than me.

Zellweger wanted to eradicate the church and start from scratch. I could see in his eyes that he was a maniac. Here, I, a serial killer, am calling someone else crazy.

I was playing a game of chess with him. I went a couple of steps ahead of him in my mind.

What would stop him from taking out his pistol and shooting me on the spot if I tried to get up and walk away? Could I make a move to chole him out? Maybe a few years ago, but certainly not now in my weakened condition. Zellweger would be a hero for capturing and killing the crazed John Deegan. Certainly, with his position of power, the Swiss government would not prosecute him. On the contrary, he would get another metal.

I was in a stalemate. There was no choice.

"I will listen with interest. But I will make no promises," I offered.

CHAPTER 32

Zellweger's plan was diabolical. I let him wait a week before I told him I would work with him on his plan. I knew if I said no, he would send a team to kill me and Gjuli and anyone else who was in our home. I knew too much already.

✝

As the colonel said, Pope Francis retired due to health reasons. As an aside, I thought he was a good man, but I loathed socialists, of which he was one.

The cardinals from around the world were summoned to the Vatican to a conclave for ten days after Francis' retirement. There was still time for Colonel Zellweger to work his plan.

Zellweger's design was to gas nearly every cardinal of the Roman Catholic church while they sat in the Sistine Chapel to vote for the next pope. Only the elderly cardinals, those over eighty, would not be in the chapel. They weren't eligible to vote.

The colonel had plenty of time to plan, and all the access he needed to the chapel to complete his deadly task.

Zellweger thought I was with him. I instructed him how to position poison gas cylinders in the ventilation system of the chapel, and which gas to select. I had no intention of letting such a sinister event occur. I was playing along in the hope that my chess game would end in my favor.

* † *

Gjuli and I had checked into a cancer clinic in Zurich. My treatments were to start, and the countdown to my days left on earth would begin. I had no illusions about pancreatic cancer and its sure destruction of my body. Maybe the treatments would kill me more humanely than the cancer. I could only hope.

With all this going on, a defrocked ex-priest by the name of Emilio Caserta was found murdered in Central Italy. He was caught molesting kids. Then, a gay priest in Rome was murdered soon after that. And guess how they were murdered? Correct, with a sharpened crucifix sticking out of the carotid artery. A classic John Deegan killing.

Someone, some moron copycat was trying to pick up where I left off. Or someone was trying to set me up as the murderer. I was pretty sure I knew who was setting me up. I didn't need to be a genius to figure this one out.

Unbeknownst to me, Vic and Raquel were coming after me. Vic meant what he said about finding me and killing me if I started my murder spree again. These Bronx Italians were not all talk.

Here is when Vic Gonnella took on my fraudster, fake, phony persona. Vic and Raquel pretended to be someone else. Somehow, the dynamic couple found me at the clinic in Zurich.

The next thing I know, in my weakened condition, I was introducing my dear wife to Vic and Raquel at the clinic. It turned out to be lovely. Vic asked me a few questions about the priest murders. I only knew of one. Vic filled me in on the second killing.

Vic Gonnella believed me when I told him I had nothing to do with these two dead priests. There was no way this old, decrepit bastard could have done these two priests. Vic had figured that out on his own.

* † *

To make a long story short, my treatments were started. I was feeling pretty good. Those Swiss doctors mean business. I had to beg them to let me go to Rome for a few days. They relented after I agreed to make daily trips to see a colleague at the Agostino Gemelli University Policlinic in Rome. Ironically, this is where the popes go when they are ill.

Gjuli and I then went to Rome.

The Conclave was about to begin. I designed the gas cylinders, the ones Zellweger, his dreaded associates, and a guy who called himself John Deegan were going to install in the sub-basement of the Sistine Chapel. I was amazed to learn that the first Conclave to vote at the chapel was in 1492. I love history. The antiquity of this place enthralled me, but at that moment, the danger took precedence.

It was Zellweger who had killed these two priests. Go to find out, he killed them both with his own hand, but that information came much later.

You see, Zellweger was brilliant. He didn't get to his position in the Swiss Guard for nothing. He figured out, using master chess player moves, either the cancer would kill me, or law enforcement would do the job. He was ready to tell them where I was at the appropriate time. John Deegan would be out of his way. The old double-cross at play.

With John Deegan dead, Zellweger could blame me for killing the cardinals at the Sistine Chapel with his agent of death. Deadly hydrogen cyanide gas. Which was my suggestion to the colonel.

Now, at the moment of truth, when the head cardinal kicks everyone out of the Sistine Chapel and the Conclave begins, Zellweger was dramatically in the sub-basement, ready to turn the switch which would release the poison gas and kill all the cardinals. Case closed. There would be no white smoke in St. Peter's Square. The Roman Catholic

Church would now be in the hands of Zellweger and other sickos.

I was a few feet behind him. Well, it wasn't me per se. I was disguised as a worker in the chapel. A really good disguise, if I may brag a bit.

Zellweger turned the switch, and the gas hissed from the valves.

This is where I almost wet my pants from laughing.

No choking, no screaming, no moaning from upstairs in the chapel. What we heard was laughter. Waves of silly laughter. It sounded like a college frat party.

I stood in front of the colonel, who looked dumbfounded. He was stone-cold quiet. I went off on him.

"Colonel, I knew you were fucked up the moment we met on the shores of Lake Lugano. I just didn't realize to what extent."

Zellweger tried to open his mouth to speak. He sensed I had beaten him at his own game of double-cross.

I'll never forget exactly, word for word, what I said to the colonel.

Protossido di azoto, gas esilarante. Nitrous Oxide you stupid fuck. It's also known in some places as laughing gas. There is just enough gas in these containers to get these old men a little high and remove any anxiety they may have. Some of them will laugh their asses of for a few minutes while some will take a quick nap. The worst these fucks will feel is a bit confused.

I put the laughing gas into the cylinders myself.

The world would never know the cold-blooded murderer John Deegan, the hated anti-Catholic sicko, had saved the Catholic church from chaos and perhaps worse.

At any rate, I needed to get back to the Swiss clinic to let those doctors have their way with me.

Perhaps God, Jesus, Baby Jesus, The Holy Ghost, and whomever else is power would see to it that one of their assholes, John Joseph Deegan, would get to live a bit longer and do some other work.

CHAPTER 33

Well, I beat pancreatic cancer thanks to God, Gjuli said, and the great oncologists in Zurich. I was grateful only to the science.

The five-year survival rate for cancer of the pancreas is about 13%. Unless there is metastatic cancer, then it drops to 3%. My odds were not good, but when I left the clinic, I was cancer-free. I was pretty much ready for the casket to be honest.

Gjuli said I was given a second chance at life. There was no way she was going to let me out of her sight, so it seemed my galivanting around the globe to continue my chasing of real bad guys was coming to an end.

I watched Vic Gonnella and Raquel Ruiz from a distance as their company, Centurion Associates, grew into an internationally recognized private investigation and security firm based in New York City, with offices in Europe. I'd like to think I played a significant role in their success. There goes my runaway ego.

Look, they chased me all the way from the Bronx to Europe, where I had escaped by the skin of my teeth. No one except me, Vic and Raquel knew what really happened. Vic could have easily taken me in or put a bullet in my brain. He let me go.

Then there was that case in Philly where I handed it to them on a silver platter. Then there was the Vatican incident involving that maniac zealot Zellweger. Vic and Raquel got credit for that one, too.

It had been years since the Vatican thing. Gabriella Gonnella was born.

Vic and Raquel had become wealthy, but I still set aside enough money for Gabby in a trust fund, ensuring that she and five generations of her heirs would never have to worry about financial concerns. Flying private jets wasn't the only benefit of having big money. I had come to love these people. Besides, who was I going to leave my billions to? The Catholic church? The Boy Scouts? Some Yeshiva in Brooklyn?

I had taken care of Gjuli's future and her Bronx Albanian family as well. They were not just on the dole. I arranged for them, through a blind LLC, to own ten apartment buildings in the Bronx. They still had to work the properties and new landlords, and they loved it.

Vic and Raquel were now in a position to pick and choose the major cases they wanted to be involved with. Their fees were extraordinary, and they deserved it. Can you imagine two Bronx cops, counting hours and working toward their pension, had become multi-millionaires? Only in America, as they say. I was proud of their success and how I brought them to it.

I was feeling great, even young again, since I dodged the cancer bullet. I was eating right, taking long walks, and doing some light exercise, and enjoying my home and my wife. I enjoyed my home and relaxing.

Boredom crept in with its unrelenting, nagging demands. Despite Gjuli and her mandate that I was to stay put, I found I felt smothered, a prisoner in Switzerland. This is what happens to a normal man, let alone a genius.

I had to get back in the game, and the diversion for me was to do something with Vic and Raquel. I missed them enormously, and I wanted to meet Gabriella.

* † *

I saw my opportunity to use my brain following Vic and Raquel on their mainframe.

They were hired by Dominican Republic bigwigs to help solve a case in their resort town of Punta Cana.

There was a killer, yes, a serial killer taking our Venezuelan chicas. Chica means girl in Spanish. It also means prostitutes. Whoever was killing these chichas had a serious problem. And whoever it was was very good. A few murders occurred, with no clues left behind. The local cops and the national police were hopelessly lost.

Vic and Raquel brought Gabriella and her grandmother, along with a tutor, to Punta Cana, thinking it could be a working vacation for the family.

They never expected John Deegan to follow.

†

Vic and Raquel were at a fancy dinner in Punta Cana. She looked like a movie star; he looked like James Bond. The couple that the paparazzi loved to follow.

Here is where I had some fun.

Later that night or in the morning, I can't recall exactly when, I called Vic on his cell.

"Vic, you both looked great at the gala," I said, or something like that.

Vic called bullshit.

I told him he really enjoyed the Peking duck. He lost it.

I told him I was disguised as one of the servers. He lost it again.

Now I played a bit with him.

"I never expected you to apprehend this killer in less than a week. As an old friend and advisor, I must tell you that the killer is right under your nose."

"Stop wasting your time on the dentist of the chicas. He's not the killer," I informed.

Vic said I didn't know shit and reminded me of what he said in Rome. I am not his friend. A bit insulting, but I get it. I'm still a serial killer when you peel back the nice guy wrapper.

Aside from the weird dentist. they had another potential killer by the name of Lenny. A real sex disgusting degenerate. He had a habit of roughing up the chicas.

"Oh, Vic...Lenny ain't the guy neither," I said in my Bronx accent.

Vic gave in. He said something like we have worked well together. He was softening.

"So, I guess I have a job?" I stated.

"Who said anything about a job?" Vic hollered. He lost it again.

I had already decided on who the killer was. I needed some surveillance of the home where my supposed killer lived.

I disused myself as a photographer from an Irish magazine. Brogue and all. I bought a couple of expensive cameras and got the shots I needed. They would come in handy later.

* † *

After about 2 or 3 more Venezuelan chicas were found murdered, mostly all in the same fashion, a terrible thing occurred.

Some hot-shot, low-life Dominicans decided to kidnap Gabriella. They captured the child and her tutor. A young woman named Theresa.

Big mistake.

I will admit my heart was in my mouth, but I knew they wanted money, of course. The young child of rich American parents. A good opportunity to earn a stable income that would last for ten years in the

Dominican Republic. They could care less about the hookers being killed.

Vic and Raquel were insane. I was already insane, so what the hell? Vic blamed himself for bringing his daughter on the trip. I couldn't blame him for feeling that way. I assured Vic and Raquel I would bring Gabriella back, safe and sound.

Now I went into Deegan genius overdrive.

My hunches were usually good. This time, my intuition was spot on.

I went to the worst neighborhood near Puna Cana, in a town called Bavaro. It took some time and a few bucks, but I found one of the kidnappers.

I took this hapless bastard; he turned out to be a sergeant of the police who was working with us on the murders. I bound and gagged him, took him out to the forest, and reasoned with him. If you believe I reasoned with him, you are sadly mistaken. I tortured the prick. It took me some time, but he eventually rolled over on his pals. I don't care to remember if it was before or after he shit himself.

I now had an address. There were four of them in total, including the now-deceased sergeant, whom I dispatched when I received the information I needed. Yeah, I made a deal to free him, but I had lied. I'm a bad man. But I slit his throat neatly and quickly.

I had the address where Gabby and her tutor were being held captive. I disguised myself again as a local. With my Spanish, I jumped into a Dominos game with a group of old men across the street from the house where the bad guys were held up. I let the old domino players win.

I was able to watch the house closely for a bit. Then I pounced. The three villains were taken out in John Deegan, the special ops specialist, fashion. There are a few things you learn in life that you never, ever forget.

I was scratching at the back door as a cat or dog would. I scratched a few times until I heard a voice.

"Go see what that is."

Some guy walked to the peeling, paint-starved, wooden door, looked out the door's window, and saw nothing. I then reached my hand around, scratching low at the door.

The idiot criminal pulled open the door, saw nothing, and stepped out into the decrepit yard for further investigation.

I then sprang on him, pulling the criminal by his arm onto the ground. Without thinking twice about it I slit the guy's throat, severing his jugular vein in a spray of blood. He was dead without making a sound.

Then I saw Theresa, Gabby's teacher. She lay on a mattress, nodding off next to the sleeping Gabby. I put my hand gently over her mouth, she tried to scream, and I whispered some reassuring words to her.

"Stay very quiet, young lady. I'm here to help you. I'll be a few minutes. Don't stir, Gabriella."

Theresa nodded her head.

I moved silently toward the next room. Long, multi-colored beads on the door separated the two rooms.

One of the bastards was playing a mindless game on his cell phone, the third gangster was asleep on a ragged sofa.

I moved quickly through the beads. The guy tried to jump to his feet. The element of surprise worked wonders. I stuck the long, thin knife I had used on the guy in the woods into the thug at the base of the back of his skull.

There was a familiar feeling of a man's body trembling through the blade. His spinal cord was severed, and he fell dead into a heap onto the bare, wooden floor. I slowly wiped the blade on his shirt.

The third goon never stirred. I moved deliberately toward the chair while he slept. This was the only time I spoke during this piece of work.

"Cuno, rise and shine, sleeping beauty, I uttered.

When he tried to stand, I tore out his thorax with a circular motion of the blade, which had killed all four of the kidnappers.

Needless to say, Gabriella was back with her parents that day. Theresa too. A bit hungry and dehydrated but unharmed.

But I must share with you the moment I let Vic and Raquel know Gabby was safe. I handed a new phone I picked up along the way to Gabby. The conversation went something like this:

"Hi daddy!"

"Gabriella? Baby! Oh my God! Where are you?"

"I'm in a car with Miss Theresa. We are coming home.

"What car? Whose car?"

"Your friend, John. Here, hold on, he wants to talk to you."

"Vic, all is well. She is unharmed, as is Theresa."

Raquel could hear the conversation. I heard her cry out.

"Jesus Christ, how? How did you find her? Where was she?"

"That's a story for another day. I did have to break a promise I made, though,"

"Promise? What promise?"

"You have so many questions, Gonnella. We will be back within the next twenty minutes or so, then I must run out and tend to some unfinished business."

"Oh my God! I...I don't know what to say!"

"Just tell your cook to make some chicken fingers or whatever kids eat these days. Gabby is famished. Get some ice cream, too. Ice cream is comfort food, ya know. Theresa says hi."

I dropped Gabby and Theresa outside the White House, where Vic et al were staying. I drove away quickly.

That was so much fun.

* † *

My sixth sense told me to get out of the Dominican Republic.

Vic kept trying to call me. I finally answered from the veranda of our home in Lugano, with Gjuli sitting next to me. It took her an hour to stop yelling at me.

"You're back in Switzerland?" Vic screamed.

I told him how beautiful it was looking out at the lake. I put Vic and Raquel on the right track to find the killer of the Venezuelan girls.

I felt like the lion who takes the cubs out to teach them how to capture their prey for food.

Naturally, I was right about the surprise killer.

CHAPTER 34

Throughout much of my life, I have had flashbacks. I don't mean just a tiny thought that ran through my head.

I'm referring to vivid recollections with vivid colors, sounds, and tastes. The flashbacks were real. I would be sent back in time and recall every detail as if I were there.

I suppose they are like seizures. No warning, no advanced indication that the remembrances were coming, and nothing could stop them. They just happened. It was as if I were in a trance.

One minute I would be doing a billion-dollar deal in my business, then wham...a flashback would hit, and I was done for. They didn't last very long in real time, but in my mind, the episode could be for hours.

The people who worked for me could see it in my face and covered for me brilliantly. They would pick up where I left off and let me return as if nothing had happened. Interestingly enough, my associates would never ask me about why I suddenly went blank. I suppose it was their way of working with the genius. Who knows.

Luckily, the remembrances didn't come very often, but when they came, they showed up with a vengeance. I never went to see a medical doctor, a neurologist, or a psychiatrist. I probably should have gone to all of them.

One of my recurring flashbacks was when I was in the second grade, around the time that Father O'Gorman was molesting me.

I was in class at St. Martin of Tours School, in the first row, first seat. The sicko I had for a nun was a real segregationist. Your seat was determined by your grades. Of course, being the chosen one, the student most likely to enter the clergy, I had the first position in the class.

The first row was mostly Irish kids like me, save one Italian boy. In my evocation, I could see all the students. Mary Anne Kelly was behind me, then Nancy Boyd, Elizabeth Mc Mann, Joseph La Russo, and finally Richard Atwell.

The girls all wore their blue and white St. Martin of Tours pleated skirts, featuring the SMT insignia on the left front of their uniforms. The boys wore dark blue pants, white shirts, and a SMT embossed blue tie.

Those of us who were in the first row were the smartest kids in the class and the most envied of all the kids. The second row consisted almost entirely of A students. Solid B's with the possibility of moving into the first row with hard work and prayer. They had a somewhat better chance of being acknowledged as bright pupils.

The third row was relegated to the C students. Mostly cut-ups and the most likely to get smacked around by the looming nun, who seemed to enjoy the corporal punishment.

The fourth row was some C students, but mostly they had borderline D grades. They were hopeless. They could work their way into the solid B students, but it is highly unlikely. Most of these kids were immigrants and first- and second-generation Italians. Some spoke broken English.

The D row was the row of the helpless and hopeless. They were the most likely to be expelled and sent to the island of public school, also known as the devil's island. They were mainly Puerto Rican, and a few black kids.

So, I was the academic and religious leader of the class. The two girls sitting directly behind me were blonde-haired, blue-eyed lassies. Their mothers were very involved with the church, particularly with the Holy Rosary Society or the Sacred Heart of Jesus Guild. Paul La Russo's father was the local undertaker and poured money into various church charities, tipping the priests well for the funeral masses they performed. LaRusso was no more intelligent than the kids in the C row, but money talked. Richard Atwell's mom was a dame of the church. All the priests and nuns loved her because her brother was a Jesuit priest.

This particular flashback was interesting, if not bizarre. But it was as true as my name is John Joseph Deegan.

We sat at attention, waiting for our report cards to be distributed. The nun had the tan 4X6 inch cards, in order of our seat assignments, double wrapped in a rubber band.

We were all waiting, our hands folded in prayer with our palms together and our fingers pointed up to heaven, in absolute silence.

Father O'Gorman would arrive any minute to hand out the good news for some and the bad news for others.

Sister sat at her desk in the front of the room, fingering her huge set of black rosary beads, which were wrapped around her waist like a pious belt.

The front door to the classroom was closed. In the silence of the room, the growling stomachs of some of the kids who didn't have breakfast could be heard.

Abruptly, the door swung open and was filled with Father O'Gorman in his black priest's outfit and black cape. He wore his angry game face. He also wore a four-cornered black hat that was slightly askew.

Sister rose quickly from her desk and would immediately hit the clicker she kept in her hand. When the priest entered the classroom, the clicker went off, and we all stood. She clicked it again, and we all knelt on both knees. O'Gorman then dramatically surveyed the students. He blessed us in Latin with a quick sign of the cross. We all blessed ourselves. The nun clicked again, and we rapidly returned to our seats.

Sister removed the rubber band and handed the report cards to the snarling priest.

His face suddenly turned to a wide, toothy smile.

He held the cards in his consecrated hands like they were some sort of religious icon.

"John Deegan. Come in front of me, John. Hmm, let me see," the priest announced. He proceeded to read every A on my report card. They were all A's, both front and back, for the actual grades by subject, and then to the rear of the card for behavior issues.

"Excellent. Perfect once again, John. Tell mother I'll be around to see her."

He handed the card to me and winked. We both realized the wink was meant for our secret.

"Mary Anne Kelley, front and center."

The little girl went up to the priest. She curtsied.

He read Mary Anne's grades as he did mine.

"You have certainly made your family proud, Mary Ann. Please tell your parents I said today's Mass for the repose of your grandmother's soul."

He went down the first row with more of the same. Smiles, congratulations, and a personal message to the parents.

My stomach went into knots because I knew what was coming after row B.

Row B was much of the same, except, "Sister tells me you can do better. We are expecting improvement by next grade period." Or "You have trouble in arithmetic, I see. Work harder."

Row C was devastating. O'Gorman was no longer smiling. The nun was wringing her hands in a circular motion with almost a strange, sadistic smile on her Dominican habit-encircled face.

There was only one girl in the C row. She didn't get smacked around. Just chastised for not keeping her mind on her work. The priest ridiculed her for her unkempt appearance. Her uniform was not ironed properly. Her face went from pale to scarlet in seconds.

The boys were a different story.

O'Gorman would butcher the Italian names badly. I'm certain it was intentional. Romano would be Ramayna. Ferrara would be Fenada.

As he read the letters on the report card, mostly C's a couple of D's, the hopeless boys would be standing in front of the enormous black enveloped priest. O'Gorman's right hand flew from under his cape to a flurry of hard, open-handed face smacks.

Red-faced from the blows and the embarrassment, the boys, heads bowed in shame, wobbly returned to their seats.

Sister what the Fuck was almost orgasmic. She loved the brutality. I felt so bad for these kids that I would almost cry. It was terrible. My stomach was in knots.

The D row was an atrocity. For one poor kid, a dark Puerto Rican named Pedro Diaz, O'Gorman rained blows upon him, practically following the helpless child back to his desk while he beat him.

The nun was giddy with pleasure.

When he handed a Puerto Rican or black student their report card, the look of disdain on his face was obvious.

After the last face-smacking, sweat ran from the priest's hat down his face. Sister offered him a napkin and a cold glass of water.

As O'Gorman started to leave, I had a prearranged job to do.

"Father O'Gorman, may we have your blessing?" I uttered.

"Of course, John."

The nun clicked again. We stood. Clicked again, we knelt. O'Gorman, this time in an exaggerated flourish, blessed the happy A and B row students as well as the wounded C and D row kids.

O'Gorman was off to terrorize the next class.

The now-moist nun shut the door behind the pedophile priest.

Sister turned to the C and D row and with a reddened face announced:

"You've embarrassed me for the last time!"

There were several other repetitive flashbacks.

Another flashback was from one of the earlier grades. It could have been first or second grade. I don't remember right now, but I'm guessing it was the first grade.

Polio was a scourge of children. I remember kids in leg braces and seeing some in iron lungs. Any still water, like a puddle in the gutter, we called polio water.

The injections were given at school.

A doctor, dressed in a dark suit and tie, and a nurse, wearing a white hat and uniform, were stationed at a desk in one of the classrooms. The nuns lined up each class, by size, outside the room. The boys all had to raise their white shirts above the elbow. One at a time, the nuns would make us enter the room alone. While waiting my turn in the hallway, I remember my knees shaking so badly I thought I was going to collapse into a heap on the floor. A few of the girls did just that. They fainted away in the hallway or when they got to the doctor. Most of the nuns were not at all understanding. My nun, Sister Jarlith, was the best. She leaned down and whispered to me, "Now, John, just count to ten and it will be all over before you reach ten."

When I was sent into the room, my entire body was shaking.

I remember seeing the needle as the doctor drew the vaccine from the small vial. It was a long glass tube with a needle that looked as long as half a 12-inch ruler. The nurse put a cotton ball on my arm, and I could smell the alcohol. The doctor then took my arm and lowered the needle. I looked up at the crucifix on the wall and counted to ten, out loud. I didn't hurt as bad as I imagined but it hurt like a son-of-a bitch later. And it itched like crazy. Back in class, when all the kids were scratching their arms, the head sister would come in and remind us all not to scratch. She said we should think of the suffering Jesus had on the cross. What a morbid fuck she was.

I need to rest now because this memory talks a lot out of this old man. There were many more.

CHAPTER 35

As I'm sitting here in Lugano, looking at the lake and Mount Tit, enjoying the scent of roses and honeysuckle when I was hit by those flashbacks.

This time, they came in a collage of memories.

The smell of Father O'Gorman's alcohol breath and rancid body odor as he kissed me. The feeling of his large, wet tongue in my mouth would make me gag to the point of vomiting.

Then there were the treacheries of Sister Lauranteen. My fourth-grade teacher, whom I am convinced today learned torture techniques from the Japanese of World War II.

Sister Lauranteen had a pretty, almost angelic face, which was encased in a white tunic, a white scapular, a black veil, and a black cappa. When this obscene nun went into hurt little boys' mode, her face and eyes turned into evil personified. The transformation occurred daily. There was never a warning.

Whatever the boys in class did, whether it was forgetting to bring the weekly envelope to mass with a donation on Sunday or pushing another student during recess, this maniacal man-hater would make the boys raise their pant legs above their knees and kneel on uncooked Uncle Bens converted rice. The rice was poured in two neat dollops on top of the terrazzo marble floor.

Sister Satan, as we called Lauranteen, for other minor indiscretions, would make the boys hold out their hands, palms up, while she went from over her shoulder with a wooden pointer and would whip it down on the poor kid. If the student pulled his hands away, which is a normal instinct, he would get two additional shots.

I, being the best student in the entire grade, and the most compliant as well as the chosen one for the priesthood, of course, never felt this maniac's wrath. She looked at me with adoration, like when she saw a photo of Pope Pius XII.

Another of the group of flashbacks was the nun who lined every student up by size in the darkened hallway before anyone could enter the class first thing in the morning. Her objective was to determine who did their homework assignments the night before. Naturally, my fellow first rowers and I were hustled into the room because we always did our homework. For those who didn't do the work, usually the C and D row victims were lined up on the opposing wall like the Nazi's lined up people about to be shot. When she finished, the condemned were marched into the stalag, sorry, the classroom, and felt the sting of the nun's pointer on the back of their legs. Three shots each. I couldn't watch. I, the guy who untimely became a killer in the army and a serial killer in civilian life, could not look at this abject brutality.

I recalled the one nun, I can't see her face in the flashback, who would drag her male victim by his upper lip or by his sideburn up to the blackboard to do an arithmetic problem. If the hapless child made a mistake, she would smash his head against the blackboard, usually leaving a stain of the Vitalis or other grease they used in their hair. (I always had a crew cut until high school). To add insult to injury this snake with tits would call on one of the A row students who would finish the arithmetic in seconds. The poor student was ridiculed in front of the entire class.

Is there any wonder that children from my era, who attended parochial schools in the inner city, when they were able to make a choice, stopped attending church? Between the pedophile priests, the corporal punishment, the demand for money, which most of the famines didn't have, and the guilt they imposed on us every day, why would we look to Catholicism for any comfort?

My generation went from the Mickey Mouse Club and Andy's Gang to Zoloft and Xanax in twenty years.

I awoke from this flashback, soaked in perspiration and shaking.

CHAPTER 36

Maureen Deegan, my devout Catholic mother, thrust me into the church like a pile driver.

There was never a doubt in her mind that I would be a priest, a preacher of Christ, her Lord and Savior.

Mom also pushed the Catholic guilt, which apparently, she had suffered as a child, upon me.

For years, I had lived with the guilt that Father O'Gorman and later Bishop Peroni had sexual relations with me. I never thought it wasn't my fault.

The day I slaughtered O'Gorman in his confessional was the last day I allowed guilt to smother me the way it had.

Through all the torture and killing I committed in Special Ops, through all the notches in my belt as John Deegan, the serial killer of people who have harmed children, right up until today, where I have killed those who deserved their lives to end, I only have guilt in one aspect of my life.

That is the shame I have about how I affected the life of Gjuliana Bashkimi, now my wife.

Gjuli came into my world sometime during my freshman year at Tolentine High School.

Most of the girls at Tolentine back then were cutesy, freckle-faced Irish teens. Some had the Kennedy family high foreheads and gummy smiles. Others had a washed-out look, putting them in the hands-off category for 99% of the boys.

In my homeroom class, Gjuli walked in with our assistant principal. Her family just came to the United States, being helped to expatriate by the Roman Catholic Church. In her hands were a notebook and a Bic ballpoint pen. Gjuli, with a very foreign name, wore the Tolentine blue pleated skirt, which fell well below her knees, a pair of white socks that went a little past her ankles, and a worn-out pair of brown loafers.

I had never seen, with my own eyes, a girl as beautiful as Gjuli. My mouth hung open like the clown face at the mini-golf park.

Most of the girls I had seen in school and in the neighborhood were blonds, except for a couple of Italian girls at St. Martin of Tours elementary school. Most of the Tolentine girls could have been models for Air Lingus. Blond, what we called dirty blond, or light brown hair with smooth, rosy complexions, was the norm.

I had never heard of Albanians until that day in 1964. Sometimes my mom used to say to us before we ate dinner, "You look like a bunch of starving Armenians." She was referring to the genocide in the early 1900s when the Turks tried to wipe out an entire race of people. I'm sure she had learned that phrase from her mother or grandmother.

I quickly learned the difference between the two nationalities. Albanians, as I would find out, were a different sort of people I had ever encountered.

Gjuli's piercing, large, dark eyes and her brown flowing hair complemented her olive skin. Although she should have been apprehensive or even nervous entering a new school mid-semester, Gjuli looked almost elegant when she entered the classroom. She walked in with her head held high, with perfectly erect posture. There was an air of confidence I had never seen in a girl before.

I wasn't much into checking out girls in those days. Remember, I was being sodomized and I had no real sexual urges like a usual thirteen- or fourteen-year-old boy. I did notice that Gjuli looked more like a grown woman than the mostly flat-chested Irish girls at Tolentine.

Gjuli spoke no English except a few words like hello, goodbye and good.

Her father, Sokol Bashkimi, was from Kelmend, Albania, a Catholic stronghold. I learned later that the Turks (those dreaded people), back in the 1400s, forced the mostly Catholic Albanians to become Muslim. Most Albanians capitulated and converted. Those who didn't, under threat of horrible economic sanctions pushed upon them, were staunch Catholics for hundreds of years.

Gjuli was now in a school where only English was spoken and there were no tutors in those days. Naturally, being the brightest in the school by a few points, I was asked to help Gjuli learn English and hopefully assimilate into American culture. I must say, the project challenged me.

Teaching her English was easy; she is very bright. Assimilation was another thing. Nearly impossible with her Albanian culture and rules, which are steeped in the long-ago past.

Gjuli and I were together constantly. I helped her learn English and improve her reading skills. We would spend hours together after school, but I wasn't allowed to walk with her on Fordham Road to Davidson Avenue, where she lived, just a block from where I lived.

Her unfriendly-looking father and brothers would have gutted me like a lamb.

As we got to know each other, I can tell you that, without a doubt, Gjuli wanted to kiss me on many occasions. She had this look in her eyes that beckoned me to come close to her.

I was not inclined to do any of that. I wasn't sure if I was a homo because of the abuse I was suffering. I guess I was asexual at that point, which I was for the greater part of my life.

Gjuli would sneak out of her apartment on weekends. She lied to her mother, telling her she was studying with friends at school. Gjuli would come to The Aqueduct and sit there for hours upon end watching me play handball or basketball. Whenever I glanced over at her, those big, dark eyes would be looking at me and only me.

As time progressed, Gjuli was smitten and in love. Everyone at Tolentine thought we were boyfriend and girlfriend. If you saw John Deegan, there was Gjuli Bashkimi.

I had zero sexual urges toward Gjuli. I had no yearnings at all. If I got an erection at night in my bed, or when I woke in the morning, it wasn't because I was thinking about Gjuli. It was only a physiological reaction. I would concentrate on my statue of St. Michael the Archangel on top of my dresser or the hanging wooden crucifix on my bedroom wall. I prayed the erections away.

My senior year, when Gjuli and I had turned eighteen, I knew exactly how she felt about me. Gjuli told me she was deeply in love with me and wanted to take the next steps. I was petrified. I didn't have the same feeling about sex as she did, but I did love her. I loved her as a friend and reveled in any of her accomplishments. Gjuli was an honors student. She was going to Fordham University in the fall and hoped that I would be going there as well. Most of the kids from Tolentine attended Fordham or Manhattan College to continue their education in Catholic schools. It was, in many cases, tradition.

Then I dropped the bomb on Gjuli. I was accepted and committed to Villanova University in Pennsylvania. With the help of that dammed Bishop Peroni, I would be leaving soon to spend the summer semester there and would stay at Nova and study for the priesthood.

Gjuli was crestfallen.

She understood what that meant. I had chosen, instead of being with her, a life of celibacy, never to be married, and a life of religious devotion.

Instead of a summer at The Aqueduct playing sports or taking the bus to Orchard Beach, in the Bronx, I would be at Villanova with all the soon-to-be priests.

She begged me not to go. She pleaded for a life together with me. She cried incessantly when she saw me. When I told her to find a nice Albanian boy to marry, her family had several lined up for an arranged marriage, Gjuli's eyes became rage-filled fireballs.

Our goodbye was sad. I promised to keep in touch and see her on breaks when I returned to the Bronx for holidays, but the looming priesthood gave her no comfort.

Sure, I felt guilty, but there was nothing I could do about it. The so-called 'calling to the priesthood,' if I had it at all, was not as much of a determining factor as my fear of intimacy. As a matter of fact, I felt no calling at all. My mother's determination for me to be called Father Deegan, and my being the chosen one since birth, set me on this path. It was my destiny.

* † *

I received daily letters from Gjuli while at Villanova. Her letters went from informational about her Fordham studies and neighborhood gossip to, after a few months, steamy, sexually packed tomes.

After a while, I stopped writing back to Gjuli. But

her letters kept pouring in. At some point, I stopped opening them.

More guilt crept in. When I went home for the holidays, I never even called Gjuli. She would stop by around the holidays to see my mother, who gave her a less-than-welcome feeling. Maureen Deegan wasn't about to let any 'trollop' get in the way of my ordination. To mom, my future was clear-cut.

* † *

My guilt ran even greater when I left the seminary at Villanova to join the military. I was home awaiting orders and briefly saw Gjuli. Once again, I rebuked Gjuli's advances for some crazy idea of fighting for my country. Gjuli wanted to move in together. I still never had sex with a woman and had no natural urges to do so.

Again, I would be gone for years at a time in a place I couldn't even talk about for reasons of national security. I still received Gjuli's passionate letters through a secret Pentagon address. I would occasionally reply, without making any promises or showing any passion.

In Gjuli's mind, at least the celibacy thing was gone, but she had no idea about my sexual issues. I was mentally ill, if I may say so myself.

* † *

When I left the service and started in the financial world, it was more of the same. Gjuli was not on my agenda. That sounds callous and mean, but there was no way I would share a residence with her for the same intimacy issues.

All the while I made my fortune, I still felt guilty. Guilty that I loved her, but I couldn't share my life with her or anyone.

As they say, Gjuli held the torch for me from the time we were teens. Is that loyalty or some kind of punishment she needed to experience?

Gjuli was more gorgeous than ever, and I'm certain she had her suitors, but she kept thinking we would eventually be together.

Then I went through my vengeance period. Gjuli had no clue what I was up to. No idea I was the killer with the sharpened crucifixes on the news. At least not until the cops came to her door one day and wanted to know what she knew about me and my whereabouts. I'm happy that I wasn't a fly on the wall to see the devastated reaction he must have had.

Finally, when we were well past middle age, Gjuli and I got together in a swank hotel suite in New York City.

The intimacy was not easy for us. Here I was, nearly a virgin old man.

Gjuli was patient. She was loving and now understood why I had behaved the way I did.

To Gjuli, I wasn't the most wanted serial killer on the planet. I wasn't the cold-blooded murderer the rest of the world thought. To my darling Gjuli, I was still the American boy she fell in love with at Tolentine High School.

We live in hiding from the world, surrounded by luxury. Two kids who met in the Bronx and waited for the time we could finally be together.

Each time I leave her, the guilt comes to me in torrents, but I still must do my thing to stay sane.

Gjuli was used to being alone, but our hearts became one, just in the nick of time.

I promised to be with her for the rest of our lives.

CHAPTER 37

I was never much into politics. Sure, I donated big checks to the Democrats and Republicans and Independents, but I thought they were all full of shit. I played them like a deck of cards. Everyone loved John Deegan. They loved my damned money is what.

Can you tell me what has hurt more human beings in the history of our earth more than religion and politics? Forget it. There is nothing.

The more the politicians came sniffing around with their toothy smiles and phony glad-handing, the less I liked them. In my business, giving the money was a necessary evil. I never asked them for a favor and was never disappointed. Every time these politicos left my office, I had an urge to take a shower.

Here is what I think in everyday terms about politics and power.

When I was a kid, everyone hated the Japanese. Look where we are now with Japan. We turned them into a superpower without nukes. The Russians were our ally and friend until they became something else.

Now look where we are. On the brink of World War III.

The Nazi's were our sworn enemies until we devastated them. Then we rebuilt Germany into a leading economic power.

As a young man, we were slaughtering Vietnamese by the droves. Now we buy clothing and furniture from them, and some American people are raving about their vacations to Vietnam, praising the beauty of the beaches and the wonderful surfing. 58,000+ Americans died in that country and for what?

In Central and South America and Mexico we were killing the drug lords and other scum in both clandestine and open operations. Until we allowed them, and their deadly drugs to enter the United States to the tune of twenty million people. Lunacy.

To me politics is a sham.

Now, the fanatical Arabs are the bad guys.

* † *

Gjuli was homesick for her family. They weren't getting any younger, neither were we. Besides, I had business to attend to with Vic and Raquel.

We arrived in New York City on that private jet I fly around in, accompanied by an extra valise full of my makeup and disguises.

One evening, when Vic and Raquel came home from the office, I was sitting in the kitchen of their Manhattan Townhouse. Gabby was happy to see me, and her grandmother, Olga, made me some great Café Bustello coffee. I did some card tricks and voice imitations.

Gonnella was pissed. Man was he pissed! The conversation between Vic and me was a bit testy. On Vic's part, anyway. I set him straight, but it wasn't easy. These Bronx Italian types were generally hot-headed.

"John, what in the fuck are you doing here?" Vic bellowed.

"Not happy to see me, Vic? It's been a while since Punta Cana. That was some case we solved down there. Got to get back to the Dominican one day."

"John, we come home from a real busy day, all kids of shit going on. We were looking to have a nice, relaxing family dinner, and here we find you, a serial killer, with our family. Really?"

"C'mon, Vic. I'm so much more than a serial killer, and you know that."

"Yeah, I get that. But the fact is, you did kill all those people. Not the ideal situation if you catch my drift," Vic seethed.

He had a point.

Vic asked what I was doing in New York. Of course, I played coy at first, explaining that Gjuli missed her family. He didn't buy it.

Then I dropped the bomb: my real reason for joining my wife on her Albanian family reunion. I didn't go for the roast lamb and homemade pita.

"Vic, my timing is perfect. You're going to need a lot of help finding these Arabs."

"Which Arabs are you referring to, Deegan?" I could see in his eyes that Vic was taken aback.

"Let's just say a little birdy has told me about the reservoir fiasco."

I had learned from my eavesdropping and my other secret sources that the governor of New York, an old friend of Vic's, called him into a secret meeting on a case that could have had a massive impact on New York City.

You see, the Ashokan Reservoir in upstate New York supplied most of the city's water. And guess what? There is basically only one pipeline into NYC. Not good. Especially when intelligence uncovered that the crazed Arabs were going to blow the pipeline to smitheries.

I wanted in.

I had to give Vic the skinny on what I knew about the situation. The United States, under President Donald J Trump, sought out and killed the leader of a fundamentalist group by the name of Major General Qasem Soleimani.

Trump, in his dramatic fashion, bragged about the Soleimani killing in an address to the nation. The Arabs, of course, were furious. They wanted another Word Trade Towers statement.

I used history to explain to Vic what was on the Arab mind.

"This group is especially dangerous, my friend. They have long memories, going back to the days of the Crusades. Arabs never forget a thing, Vic. Pope Urban II started the whole mess in 1099, but the

Muslims came out on top. The Muslims viewed their enemy, which is now us, as filthy, unwashed barbarians who wanted to capture their land and fuck their women. The problem is, they were right. The biggest problem, however, is that they still think that way. At least, the fundamentalists do, and that's who you are dealing with. A never-ending war."

For the first time, Vic didn't react to my calling him my friend. And I had his rapt attention.

†

A few days passed, and I had already begun my investigation. I disguised myself as a Muslim and headed into their turf in Brooklyn.

Vic was having a difficult time processing the situation and had no idea where to start. I guided him accordingly.

One of the problems was that there are so many Arab factions in New York City, it was like looking for the proverbial needle in a haystack thing.

I couldn't figure out who was who on my own. Although I would soon find out where these bastards were hiding. The CIA actually had a competent hand on things.

Behind every fanatic, there are ten behind him.

The Supreme Leader of Iran, Ayatollah Sayeed Ali Khamenei, ordered his Brigadier General Esmail Ghaani, the Commander of the terrorist group called the Quds Force, to exact revenge directly against the

United States, using any means necessary to cause panic and chaos in the United States.

Ghaani had sent Arash Hasham Hoosmand, his next in command, to mastermind a blow against the American people. There was absolutely no clue where Hoosmand and his jihad crazies were held up. They prayed five times a day for the destruction of America.

There was also a well-known Imam in the mosque of an all-Arab neighborhood in Brooklyn. The Imam was quite vocal, as his father was before him, about the Ayatollah saying negative things about the regime in Iran. Big mistake. The Quad Force made an example of him. He was slaughtered like a lamb inside the mosque.

NYPD put a command post there to investigate the killing and to show a police presence. I was already working in the area. Remember, I play chess.

This is where I had some fun. I was dressed as an old Arab. White beard, authentic long Arab outfit. Perfect from head to toe. My Arabic was excellent, thanks to my training with the CIA, so I was able to make friends with some of the locals.

Vic and Raquel were in the police command center, trying to gather as much intelligence as they could.

Interviewing the locals would get them nowhere. Everyone was deaf and dumb. An American cop had no shot. They saw nothing, heard nothing, and didn't move the needle on any leads. NYPD detectives came up with, as my Italian friends always said...u gatz.

Vic and Raquel were now canvassing the neighborhood. They were used to this kind of thing from their NYPD days.

Vic and Raquel approached me while I was sitting outside the café. They had absolutely no idea this old Arab they were about to meet was me.

Knowing an old Muslim man would not speak to a woman, Vic did all the talking.

Vic asked me some questions. I pretended not to speak much English, but I played along with some words, just enough to show him I understood what he was asking. Vic stopped wasting his time and he and Raquel returned to the command post. I followed.

As the coroner was taking the Imam's body out on a covered gurney they heard a familiar voice behind them.

"I told you that my help would be needed," I said.

When they turned around, they were both stunned to see it was me in the long white beard, in the Arab regalia They almost shit themselves.

So, my two now willing pupils, Vic and Raquel realized two things. I was three or four steps ahead of them and I could be anywhere and be anyone I wanted to be.

To me this was just a game. Sure, I didn't want to see panic, suffering and ultimately massive death in New York City. I certainly couldn't abide by these fanatics attacking my city as they had twice before. But it was still a game.

I'm getting old and the energy level has lessened. Part of my plan was to uncover when and where the maniac would attack, give the information to Vic and Raquel and be gone for a while.

I seriously thought this may be my last trip to the United States and I would just relax and deal with that boredom bullshit.

* † *

I met this guy in a Yemini café. He was one of those people you meet in life that wants you to believe is connected somehow to bad guys. You know the type. The Italian guy who pretends he know all the mafia families. The black guy who says he's tight with JZ and Puff Daddy. The Irishman who knows top IRA assholes.

This guy was known as Mir. And it turned out he did know these crazies. He said he delivered food to them. So, I followed. Bingo!

I had to go see Vic and Raquel and change my disguise to a smelly homeless guy. As fate would have it, Gonnella was targeted for death by Hoosmand.

This nobody homeless old dude finished off the two assassins in front of the Gonnella-Ruiz Townhouse.

A couple of more notches in my belt for justice and for my country.

It was time for me to collect Gjuli from her family and return to the safety of Lugano. I had showed Vic and Raquel how to hunt. They had learned to play chess instead of checkers. I had put them on the track to stop the bombing of the pipeline from the Catskills to New York City. Just think of the shit that would happen if millions and millions of people couldn't turn on the faucet in New York City and get water for drinking, cooking, bathing, sterilizing. Madness! The Ayatollah and his deranged fundamentalists would have made 9-11 look like child's play.

†

I watched the next few days from afar. It was a bit touch and go but the good guys won, and the bad guys died.

The New York governor was locked and loaded for the White House now. Vic and Raquel were set at the right hand of the father and me, John Deegan and my beautiful wife Gjuli were back where they belonged among the honeysuckle bushes at Villa Cielo.

CHAPTER 38

The last time I was in New York City, I think it was when I worked with Vic Gonnella and Raquel Ruiz on the Arab pipeline gig, I decided to go up to the Bronx and see my old stomping grounds.

I had hired a driver who drove a gigantic SUV. I think it was a Cadillac Escalade.

Wearing my Arab old man garb, long white beard, and all, we headed for the Bronx. I wore the disguise as I was afraid former neighbors or schoolmates would recognize me. It would be something if I were seen and reported to the cops. I could just see the headlines in the New York Daily News. "Right Under Our Noses. John Deegan Caught in The Bronx."

It didn't take long for me to realize there were no leftovers from the old days hanging around anymore.

The driver knew the Bronx well. We went up the Harlem River Drive and over the Third Avenue Bridge onto the Major Deegan Expressway. It looked pretty much the same. Even the road construction looked as if they had accomplished nothing since I left.

Turning right onto Fordham Road, I felt my hands get a bit moist with excitement. Then reality set in.

I wanted to see Manion's Bar, the focal point for the heavy drinkers, including my dad. It was on the right side of Fordham, about three blocks up from the Deegan. It was now a Botanica. I hadn't seen a white person, but it was early morning. Across the street, behind 12-foot iron security fences, was the Fordham Hill Apartment complex. It looked the same.

Next stop was a right turn on Andrews Avenue, where Tolentine High School was the anchor for that neighborhood. The school was closed down. The building was there, lots of graffiti on the outside walls, but Tolentine was no more. I couldn't believe my eyes.

My stomach churned when I thought about Bishop Peroni. I so much wanted to kill that man, but he was dead before I started my crusade. I almost went into a flashback, but for some reason, it left me.

We went around a few corners, and there stood St. Nicholas of Tolentine church. I always thought of it as a majestic building. It still was. I could see my mother walking up the steps of the church to attend Mass and receive communion. It didn't give me any comfort. For a second or two, I wanted to get out of the car, go into the church, and light a candle for my deceased parents. Then I remembered what the priests did to me and how brutal some of the nuns were. "Fuck that!" I blurted. The driver asked me what was wrong. "Nada" was my reply.

I couldn't believe how filthy the streets were. Back in the day, the streets were spotless. Everyone swept the sidewalk and the gutter, throwing anything that didn't belong into the garbage. Now, I saw papers, bottles, cans, you name it, strewn all over the street.

When we got to Grand Avenue back in 1960, it was almost like a fancy neighborhood. Not many cars were parked on the street, and there was no garbage anywhere except in garbage cans lined up neatly by each building superintendent. It was a quiet street with good neighbors. Primarily Irish, with some Germans, a handful of Italians, and Jews, but all predominantly white.

As I drove down Grand with my driver, I was stunned by the transformation. Cars are parked everywhere, some on cinderblocks, with the tires gone. Like Fordham Road, the street was a garbage pail. All kinds of refuse are on the sidewalk and in the gutters.

We passed my building. I had to fight back the tears, thinking of my parents and my siblings living together as a family all those years. I recalled the pretty Puerto Rican lady who lived on the first floor of our building. She lived there with her two sons and her Irish fireman husband. We often heard the screaming and banging from downstairs. He would yell, she would scream, and the kids always cried.

They separated. She had an order of protection because of his physical and verbal abuse.

It was around 2 A.M. one early morning, about the time when Manion's bar closed. The fireman husband came banging on the door. The incessant banging and screaming in the downstairs hallway woke the entire Deegan family and likely everyone else in the building. He said, 'I want to see you. Who is in there with you, and what other things are garbled?' He began trying to break down the wooden door. I recall that he was a large man.

Suddenly, a big bang sound came from under us. It shook our apartment. We heard moaning and more screaming from the woman and her kids. The lady had taken a shotgun and blasted the fireman husband right through the door. He died at the scene. We said a decade of the rosary.

Driving down Fordham Road towards Webster Avenue, my tears started to come.

In my day, there were beautiful fashion stores, shoe stores, and bakeries, as well as a great movie theater called the Valentine. A great hot dog spot, and a big store called Alexander's.

Aside from the piles of refuse in the streets, every store I knew was gone. It was like a foreign country to me, except for the clothing stores, which all had bins on the sidewalks piled high with bales of cheap merchandise. Every store like that had a man on a twelve-foot aluminum ladder looking down on the shoppers. They were on the ladders to prevent theft.

Latin music blared from almost every store. Fordham Road went from clean, solid commercial stores with a sophisticated flair. Now it was a Gypsy-like bazaar.

If I walked down the street without my disguise, I would have stuck out like a sore thumb. With the Arab garb, I would have blended in.

Change is the only thing in life that is constant. I understand that. The change to this once clean, vibrant, and safe area of the Bronx was impossible for me to process.

The big department store, Alexanders, had a new name; the Valentine was now a Pentecostal church, and Gorman's Hot Dog store was gone.

The driver went down Fordham Road. There, stood Fordham University on the left, behind high iron fences. It looked better than ever. Those stone buildings are magnificent.

I thought of Gjuli and how she had gone there and begged me to join her. It was a short bus ride down Fordham Road for us. We could be together. We would study together; we could live together. We could live happily ever after.

I instructed the driver to take me back into Manhattan but not to take Fordham Road back to the highway. I could no longer look at the devastation.

In the Escalade, I started to think what if. What if that creepy Father O'Gorman never molested me? What if I resisted my mother's demands that I go to the seminary and become a priest? What if I went to Fordham with Gjuli? What if we had kids? What kind of dad would I have been? What if I didn't run to the army and become a trained killer?

I could have gone to Wall Street, and because of my intelligence, I would still be extremely wealthy.

It suddenly dawned on me how one pedophile, I don't care if it's a priest or a dad or an uncle, or anyone, has the effect of devastation, not only on the victim but also on their family. This knowledge is devastating. Not only does the victim's life change, but everyone in the sufferer's orbit is damaged.

Notwithstanding what the rest of the world thought, I was glad I did what I did.

Part of me wants to do it again... and again, and *again...*

CHAPTER 39

Some time had passed since my last contact with Vic and Raquel. It had been more than some time, actually. I had no guilt for what I had done in my life, but I was sensitive to the fact that I was still a killer.

I got the feeling I was wearing out my welcome with the dynamic couple, so I intentionally stayed away. Other than cryptic holiday or birthday cards, there was no communication. Vic and Raquel knew where I was and how to reach me if they needed to, but that's the way it is with people sometimes.

Their company was flourishing to become one of the biggest investigation firms in the world. The press constantly interviewed Vic and Raquel. They were often quoted when asked about a crime. If there is a major situation somewhere in the world, Vic and Raquel would be asked for their ideas and opinions.

From time to time, there was interest in me online and in the media. There was even a John Deegan page on Facebook. Where did they think John Deegan was hiding? Did they think Deegan was still alive? Will Deegan kill again?

To their credit, Gonnella-Ruiz never strayed from
the script. Deegan was a genius with a message,
which is what Vic and Raquel would say, but nothing
to give away to those who were trying to track me
down. I appreciated their sense of loyalty.

The famous couple was also raising a daughter the
best way they knew how. I wasn't the ideal person to
have around, I get it. I imagine there wasn't a day
that went by that Vic and Raquel didn't think about
me. As I them.

* † *

Gjuli and I were living our best lives in Lugano. I
was cancer-free, which was miraculous. I had beaten
all the odds. Well, the doctors and science had saved
me. Gjuli would always say it was God's hand that
saved me. She always prayed to whoever she prayed
to for her thanks. I didn't argue with her because I
always admired a person's faith. After all, my fight
with the Catholic Church had nothing to do with
dogma or belief.

To show you how much Gjuli loved me, and how
selfless she was, my wife knew when I was getting
bored and restless. It wasn't that often anymore, but
it still reared its ugly head. I suppose I had some
physical tell Gjuli would pick up on. Perhaps I was
distant, maybe I sighed more than usual, or better
yet, Gjuli had a sixth sense for these things.

Gjuli hinted she wanted to see her family again.
Her cousins invited her to their home in Yonkers,

New York, right outside the Bronx border. She wouldn't leave me, but said she really missed the family. She knew I would move heaven and earth for her, so it was time to pack our bags.

I never had friends. I didn't trust anyone because of the abuse. So, in my old age, I didn't miss friendships. Now I couldn't trust anyone.

Every day, usually in the early mornings and late evenings, I would scan my computer for some activity of interest to me. The hacks I created for various law enforcement agencies were helpful. I can tell you it wasn't sports, business, or politics I would spend any of my time on. I liked listening to music too. So did Gjuli. We spend a lot of time listening to a wide range of music, from Beethoven to the Beatles.

I keyed in on activity in the Vatican, which would make me sick to my stomach. There was nothing I saw in the Catholic Church that didn't reek of deceptive, duplicitous, phony bullshit.

I also kept an eye out for crimes that interested me. Mostly unique murders that were committed in the United States. On any given day, I would be following 4-5 serial killer cases. And at least that many of potential serial killer situations.

One case in particular had caught my eye. I immediately knew it was my ticket back to New York.

I broke the long silence and called Raquel. We had a cordial and at times comical call. I pretended to be an old Jewish woman saying, "You never call, you never write." Raquel cracked up laughing.

Raquel sounded happy to hear from me, but I could tell she was stressed. I trained myself to always listen beyond just the person's voice. I asked her what was wrong. She blamed the COVID-19 epidemic. Like everyone else, the uncertainty was hovering, especially when it came to her mother, Olga. COVID-19 was especially dangerous to the elderly. And of course, Gabby. Young people were not out of danger from the pandemic.

I asked to speak with her and Vic together. Raquel put Vic on speaker.

"Hello, Mr. Deegan, how are you?" He sounded happy to hear from me.

"I guess I'll be coming to New York soon. I see a new case on the horizon," I blurted.

"You have a new case? Is the FBI and Interpol aware of this?" Vic said with a sly laugh. He was being his usual sarcastic self, always reminding me of my criminal status.

I could be sarcastic, too.

"No, you two have a new case. Aren't you aware of your surroundings?"

Silence. They had no idea where this conversation was going.

I informed them that someone was targeting Hasidic Jews with a high-powered rifle in Rockland County, New York.

Now I've dropped more information and my prediction.

"Two dead, forty-five minutes from your lovely home. Shot by a sniper. Satmar Hasid. Your phone will be ringing any time now."

They knew, as I did, the FBI needed three murders with the same M.O. to consider it a serial killer.

I told them I was disappointed they didn't know what was happening in their backyard. Then came my prediction.

"Here's how it's gonna work." I offered.

I told them, whomever is doing it, the local yokels and the FBI were useless. They need you two to solve the case and maybe save a few lives.

I told them I wanted in.

Raquel said they were not interested.

I never took no for an answer in my business. I pushed it with more salient predictions.

"Excuse me, it will play out like this. The Hasidic community will be in sheer panic, especially after the killer shoots another one. And he or she will. The FBI will say it's a hate crime, the news media will be all over this like stink on shit, maybe a copy-cat or two, then your friend the governor will get the call from the Rabbis reminding him who is really in charge with the votes, then he will cry uncle, call you and I'll already be up there figuring things out."

I told Vic and Raquel I would be seeing them in Monsey, New York, soon and hung up.

It didn't take a genius to figure this out. But it helps. As things turned out, I was right all along. Shocking!

Gjuli and I had a smooth, comfortable trip to New York. She had an additional suitcase of presents for her family. Me with a suitcase of disguises.

I called Vic after Gjuli was settled in with her family. I was staying in a hotel in Manhattan under an assumed name, a disguise, and fake documents.

Vic laid a bomb on me, saying Raquel would not be joining the investigation. She had an unhealthy fear of being around the Hasid's. Their community was rife with COVID-19. Maybe it was not such a bad concern on Raquel's part. It took some cajoling, but Raquel finally joined Vic a day or so later.

I was already on the job.

Like the good cops and investigators, they were the dynamic duo, and they went to the scene of the shootings in Monsey, New York. The first shooting was right outside a big food store where the victim shopped before he was clipped right on the street.

Vic and Raquel entered the store and were amazed at entering a foreign world. The announcements and the signs were all in Yiddish.

They asked what the food was on a steam table. An elderly man, dressed all in black with his payas coming out from under his hat, and speaking in a thick Yiddish accent, helped them with the names. The Yid was me. They never knew it. Once again, I fooled them.

* † *

Long story short, the killer kept shooting Hasids on Friday night around the area. He was called the Shabbos Killer for doing the murders on Fridays, the beginning of the holy sabbath.

I didn't stay long in Monsey. I had other fish to fry.

Vic had given me the ballistic reports he received from either the FBI or the local cops. I don't remember who gave them to Vic now. I knew I had to stay one or two steps ahead of them all.

The next thing I knew, with the other information I had gathered, I went from New Jersey, where I had used a businessman's disguise, and then followed a lead to Pennsylvania, where I had purchased a Mennonite outfit to blend into the community. I was on the lookout for a company or person that made the kind of projectile that was used in the shootings.

I gave my whereabouts to Vic and Raquel, who came running. I knew they would not divulge my plans.

The shooter turned out to be the son of the manufacturer of the bullets. The kid's father died from COVID. The kid blamed the Hasidim because his father did business with them near Monsey, caught the virus, and died. He was all alone in the world now and mentally challenged.

It wasn't a hate crime, as the FBI was saying. It was a revenge crime committed by a mentally unstable young man.

Through a thorough investigation, I had led Vic and Raquel to the boy's home (his name was Edward Olsen), where he was held up. It was now going to be in the hands of the local police, with Vic and Raquel in the center of things.

With the cavalry coming, I had to make my getaway.

Once again, I helped close an important case for the Gonnella-Ruiz team. Once again, I taught them to think outside the box.

They saved some lives, of that, I am sure. Unfortunately, it cost young Edward Olsen his life.

I'm sure that to this day, the outcome haunts Vic and Raquel.

CHAPTER 40

Aside from being repeatedly sodomized and forced to do oral sex as a child and later as a teen, my time in Catholic schools was academically rewarding. Of course, if I had to do it all over again, I would have bit that pedophile Father O'Gorman's dick off and been summarily thrown out of St. Martin of Tours.

The nuns always brutally threatened the C and D row students with expulsion and being sent to the animals at the local public schools. I would have preferred to go to P.S. 57 on Crotona Avenue, a block from home, then to be raped on a weekly basis. Many of the Jewish kids in the neighborhood attended P.S. 57 or P.S. 92, and went on to high school at Columbus, Dewitt Clinton, or Theodore Roosevelt. Roosevelt was the closest and the worst of the three. Those Jewish kids somehow went to good colleges and became professionals, such as lawyers, doctors, or accountants. Their parents valued education and helped them every step of the way. The public-school students weren't tortured by nuns, and as we said in the army, they were not FUBAR. Fucked up beyond all recognition.

I felt bad for the students who had poor grades. Beyond the beatings and ridicule that rained on them, they had to live with walking around feeling like they were stupid losers. That kind of handling of children is life-changing. What that kind of treatment does to a child's psyche is nothing less than immoral abuse, at the very least.

Being the chosen one, I would never be able to try to break away from St. Martin's or Tolentine for fear that it would have killed my mother. If I dared to tell her what O'Gorman was doing to me, he had convinced me that some tragedy would befall her, and she would never have believed me.

A pedophile priest would know all about manipulation. He was God's representative to us on earth. I was trapped, and he knew it.

Pedophiles always found a way to get to the weaknesses of the child they groomed and ultimately abused. In my case, it was my mother, her devout faith, fear of losing her, and for the safety of my siblings. At eight years old I had no idea what a penis was for other than peeing.

* † *

I found the work in school to be easy. I was truly gifted. I would hear or see something in school just once, and it would be embedded in my brain. I was just like a sponge. When I read something, it was locked in. I never really had to study as the information was always there in my brain.

I remember one nun who would not give me 100 on any test. She said only Jesus was perfect, and there had to be something about the subject I didn't know. Mother needed to sign the test papers. When she caught wind of this nun's edict, she made a B-line to the convent. The Mother Superior changed the nun's theory on perfection. After all, I was John Deegan, the clean-cut, well-scrubbed future priest of the school. The 100's then came in waves.

I was always the altar boy who walked down the center aisle of the church during a procession, carrying the long candle next to the priest who carried the large crucifix. I was always on the altar for the 10 o'clock high Mass. I rang the bells during the consecration of the host perfectly. In the school, after lunch, I was the boy who rang the bells for the daily Angelis. And I rang the bell at the perfect time, all the time.

If, on the off chance, I was not perfect at something, the nuns would see that I was. It was their job to bring me along, preparing me for a life of poverty, chastity and obedience.

* † *

One of the repetitive flashbacks I have had was during the Soviet Union-United States conflicts in the late 1950's. It seemed as if nuclear war was going to happen at any time. There were bomb shelters throughout the neighborhood, usually in the basements of buildings. It was a given the Russians were sure to bomb us. They were the evil empire. They were controlled by the devil himself. The Russians, we were told, were atheists with no need for Our Lord Jesus Christ. From time to time, the class was sent into the hallway, where we were huddled together, told to sit, and put our heads between our knees to pray. I recall tightly squeezing my eyes shut and practicing for the coming bombs. If I prayed hard enough my family and I would all be saved from those cretins in Russia. Who the hell does this to kids? More mental stress, abnormal teaching, and guilt that no one needs in their formative years.

The flashbacks came and went, always leaving me upset and jittery. Even now, as an old man, when the remembrances come, they come with a fury. Sometimes they pop up, and for some reason, they vanish quickly. Other times they linger and the details are so realistic; the fear and disdain of the dream makes my adrenaline surge.

One remembrance was when I was serving Mass. The old Irish priest, Father Boyle, was serving communion. In those days, everyone received the host while they knelt at the marble railing around the altar. The priest would say a prayer to each person, making the sign of the cross with the host before putting it on the tongue of the parishioner.

Father Boyle's hands always shook. At that time, I thought he was just old or maybe sickly. The truth was that the man was a hopeless drunk.

I was the altar boy, standing next to Father Boyle, holding the gold-plated plate under the communicant's chin in the event the host would fall. On this day, the consecrated host dropped from an older woman's tongue, and I moved the plate to catch the wafer. It fell on the marble floor next to the railing. I let the holy body of Christ hit the floor.

Boyle gave me a disgusted look through his yellow, bloodshot eyes. It was my fault. Now, a big ceremony had to take place with the priest praying over the fallen wafer like his mother had just died. Another priest came out. It was the kindly Italian priest, Father Monteleone. He moved me aside and patted my head. He whispered to me it was just an accident. The two priests said some somber prayers, and Father Monteleone removed the host from the floor, placing it on white linen and then into a chalice. I could feel the reddening of my face and neck. It felt as if everyone in the packed church was looking right at me.

After Mass, Father Boyle wasn't so bad. He told me to say an entire rosary at the altar after all the Masses for the day were finished. Kneeling on uncovered marble for the duration of the rosary, I guess about 30 minutes, was torture. It could never be the inebriated priest's fault, so it had to be mine. It bothered me for months.

There were some good flashbacks, however. A tradition in my family was that after any of the kids had their first holy communion, we would all go together to the Howard Johnson's restaurant on

Southern Boulevard to have a bacon and egg breakfast. My dad didn't have a drink the night before so he could get up early the next morning. For my first communion, there were only four kids in our family. We walked from St. Martin's to the restaurant, my mother beaming with pride. We were all together eating in a restaurant. As a family, we never went out to eat, except for the first Holy Communion. Eating in restaurants was for rich people. It was a reward and a special treat to eat out for everyone in the Deegan family, including Dad. In the flashback, I could taste the crispy bacon and the chocolate milk. We were all so happy.

I wasn't yet encumbered by the guilt of being Father O'Gorman's butt boy. That didn't happen until second grade.

CHAPTER 41

Of late, I've been reminiscing in my mind about my crusade, my mission in life.

I'm on my veranda overlooking the beautiful lake here in Lugano, Switzerland. The aroma of honeysuckle and roses here is amazing. The air is so fresh and clean, I can't think of anywhere else I'd rather be. I can stare at the mountains surrounding Lugano for hours on end. The serenity the whole area brings me is so pleasurable that I forget some of the things I've done in my life.

Gjuli is inside the house, cooking homemade Albanian pita. She's working with our chef on some outstanding Italian dishes with a Swiss and German flair. There are times when I shoo everyone from the kitchen to make the famous Aunt Millie's sauce. I still have the recipe embedded in my brain. To me, that sauce is comfort food.

Every minute I spend together with Gjuli is a blessing. I left her alone for so many years, and I feel I can never give her enough. I don't mean things. Gjuli could care less about living in luxury. She often tells me that if we had an apartment back in the Bronx, it would have been enough for her so long as I was there. No one in my life looks at me the way Gjuli does. The love and devotion she has for me sometimes moves me to tears. But even after the years we have been together, I still have an iron barrier surrounding me.

I occasionally attempt to be romantic, but I will confess that is very difficult for me. For decades, I chose to be alone. I chose to put up walls around my feelings and reject any friends or intimacy.

I don't have to explain my feelings to Gjuli. She is very loving and patient with me because she understands the pain I went through as a young boy and as a teenager. She realizes I left the seminary because of the deviates I encountered there and how my faith was destroyed. If I ever had any. Looking back, my faith was more of an obligation than a conviction.

We mostly spend quiet time together. I don't ever brood about my past, but the awful things I experienced are always just a thought away...like my flashbacks that come and go without warning. I can be triggered by a word, a photograph, a religious icon or simply by looking at something beautiful. I often feel guilty when I'm enjoying life.

Gjuli avoids talking about Grand Avenue, Tolentine, the Bronx, and the Aqueduct, so as not to trigger me with bad thoughts about the underlying negative experiences I had. If I am in an especially good mood and bring up the Bronx or mimic our teachers, she's my best audience. Some nights, when we share a great bottle of wine or an after-dinner aperitivo, I go through my repertoire of imitations. From Franklin Delano Roosevelt to John F. Kennedy to Ed Sullivan introducing Elvis Presley, to Jimmy Stewart and James Cagney, I do a stand-up routine that makes Gjuli belly laugh. And she laughs at the same old routine every time I do it. I need some new material to make things fresh.

Just the other night, I asked Gjuli out on a date. We visited an incredible trattoria in Lake Como. We had been there a few times before, and Gjuli loved it. It's a small place off the beaten path, with a view of the lake through a row of enormous pine trees. The spot is run by a Lombardia family with roots going back to the Middle Ages in Germany.

Naturally I had to wear a disguise like I do whenever I leave the house. I looked like a professor of English literature, complete with a tweed jacket, dark jeans, and maroon-rimmed, tinted glasses. My gray hair was slicked back, and I wore as ascot on my neck tucked in the collar of a wrinkled white linen shirt. Our driver took us on the short ride and patiently waited in the car outside the restaurant. Our staff thought I was a wealthy eccentric with a flair for the dramatic, not a killer in hiding. We use the driver because I can't see so well at night anymore, and we like to have some wine with our dinner.

The place is called Longobardus, the old Latin name for Lombard. There is no menu. They tell you what their chef, who is the matriarch of the family, cooked for the evening. When the waiter describes the available selection in his soft, melodic voice, it sounds almost poetic.

When we go out for dinner, we generally order two different dishes for each course, allowing us to share and experience different tastes. They have a short wine list, a few super Tuscans, but mostly bottles from Lombardy, but we prefer having two carafes of homemade house wine. One white and one red.

I made sure there were colorful wildflowers brought to the candlelit table for Gjuli. This is as romantic as I can be. I didn't have much experience in this area, as you can well imagine, knowing my past. Gjuli appreciates each gesture I make, such as holding her chair when she sits or when I stand when she goes and returns from the washroom.

This night, as luck would have it, two Catholic priests in their black suits and Roman collars came for dinner. They were seated not too far from us. The trattoria has just eight tables. Gjuli looked at me, and her big, dark eyes suddenly looked sad for me.

I smiled and said, "Non á niente amore." It's nothing, my love.

We ignored the prelates for most of the evening, or at least until most of the wine was gone. I gently pulled Gjuli close to me and in my best Humphry Bogart impersonation, I whispered, "I need to go out to the car and get a couple of my crucifixes." Gjuli laughed so loud that the whole place looked over at us.

After an appetizer of homemade salamis and an

amazingly sharp local cheese, we enjoyed an incredible meal of homemade fettuccini with shaved Grana Padano cheese in a wild boar sauce, as well as a creamy, bright yellow polenta with stewed pork and white truffles. It was heavenly.

We finished our meal with some delicious homemade desserts, ripe fruit, and a couple of cups of espresso. Two flute glasses, halfway filled with a limoncello pistachio liqueur, are presented as a compliment from Mama, who waved at us from the kitchen.

There is no check. The waiter whispered the amount owed in my ear, holding his hand near his mouth like we were part of a secret society. The place doesn't take credit cards, which was fine by me. I always pay cash.

The ride home was beautiful. We left the car windows halfway open and enjoyed the fresh, slightly chilly air with the scent of the lake wafting through the car. The road from Lago di Como and Lugano, Switzerland, is narrow and curvy. The left side was all gray walls and rocky hills. To the right, the moonlit dark water of the lake was like a Renaissance painting. On the opposite side of the lake, light from some of the homes twinkled like the stars. When we reached the Swiss border, the two military guards on duty waved us through.

We arrived home just before midnight. Gjuli put some soothing jazz on the sound system and went to the bedroom. When she returned in a beautiful, long, silky magenta robe, I knew she was not interested in going to sleep. I smelled her favorite French perfume. That was always her subtle signal.

I poured two glasses of vintage Port into two crystal glasses and told her how beautiful she was. She was always beautiful from the day we met. Now, how's that for romantic? And it did it in my own voice, although I did consider using my Sean Connery impersonation. We chatted about how good the food was and what a lovely evening it was. Gjuli never mentioned the two priests. Nor did I. We both knew that was a subject that could possibly trigger me.

After the glasses were dry, we made our way to the bedroom. For some reason, I had butterflies in my stomach. Not a good sign. At times, my flashbacks were preceded by the butterflies. This would not be the most opportune time for me to go into a trance to visit the past.

I undressed and went into the shower. I was stalling. Knowing Gjuli wanted to be intimate, that wasn't fair to her. She never overtly asked me for sex. She was too loving and subtle for that.

I took my time in the shower. I knew Gjuli wasn't going to fall asleep, but I lingered in the shower, feeling the warm water from five jets coming out of the wall. The overhead nozzle soaked my head and shoulders. I washed my body with a honeysuckle-scented soap. I washed twice. I rubbed my head with a sandalwood shampoo I was fond of from Italy to get the pomade I used to slick my hair back. I washed my hair twice.

I dried myself off and put on my favorite worn light blue terrycloth robe. A couple of deep breaths, and I approached our bedroom.

Gjuli was like a vision, leaning on her elbow, just smiling at me. She was under the bedding, no longer wearing the robe.

There were times when we made love that I couldn't perform. Either my thoughts of the priests molesting me and of my learned fear of intimacy or...let's face it...my age somehow got the best of me. I was determined to fight off the demons in my head this night. My wife deserved it.

I cleared my head, and a bit of foreplay put both me and Gjuli in the right mood. We made love with our bedroom windows open, listening to the calm lapping of the lake water against the shore.

No joking, no impersonations, no voices, no disguises. I was finally able to be me, John Joseph Deegan.

We fell asleep in each other's arms...

CHAPTER 42

Flashbacks from one's past are common as one grows older. For me, growing up in the Bronx was very interesting, to say the least. A story I can continue to tell and add to.

The old neighborhood, Clinton Avenue in the Crotona section, was a melting pot. Everyone who lived there, in those 5 and 6-story walk-up buildings, seemed to be in the same boat, working from paycheck to paycheck.

My dad had a good, steady job, but there was little left over at the end of the month for anything extra. But we didn't ask for anything, likely because we didn't need anything. My parents didn't have a checkbook until the early 60's. Rent and food were paid in cash. Yes, this was normal back then. Nobody back then could even think that we would do it differently.

Gas and electric bills were paid in cash at the bank on Tremont Avenue. Tuition was paid in cash at the school. There weren't many other bills to pay, except life insurance, and the agent would come around and be paid cash for that, too.

I'm sure my parents worried about money. We kids had no idea about any of that. Back then, in the 50's and 60's the men went to work, and the women were called housewives. They stayed home with the kids, cooking and cleaning, doing laundry, and ironing their clothing. Times were different and for the youth from now strange.

Television at that time featured numerous cigarette and car commercials. It wasn't like today when images of happy people flying to the Caribbean or other places around the world show that this will make you happy. You need what they are selling. A new car was out of the question for the Deegan family, so a good used car was a great luxury. Dad had an old Studebaker, but he mostly took the train to work. The car was used to visit a relative who lived on Long Island or to take Mom to the hospital to have a baby.

Life was simpler than it is today, and in many ways, it was better.

But my life, the life of John Joseph Deegan, was not so good at all. It was idyllic living in the Bronx until Father O'Gorman changed me forever.

The streets were always clean and safe, and everyone looked out for one another. The street games we played were good, clean fun, and taught us to be competitive. We called the beat cop Uncle Jim, and as he walked by, he whistled and twirled his nightstick. Occasionally, there was a police raid on some of the Italian guys who played dice between parked cars in the middle of the block. That was the extent of the crime we saw.

At least until the Puerto Rican influx into the Bronx changed the neighborhood, but that's a story for another day.

After I was molested, nothing was ever the same for me.

Dad wasn't affectionate or demonstrative with the kids. Mom was, and she would always be hugging and kissing us. After my situation, I was no longer comfortable with her embrace and did what I could to avoid it or get away from her as quickly as possible. When mom's sisters visited us and wanted a hug and a kiss, I dreaded the closeness.

I kept my distance from any sign of affection from anyone.

When we moved to Grand Avenue, and I was away from that creepy priest for a little while, I never let my guard down.

At my dad's wake, when the uncles and male family friends wanted to hug me and tell me it was going to be alright, I thought I would be sick to my stomach. I slumped down like a dishrag.

Bishop Perone set me into a deeper hole than I thought possible. There seemed to be no escape for me from the abuse of these two so-called good and holy men.

At Tolentine, when we had gym class, we were supposed to take showers afterward. I did everything I could to avoid being naked with the other boys. One of the brothers, another sick clergy, would sometimes get a metal folding chair and watch us in the shower. I was forced to shower when he was around. I would run into and out of the shower, barely getting wet, making sure my back was always facing a wall. The same thing happened when I was on the freshman basketball team. I never showered. I would have a bottle of Ban Roll On deodorant, and that was as far as I would go to refresh myself and not stink. One of the guys said I was taking a Polish shower. I wanted to shove the deodorant bottle down his big mouth and into his throat.

The other boys would snap towels at each other and move around the locker room, undressed, proud of their manhood and content in their skins. They would call each other homo's and allude to getting banged in the ass. Imagine for a moment what that did to me.

I never physically enjoyed what those clerics did to me, not for one second, I swear that on the souls of my parents. But I wondered if I was a homo because of the activity in which I was forced to partake. I was emotionally trapped. When one of the guys, as guys at that age often did, would say suck my dick to someone I felt my face redden and those hated butterflies came to my stomach with a vengeance.

Gjuli, unbeknownst to her, put a lot of pressure on me in my last years at Tolentine. She wanted to be intimate and make moves on me, trying to kiss me or get close with her body. I had to attend school dances. I would have rather gone to the dentist and had a root canal. I wanted nothing to do with that.

She wanted to experiment with sex, and I wanted to scream, "Leave me alone, will ya?" Instead, I just went into my shell and got away as fast as I could.

Other girls at Tolentine would flirt with me. They thought Gjuli and I were a couple, but despite that, some of the girls still wanted to make out or more, but I didn't allow any of that nonsense. Sex with filthy and dirty to me. When the girls hiked up their pleated Tolentine uniform skirts after school hours, I could care less.

In the seminary, homosexual activity was everywhere and obvious. I have a flashback of getting off the bus at the seminary and obvious gay novices would call out and say hello some in an effeminate way and others with butch voices. I heard one novice say, 'She's cute' about me. I couldn't even study in my room without being approached. And then, of course, Bishop Pig would come and stay for a day or two.

I couldn't get away from this in the Catholic world. It seemed to me that this activity was the norm.

When I was in the service there were always whore houses near the base. Guys would save their money, and the moment they had leave, they ran to the prostitutes. Not for me. I took extra on-base detail. Having sex with a woman was just not going to happen for me. When the guys came back from their assignments and told their stories about what the girls had done to and with them, I had every reason not to run and scream from the barracks.

When I started in the business world, and people could see I had a rocket on my back, the women came in droves. I had countless opportunities to date and to screw the females on the staff. I'm certain the scuttlebutt among the women in the office was that I was a fruitcake.

There was a beautiful Italian girl who lived next door to my studio apartment. We chatted a few times in the lobby and hallway. I think she said she was a model, but I never listened closely enough. She made me very nervous. She knocked one night. Wearing a too-short, too-tight miniskirt, she had two glasses and a bottle of wine in her hand. Her flirty smile said volumes. I practically slammed the door in her face.

When she had a visitor in her apartment, I could hear her bed banging against the wall and her moaning in ecstasy. I would go out for a long walk and hope she would be finished when I went home.

When I had to attend a party, it was usually in a bar or club. In those days smoking was allowed even in the office.

When my co-workers would light up and puff on a cigar, I would cringe. It reminded me of the oral sex I was forced to perform.

As you can see, none of this was normal. I was normal until that day when Father Edward O'Gorman summoned me to the rectory. He ruined my life.

But I got even... and enjoyed it!

CHAPTER 43

Vic and Raquel were making boatloads of money. I was proud and happy for them.

My experience told me the burnout factor is real, and I was concerned for their marriage and partnership. Although I have been a killer, I am not without sentiment.

I called to speak with Gabriella one day, and I was lucky enough to chat with Olga, Raquel's mother, and Gabby's abuela. That woman can talk a dog off a meat truck.

She filled me in on Gabby's schooling and the typical story of Vic and Raquel never being home. They had written a book called "Catch Us If You Can." I was aware of the book and read it with great enjoyment. As a matter of fact, I read it twice and listened to the audiobook as well. It was all about their great serial killer cases and a few other murders they had solved.

The book hit the New York Times bestseller list and made a small fortune. Vic and Raquel toured the major cities for book signings with lines around the block of the bookstores. They were also on every talk show you can imagine.

Funny thing was all the interviewers wanted to know about the John Deegan case and the serial killer's mysterious disappearance. All these years later, and I was still a significant topic of conversation. The John Deegan Facebook pages blew up. The Instagram pages went viral. There were even a few renditions of what Deegan looks like now. Very creative, and one was close. There were some John Deegan sightings at Santorini, Greece, and Amsterdam. One fella said he spoke with me outside the opera house in Palermo. I've never even been to Sicily.

Olga told me about Vic and Raquel being stressed and frequently arguing. I didn't take a genius to figure that one out. Olga also let it slip that the couple was going to Florence, Italy, on a rest and relaxation retreat. That's all I needed to hear. I was going to have some fun at their expense.

Florence is a hop, skip, and a jump from Lugano. Gjuli and I love that city, so I made it into a vacation for us.

†

It was easy for me to find out the when and where of Vic and Raquel's trip. I knew their entire itinerary within 30 minutes. I knew their arrival time and the fancy hotel they booked. I had my disguises all lined up.

One early evening, I left Gjuli alone so she could shop and feel like an Italian woman, looking sophisticated and lovely. She had plenty of Euros to spend and enjoy herself.

It worked out that Vic and Raquel were going out for an early dinner. Italians eat late, sometimes as late as 8 or 9 o'clock in the evening. American tourists often struggle to adjust to the late eating hours.

I followed the couple from their hotel as they strolled the streets and the medieval piazzas. Raquel window shopped; Vic looked bored to shit. I had to laugh when so many Americans spotted the now well-known celebrity couple. Some bold sightseers even approached Vic and Raquel for selfies. I wanted to go over to them and say, "I knew you when,' but I bided my time.

They did look smashing in their Italian clothing. Raquel would look good in a pillowcase.

They finally sat in a well-known café, Caffe Concerto Paszkowski, in the main square. I gave the maître d' a fifty euro note to sit me behind the unknowing couple.

I eavesdropped on their conversation. Raquel was talking about the things she wanted to see in Florence. She had a traveler's book on Florence with dog-eared pages. She seemed relaxed. Vic was still wound like a violin string.

I was disguised as a New York Mets fan, replete with a blue and orange Mets hat and jacket, askew white hair peeking out from under the cap, and sunglasses. I looked like any New York baseball fan on the Number 6 train in Queens, including the scruffy beard and Converse All-Star sneakers. White high-top, of course.

Vic and Raquel had no idea I was sitting a few feet away.

I took my opening when Vic said something about the Yankees.

"The Yankees suck!" I think I blurted.

The couple looked at me, and we had some Yankee-Met rivalry banter for a few minutes until I let them know they chased me all the way to Rome from the Bronx or something like that.

I had so much fun doing this.

They invited me to sit with them, but I only stayed long enough to invite them to join Gjuli and me at a great steakhouse the next evening. Surprisingly, they accepted my invitation. Well, Raquel did.

The next evening, we ate together and strolled a bit before we said our goodbyes. It was lovely. They really enjoyed Gjuli. That's what people from the Bronx do when they meet for the first time.

†

A few weeks later, I called Vic on his cell phone. I loved to rattle his cage.

I told Vic I was following another case that was brewing in the States. I predicted it was a serial killer and the case would soon be coming his way. The FBI would be on this case like stink on shit. This time, Vic listened intently and without his usual cop sarcasm. I was a little sarcastic myself when I said he wasn't paying attention like he should.

I brought Vic up to speed. There were two especially brutal murders, four weeks apart. One in New York City and the other in the city of Los Angeles. I tied the killer's M.O. together.

Vic disagreed. He didn't think killings separated by so much time and so much distance would amount to a serial killer profile. He was entitled to his opinion, even though it was wrong.

Our phone call went something like this:

"And how is my Gabriella?" I started politely as I always do.

"Growing up fast. Hey, by the way, after we had that fabulous steak dinner, we didn't see hide nor hair of you and the missus."

"We drove back north the next morning. You know I can't stay in one spot for too long. I enjoy my freedom too much," I'm not wrong.

"To what do I owe this call?" Vic sounded a bit impatient.
"I think there is another case brewing. I guess you don't follow things in the States as closely as I do. I'm always looking for an opportunity to get busy, Vic."

"Are you just looking for work so hard that you may be out on a ledge this time?" Vic queries.

"Nonsense. In the past two months, there have been murders in your city and one in Los Angeles with some common denominators. Smells serialist to me," I say.

"No idea what you're referring to. Besides that,

how do you get these things all the way from your perch up in the Alps?"

"I have friends in high places, or I just read a lot. I never reveal my sources," I teased, knowing a little how explosive he can be.

"You know better than to classify two murders as a serial killer. Even the FBI wants to see three with similar footprints."

"The FBI? Don't make me laugh. Those bureaucratic assholes have their own pot of shit to be concerned about these days."

"So, what do two murders 3,000 miles apart have in common that makes you so cocksure there will be another?"

"I'll guarantee it."

"Okay, Mr. Genius, let's hear your story."

"The next one will be in about two, maybe three weeks if I'm correct. And Vic, when have I not been correct? And, my dear young friend, after the next one, and there will be a next one, you will likely get a call from those idiots in Washington. Their profiling department with that messy woman, what's her name again? Oh yes... Gail Gain. They call her GG, correct? That's unless they've locked her up in a loony bin somewhere. There's no way they'll find this one. When they call you, please feel free to call me. I'll say I told you so, and then we can go to work," and I hung up on him...

I predicted, almost to the day, when the next similar murder would occur. I wasn't yet sure exactly where the killer would strike again, but I had the timeline right. I was right as usual, and Vic was astonished when the next killing came to light.

* † *

A wealthy celebrity by the name of Blake Du Mont was murdered in a Las Vegas hotel room. The FBI and all nationwide police systems picked up the report of the killing.

It was plain there was a national serial killer on the loose.

Du Mont was killed in the same fashion as the first two. Like with the New York and Los Angeles homicides, Du Mont had his tongue removed by the perpetrator.

In the New York City case, the young lesbian singer Lala Cole's ovaries were removed postmortem and left on her body. Gary Pose, the famous gay hairdresser to the stars in Los Angeles, was similarly killed, and his penis was flayed open like a fish and made to look like a vagina. His testicles were found in his hands.

I conferred by telephone with Vic and Raquel. I waited to see if they were good enough to find a pattern with this killer. They didn't. I was certain the FBI, if they hadn't figured it out by now, would soon.

That G.G. woman in Washington was brilliant and could pick up what I picked up quickly. Like always, I wanted to stay a step or two ahead of my adversaries; in this case, my nemesis was the FBI.

I broke things down to Vic and Raquel. They followed me in rapt attention and saw my theory unfold.

The first victim was a lesbian. Her first name begins with the letter L.

The second, a Gay man with the letter G starting is name.

Finally, Blake. Letter B. was bisexual.

LGB so far. TQ will soon follow. I suppose sometimes it takes a serial killer to know one.

The victims' deaths were all preceded by paralysis by chemical injection. Precision surgical procedures were used. In every case so far, some souvenir was taken by the killer. This fits a pattern with most serial killers. I wonder why I never did that? Maybe I should have. A nice scrapbook with items I took away from my victims. Interesting concept, don't you think?

Vic and Raquel were now my captive audience.

I proceeded to tell them my theory of who the killer was and what the motivation was. It's so good being a genius. I can't begin to tell you.

Take what is given first. The killer is a man. His size, along with some video tapes from the Du Mont and New York City scenes, verified that.

Now the suppositions. He isn't part of the Alphabet Mafia, nor is he involved in the LGBTQ+ lifestyle. His motivation was either a political or a religious statement. He hated anyone who was sexually different. He worked alone and his killings are separated by 4 weeks.

That gave us plenty of time to predict, almost to a certainty, that his next victim was a transsexual person. But where would it be? I didn't have a clue and could have just made a guess, which I usually don't do.

I narrowed the killer down to a male who had medical knowledge and was a fanatical religious individual.

I knew Gail Gain, the famous G.G., the FBI profiler, would come to the same conclusions as I had. The FBI had the same month to try to figure out the killer's next move. The FBI has faced numerous problems recently, including corruption and a lack of trust among the American people. The FBI needed something to hang their hats on. Catching the nationwide serial killer would help their image, and right now, the agency was all about how they looked in the eyes of the people.

All I wanted was for Vic and Raquel to win the race.

CHAPTER 44

The lead FBI guy on the case was an Agent Dean Salerno. Vic had no use for him. I don't think Vic ever had much use for anyone in the FBI. The way that the agency comes across to the local police departments is that they are always in charge, and the world owes them for putting their pants on in the morning.

Salerno was a smug, egotistical agency climber who wanted all the glory of capturing the serial killer. He gets this case solved, and he catapults into a big job at the FBI headquarters in Washington, D.C. Then, who knows? He could one day be the Director.

Salerno was a name that instantly triggered me. It was like ice on a decayed tooth. At the Villanova seminary, I would say 80% of the place was gay. And that's being conservative.

The seminary was more like a Cher concert than a place to study for the priesthood. It was openly and unashamedly gay.

Salerno was a short, stout, cherubic priest who taught Latin and Theology. His feet never touched the ground. He was always making passes at many of the novices, especially me. He had this thing for blond hair and blue eyes I suppose. He would poke fun at my Bronx accent and offer to come to my room for elocution lessons, to the laughs and snickering of my fellow novices.

A day or two before I left Villanova, he had the balls to come visit me. I punched him hard in his nose. The blood streamed from him like a sun shower. "How do you like me now scumbag, and how is my accent?" I yelled. He waddled away, whimpering like a little girl.

* † *

FBI Agent Salerno was no match for Vic and certainly no competition for me. G.G. in the FBI headquarters, on the other hand, was certainly my equal when it came to delving into serial killer cases.

It was during this case I decided to give G.G. a call. She answered her phone

"Gain,"

"Well, I can see you are working seven days a week on this lovely case," I say in Irish brogue. And I just know that GG immediately begins to record the call.

"Hello, Mr. Deegan."

"So, ya figured me out did ya! Kudos to you. I'm certain Salerno told you I was dead and buried now, didn't he? Have ya narrowed in on that bloody surgeon yet?" I enquired.

"I'm not at liberty to discuss an ongoing case," GG replies a little too quickly to my liking.

"I have, Gail," I reply, switching to my normal voice.

"What makes you so sure?" GG asks.

"Like you, I'm pretty damn smart. I'm even smart enough to know you hit that button on your phone to record this conversation. Hello, Special Agent Salerno and Cis Burns," I laugh.

"So, where are you predicting the next murder?" GG fishes.

"Hmmm. That tells me something. It tells me that the entire FBI, with all their technology, money, and personnel, is a beat behind me. I feel like it's a sort of game...a race to the finish line between me and the bureau," I declare.

"Tell me why you are so interested in this case."

"Great question, Gail. Just for the fun of it," Deegan is now toying with the best serial killer profiler in FBI history.

"Fun? We are trying to prevent another murder, and you are having...fun?"

"It's all in the wonderful game we call life. How about I give you a few hints, Gail?"

"Yes."

"Take a map of the United States. I'm sure your department can come up with one."

"Fine."

"Okay, now draw a line from the first murder to the second. Got it?" I toy with the idea, sounding a bit childish, but I can't help myself.

"I did. It's okay if I use a map on my desktop?"

"Okay, yeah...that's good. Now draw a line to the

latest killing. Let me know when you have that. Forget the Vegas stop. 'Cause, after all, you have to go through Nevada for California."

"Ready." GG blurts.

"Now draw a straight line up to Minnesota. Right to the tippy top of the good ole USA. Okay...okay... for now, I will give you only one hint. It won't be in any repeated states, and it's not Minnesota, either. But here is a bonus hint. The killer is from a state none of these lines pass through but he's pretty damn close. Now, that state is only three states away from where the next homicide will occur. Okay, now, Miss Gail Gain, hope you got all that. Talk soon. Buh-bye, Salerno and Burns. See if you can help out GG with this puzzle."

I ended the call abruptly. Let see if the FBI can solve this puzzle on their own...

* † *

The next murder took place in Louisiana. I found no geographic coloration in the other homicides.

A college professor by the name of Teri Arceneaux's bloated and maggot-infested and fly-infested body was found in her home. She lived alone in her family's house in the Bayou. Arceneaux was killed in the same fashion as the others. She was a male to female Transgender who was loved by her students. Professor Arceneaux was paralyzed by an injection and then killed. Her silicone breasts were surgically removed and left on her body.

Now we had our T.

At the same time, Raquel's mom, Olga, was at the wrong place at the wrong time. Despite her daughter's insistence that she stay away from the old and dangerous Bronx neighborhood, Olga went to see friends. Olga and two of her friends got too close to a drive-by shooting. Olga was knocked down and broke her hip. One of her friends took a bullet but lived.

Vic and Raquel were now focused on Olga, at least for the time being, so I was working alone until they squared things away back in New York City.

Where would this maniac strike again? And who the hell was he? I knew I had 4 weeks to solve these questions. I always liked deadlines as they made my mind work faster.

I needed to find a Q for queer somewhere with the first letter in his or her name being Q. I had to pinpoint where in the entire United States such a person existed. Back in the day, anyone who was gay was called queer. Today, it means something else.

In the LGBTQ+ world a queer is anyone who doesn't identify as heterosexual or cisgender. It also includes any person who is not lesbian, homosexual, bisexual, or transgender. Honesty, I don't know what the hell that leaves.

In the meantime, the FBI had done a very good job of discovering who the killer was. G.G. did her magic and found a person of interest. There was a boot print left at the Bayou murder, and that moved the needle. Salerno and his staff made haste and followed up on the information. I must admit they were doing a decent job of feeding all those FBI egos.

"The Surgeon," as the killer was called, was indeed a real-life surgeon by the name of Dr. Paul Vogelbach of Milwaukee, Wisconsin. As I had predicted, he was a religious fanatic.

Vogelbach was a member of a fundamentalist Christian church in Milwaukee headed by an extremist bible beater, the Reverend Christian Stewart. I came across some YouTube videos of this individual. Holy Christ, he was a real off-the-rails modern-day Elmer Gantry with his ranting and raving.

Salerno was all over the lead and brought his people to Milwaukee. There were more FBI agents and cops on the streets than Brewers fans.

They did a pretty good job with this. I knew, however, the time for the killer to strike was nearing. Not to brag too much, I do like to brag at the appropriate time, but my instincts told be to find the Q. That's where the killer would be. I knew he wouldn't be in Milwaukee awaiting capture by the FBI et al.

I had narrowed down the target to one person. I bet all the chips that I was correct.

I gathered Vic and Raquel. We took a private jet from Teterboro in New Jersey to Cincinnati, Ohio. I disguised myself as a 1960's hippy. Bellbottom pants, tied-dyed shirt, stringy white hair and open toe sandals. John Lennon tinted glasses added to my look. I was going to hit the road running.

The guy I was betting on to be the next victim was a local musician of some notoriety by the name of Quincy Davis. I chuckled at the name because it was a combination of the great musicians Quincy Jones and Miles Davis. Pretty cool name.

Quincy Davis fit the Q in queer. The guy was all over social media with the freakiest people you have ever seen. Quincy had this strange sexual vide that attracted bizarre sexual companions. He was the cover boy for Queer if there was one. In my mind, he would be the number one target for the killer. I would have bet a thousand to one I was right.

Quincy Davis was appearing late that night at a well-known jazz venue, so Vic, Raquel, and I were ready to see Davis' show. I had a feeling we would run into someone we were looking for.

Salerno and his crew found the pickings to be slim in Milwaukee.

G.G. had discovered Vogelbach used one of his accounts to rent an Airbnb in Cincinnati, so Salerno et al headed there. They were hot on my heels to collar the killer. They just didn't know I was in the mix, of course. I had put Vic and Raquel in a position of advantage.

While we were in the jazz club, a hoodie-covered, sunglasses-wearing big man walked in. It was Paul Vogelbach. He was stalking his prey. Vic wanted to pounce on him immediately. I wanted to wait and catch him in the act. I was using Quincy Davis as bait.

I don't often say this, but in retrospect, I believe Vic was right. I went against Vic's street cop instincts.

I guess I was just trying to play out the whole serial killer scenario and see what would happen. My bad.

I had egg on my face when Quincy Davis got away from us after he left the club. Now we had to find out where he lived. Suppose he was even going home. In the meantime, the FBI's G.G. had figured out the Q thing with Quincy being the target.

We got to Quincy's residence in the nick of time. Vogelbach had already given the musician the paralyzing injection.

We heard the police sirens coming close to Quincy's house. I had to make my exit, or Salerno would have caught me. That would be jail for me for the rest of my days. And Salerno would have been a hero. Catching John Deegan was the ultimate prize in the law enforcement world. I wasn't about to let that happen.

Vic and Raquel cornered the killer. Vogelbach shot himself rather than be taken alive. Quincy Davis lived, and I was back on the jet to safety.

Salerno wanted the collar so badly that he made a fool out of himself. Vic later told me Salerno was sent to the FBI's Siberia. His career and high aspirations were shattered. A dick like Salerno sometimes gets what's coming to him.

Vic, Raquel, and I won the game.

You see, to me it was all a game. Like chess, the more moves a player can think ahead, the better the chance of victory.

It was fitting for me that religion was at the core of this serial killer's motivation. Vogelbach wanted to send a message that the LGBTQ+ world and their diverse sexual orientation were unacceptable to God. My message is a bit different. Molesting children was unacceptable to God. In a way, Vogelbach and I were not very unlike one another. I did not judge Dr. Vogelbach. That's above my pay grade.

I knew this would be my last case. At least for a while, anyway.

Other than my still quick brain and my efficient disguises, I knew my fastball was gone. At some point in life, if you are lucky enough to grow old, age has a way of catching up.

CHAPTER 45

My Life, just like another 's, has been filled with ups and downs.

During the years I was working on building my career and then my business, my mind would occasionally flash back to my abusers.

The busier I was, the less chance of a flashback. The nuns used to say an idle mind is the devil's workshop. In my case, they were spot on. It seemed my past exploitation came upon me when there was a lull in the action, or if I was bored by a particular deal. This is one of the reasons I never took vacations. Even long holiday weekends made me uneasy. My work became my obsession. In a sense, making money was my comfort zone. Outmaneuvering someone and winning in a deal was rewarding.

The more I entrenched myself in the deals and the numbers that powered them, the fewer the flashbacks came. When I relaxed at all, my life would be temporarily interrupted. I had no patience for any of that.

When I went home after an exhausting sixteen- or eighteen-hour day, I would swallow some food and go right to sleep. Sometimes my dreams copied the flashbacks, but I slept through them. The dreams could be short vignettes or all-night episodes from my past, leaving me irritable and tired when I woke.

In my dreams or a flashback, my mind would replay every detail of being in the rectory with Father O'Gorman. I can close my eyes today and still draw a diagram of that nasty place. Not just the first time I was abused by him, but the many times I was forced to surrender my body. As a child, O'Gorman controlled my mind. The things he said to me left their mark. I was afraid to lose my mother or my siblings, and the pain that would have brought.

I was older when Bishop Peroni got to me, and the guilt feelings of not reporting him or otherwise stopping him last with me to this day. He, like O'Gorman, controlled me emotionally.

What if Peroni had come to me when I was the up-and-coming star on Wall Street, living in my unkempt studio apartment? Would I had stopped him? Would I had punched him in the nose like I did that fat priest Salerno back at the seminary? I was bigger and stronger than the diminutive bishop. I could have easily hurt him. But would I? My bizarre answer is... I don't know.

I detested what he did to me.

Just like when I was a young boy in the rectory with O'Gorman, I would remove my mind from the abuse. I put myself in a trans like state. It's difficult to explain the hold these men had on me.

CHAPTER 46

I will take my torment to my grave.

I'm starting to sound like a whining, simpering old man. I'm fed up with myself and the whole thing.

I feel the end of my days is rapidly approaching as my body begins to break down and succumb to the inevitable. Death is no big deal to me. It's been done. I have looked into the faces of those I dispatched as the light faded from their eyes. Often, there is a wide-eyed, surprised look, but sooner or later, we all have to go.

Nothing works the way it once did for me, except for my mind, which, for some reason, is sharper than ever. Of course, I forget some long-ago names, places, or dates because they are no longer important to me. The things I don't remember are in the back file of my mind. Sometimes when I can't pull a fact or name up, if I care to challenge myself, I go through the alphabet slowly in my head, and the information returns.

Yesterday, for example, our chef was preparing a German lunch of grilled knockwurst and sauerkraut for me and Gjuli. For a second, the aroma reminded me of passing a Jewish deli on Tremont Avenue in the Bronx, a few blocks from where we lived. This remembrance dates to the late 50's, mind you. What was the name of the deli? I'm certain a deep Google search would get it, but I wanted to test myself. It took me all the way to W, in the alphabet, to remember Witkins Delicatessen. It's not as important as the provisions of the Treaty of Guadalupe-Hidalgo, but at that moment in time, Witkins was important for me to remember.

* † *

Now, my knees, wrists, and neck are a package of pain. Occasionally, my back screams at me, and the pain shoots up and down my legs. In the last few years, I've seemed to have shrunk a couple of inches, and I'm stooped over a bit. If I stand in front of a mirror, the reflection is that of a stranger.

I occasionally get red blotches on my arms and legs that come and go, serving as a reminder that things are changing quickly.

All those badges of old age are nothing compared to my damaged past. There is no Advil to take to alleviate that pain.

There are times, like today, for example, when I feel a momentary spurt of energy and I want to get back in the fray. No, I don't want to get another 12 crucifixes and start a new campaign of terror on bad people. The vengeance in me was satisfied for the most part. But I do look for cases that I want to dive into and help solve with Vic Gonnella and Raquel

Ruiz. Of late, nothing seems to jump out at me. A serial killer here and a mass murderer there, but I see no challenges that call to me. So, I watch the world continuously change, and I shake my head in judgment.

I don't think Vic Gonnella will call anymore to say he needs me on a case. But you never know. He knows where and how to reach me, and I may even surprise him one of these days. My bag of disguises is always at the ready.

†

I long ago gave up the concept of God and the devil...heaven and hell. I'll never know if my abuse was the cause of my atheism or, as I often say, my agnosticism, to hedge my bet. I stopped saying 'God bless you' when someone sneezes, replaced by a 'salute.' God dammit is still that just because. Only God knows? is now, 'who knows'? but old habits die hard. When something is shocking, or I drop and break something, I still blurt out 'Jesus, Mary and Joseph' as that is embedded in my cultural psyche. Mom said it a minimum of six times a day.

There are days that I feel the creep of boredom pushing its way into my head. Certainly, it comes along less and less, but when it does, my boredom will still wreak havoc on my poor wife. Gjuli can see I'm restless even when I'm napping or in bed for the night. Gjuli said there is a tenseness in my face, and my shoulders shrug a bit more than usual. What can I say? I'm too long on the tooth to make any excuses about myself. This is part of being a genius, I suppose. Especially an intellect who had his or her childhood stolen. Imagine if Albert Einstein was molested by his Rabbi when he was going for his Bar Mitzvah? Bad example that. Einstein was an observant Jew until the age of 12. He didn't have a Bar Mitzvah and passed on the gifts because he rejected religious authority and dogma. Great minds think alike I suppose.

But for the sake of argument, what if the rabbi molested Herr Einstein? (and who knows if he wasn't?) Would his life have taken a different track? His destiny and humanity could have been critically different. It's just an illustration, but it gives us pause for thought.

What if a priest didn't rape me as a child and I fulfilled my mothers dream of being in the priesthood? And what if I took it, as Mom wished, all the way to the red hat? Would Cardinal John Joseph Deegan have been a compliant prince of the church, as I had been around the pious Catholics all my life? Was there a chance that I would have stepped out of line with the rest of the red-capped crowd? Would I have done anything to stop the pedophiles and gays from frolicking around in their frilly cassocks from St. Peter's Square to Tolentine parish?

Doubt it.

At my age, every year feels like six months. Every fly can become an elephant. Money and things become less and less valuable.

Sooner than later, nothing at all will matter except the last gasps of breath I take and the final flashbacks of my tortured life. Oh, those flashbacks.

I have no say in it, but I'm not done living...

Detective
Vic Gonnella Series:

INTERCESSION
JUSTIFIED
YOU THINK I'M DEAD
THE BUTCHER OF PUNTA CANA
THE PIPELINE
SHANDA
The Surgeon

Other books by Louis Romano:

ON THE SIDE OF THE ROAD

Gino Ranno Mafia Series:
BESA
FISH FARM
GAME OF PAWNS
EXCLUSION

Young Adults:
ZIP CODE

Short Story & Poetry Series
ANXIETY'S NEST ANXIETY'S CURE
BEFORE I DROP DEAD

Heritage Collection Series:
CARUSI: THE SHAME OF SICILY
IN THEIR FOOTSTEPS

True Crime:
BORN IN THE LIFE
TRUST AND BETRAYAL
JOHN ALITE MAFIA INTERNATIONAL

BEFORE I DROP DEAD: SHORT STORIES

Acknowledgements

My memory at my age is still pretty good. I must thank my memory for recalling so many stories from my childhood to the present.

My oldest and first friend in life, John Roach, the model for John Deegan, left an indelible impression on me. We talk once or twice a year, and the calls last for hours.

Vic Gonnella's character was inspired by my dear friend, Retired NYPD Detective Vic Cipulo, who helps me with all things cop in all my novels.

Thanks to Bruce Milsten for his explanation on the financial markets and how John Deegan could get so wealthy in a short time.

My wife, Mary Lynn Bologna-Romano, for dealing with my here one minute, gone the next mood while I'm writing.

And, the concept creator of this book, my brilliant muse and editor, M. Dutchy, of Spaaij Design, for her long-distance friendship.

Finally, I still miss my Jack Russel terrier Rocco. Writing is not the same without him.

About the author:

Born in The Bronx in 1950, Romano launched his literary career at 60, after years of writing urban poetry. His notable works include two poetry books, "Anxiety's Nest" and "Anxiety's Cure," as well as the mob novel "Fish Farm." His Pulitzer Prize-contending "GAME OF PAWNS" and the Vic Gonnella Series, starting with the Amazon Best Seller "INTERCESSION," have captivated readers.

Romano also writes for teens with the "ZIP CODE" series and explores True Crime in "BORN IN THE LIFE." His latest release, co-authored with John Gjocaj, is "ON THE SIDE OF THE ROAD." With a diverse portfolio, Romano continues to engage audiences from his home in Northern New Jersey.

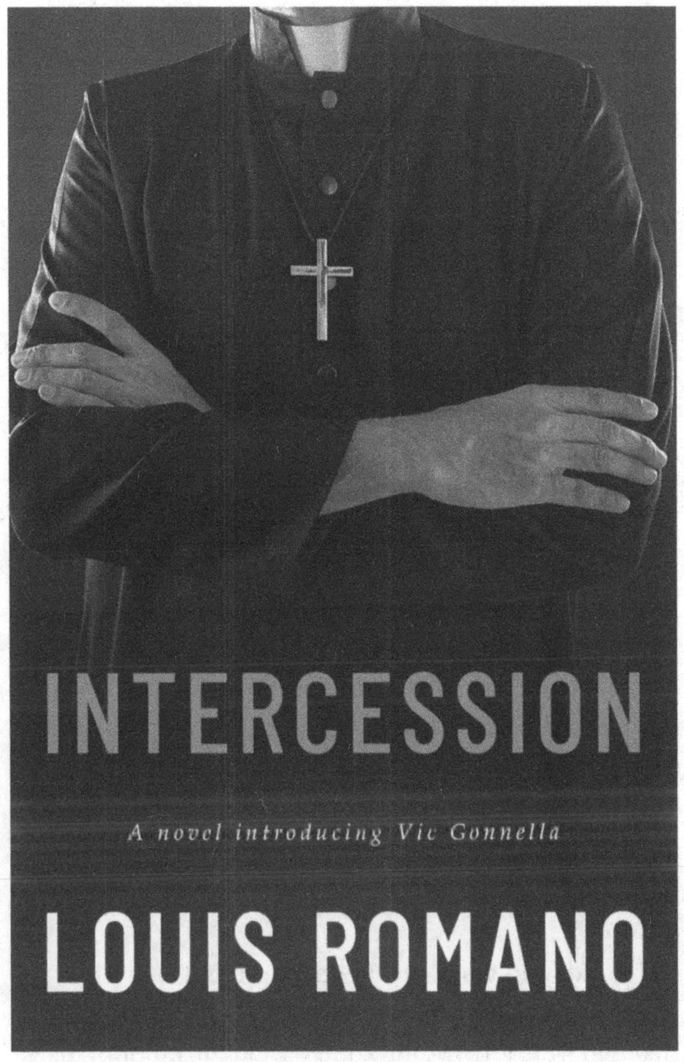
INTERCESSION
A novel introducing Vic Gonnella
LOUIS ROMANO

Chapter 1

2012, The Bronx, New York

There was a sharp rap on the door of the rectory at St. Martin of Tours Church. Father Edward O'Gorman tutted and looked at his watch. It was after 9 P.M., and visitors at that hour were not the norm. The church wasn't even getting many visitors at mass of late. Times had changed both for the neighborhood and for this once crowded but still glorious church. Father O'Gorman peered through the stained glass next to the heavy, mahogany entrance and could immediately see there was no danger, but there was certainly intrigue. A frail, old man with wispy, white hair was frantically pressing the buzzer and banging on the door as if the church was on fire.

The moment O'Gorman opened the door, the man dropped to his knees and pleaded for his confession to be heard in a church and inside a real confessional booth.

The old man was only 60 years old but had disguised himself to look as if he were in his mid-80s. His own mother wouldn't have recognized him; his teeth were almost green, and his hair was twisted and matted as if he hadn't bathed in a very long time and a razor hadn't touched his face in weeks. His hands were black with filth and his fingernails, gnarly and overgrown. Hair stuck out from his ears and nose, and his lips were chapped and infected.

O'Gorman helped the man to his feet and led him into the rectory. He was babbling about a moral conflict, an emergency to cleanse his soul of some horrible event in his life. O'Gorman, who had been a priest at St. Martin's parish since the 1950s, was retired but living "in residence" in the rectory. He had asked to spend his final days in the Bronx rather than in some lovely, bucolic home, where old priests were sent to wait for death. Father Edward's wish was granted by three different bishops and a cardinal because of their friendship with him and his many years of loyal service to the archdiocese. He had played the game very well within the Church and also had a few trump cards to use if his superiors suffered from sudden amnesia. O'Gorman knew where the figurative bodies were buried.

O'Gorman never wanted to be called monsignor and had no interest in climbing the career ladder, so his role as parish priest suited him just fine; he was happiest in familiar surroundings in a low key environment where he could behave as he pleased. When he turned 70, O'Gorman made a deal to stay on for a few more years before going into retirement. In the meantime, he'd stay in the same rectory where he had lived since he was a 28-year-old priest on his second assignment out of the seminary. He had spent only a few months at St. Anne's Parish in the South Bronx before he was moved quickly to St. Martin's. Now, he was 83 years old and spoke fluent Spanish. He had picked it up when the neighborhood became mostly Hispanic and African American in the early 1960s. He enjoyed long walks in the nearby Bronx Zoo and Botanical Gardens. His life was simple, but by the grace of God, it was exactly where he wanted it to be. His once tall and blond, good looks, marred only by a toothy smile, were long gone. The old priest was stoop-shouldered and bald with heavy, dark circles around his now dull, blue eyes.

O'Gorman was in mufti when the old man appeared at the rectory door, begging for a priest to save his soul from the fires of hell. Reluctantly, O'Gorman agreed to hear his confession. Father O'Gorman was alone in the rectory that night as there was a basketball game at St. Raymond High School in nearby Parkchester for the finals in the annual Christian Brothers tournament. The other parish priest, Father Vincent Ortiz, had gone to root for the legendary Ravens. Two of the team members had attended St. Martin's and would soon be getting athletic scholarships for college, a source of great pride for the school and parish. Both of those young men knew Father Edward very well. In fact, they knew him too well.

The archdiocese had decided to close St. Martin's school this year, and it was evident this was perhaps the last hurrah for any of the school's alum to reach for the brass ring through basketball. Sports was one of the few ways that students could escape from the poverty and danger of the area. The other ways out were death, prison, and the military. O'Gorman knew his days in residence were numbered, and he was patiently preparing for the inevitable. Sooner or later, God's waiting room in Orange County, New York or the nursing home, St. Patrick's, in the Bronx was in his destiny. What good would living in this rectory be anyway without the students, especially the boys, coming in and out of the church and residence?

O'Gorman fumbled for the key to the church's side door that hung on the kitchen wall as the old man continued to sob softly. O'Gorman threw the long-sleeved, white, linen surplice over his civilian attire and draped a purple stole around his neck so that it hung evenly just below his knees. He led him to the side of the church, and the old man shuffled beside him. They arrived just near an old grotto with the statue of Our Lady of Fatima looking down upon them. The grotto had been a popular place for First Holy Communion photographs for decades, but it hadn't had water flowing from it for over twenty years. The pump had failed, and there was no money to repair it, a sign of the times in a neighborhood where storefront churches and Santeria had taken their toll on the donations made to St. Martin. The second collection at Sunday masses had been stopped long ago as the baskets always came back empty.

Once inside, the electronic candles, which had long ago replaced the wax ones, and one security light, gave off just enough illumination for the two men to see their way to the back of the church and to the confessional that had Father Edward O'Gorman's name printed on a small, faded, bronze plaque on the light brown door.

Father Edward took the two ends of the purple stole into his hands and gently kissed the embroidered, gold crosses on each end. He then pointed for the old man to open the door to the compartment, where he would use the diagonal kneeler. O'Gorman opened the door to the priest's compartment and sat in the uncomfortable office chair that he had been using since the '50s. Creature comforts were few and far between. The confessional at St. Martin of Tours Church had the aroma of Pine Sol disinfectant and liquor. The Pine Sol was from the mop used by the once every two weeks porter that the archdiocese sent to clean up the church with a lick and a promise. The booze was emanating from Father O'Gorman. He slowly slid open the lattice.

"Bless me, Father, for I have sinned, it has been many years since my last confession."

"Go on, my son," O'Gorman responded into the pitch-black darkness, suppressing a belch from the two frankfurters and beans he had had for supper that evening.

"I have done many bad things, Father. I am sorry for what I have done and want to be forgiven so I can die and go to heaven. I killed many, many men during the war. I have not been to mass in 36 years. I have renounced my religion and my belief in Jesus Christ, our Lord."

"Let's start with the killings, my son. In service to your country during wartime, there is no sin in taking lives. You did your duty as so many men did during World War II, and God fully understands that you were doing what you had to do for the good of many." Father Edward had consoled many men who killed in war.

"It was Nicaragua, Father, that damned Nicaragua, and I enjoyed the killing of those spics. I loved feeling their lives come out of them when I choked and stabbed them to death. Shooting them was not as much fun, but I loved that too, Father." The old man's voice had become clearer and seemed younger.

"You seem a bit too old for Nicaragua. Are you sure about this?" There was concern in Father Edward's voice.

"Oh, I'm sure of it, Father. You may remember the Deegan family from back in the day here at St. Martin's, Father. A good, Irish family with a bunch of wee kids. Do you recall the name, Father...Deegan?" the old man said with a perfect Irish brogue.

"Now, see here! What is the meaning of this? Is this your idea of a joke? Get out of my church this instant," O'Gorman said as he tried to open the compartment door to get back to the safety of the rectory. It was to no avail.

"Sorry, Padre, you can't leave just yet. The door is locked, and it's just me and you over here." The accent was now Bronx Italian ruffian.

"What the... who are you? What do you want?" Father O'Gorman was shaking like a leaf.

"Just a few questions is all, Father." The voice was that of a little boy. "What? What questions? My God, what do you want with me?"

"Answer the question, Father. The Deegans, do you recall the name?"

Again in the Irish brogue.

"I do... yes, I do. They moved away many years ago," the priest said, his voice quivering.

"Ah, yes, indeed, they did, and you followed them, now didn't ya? Ya followed them so that you could help save their souls from the devil himself, now didn't ya, good Father Edward O'Gorman. Yer own people. And they had that wee boy, John, don't ya remember? Ya insisted on calling him Sean, his true, Gaelic name, remember that, Father? They were from Donegal, don't ya recall?"

"Hail, Mary, full of grace, the Lord is with thee, blessed art thou among women, and bless..."

"Shut the fuck up, Edward. Just shut your fucking mouth," the old man screamed at the praying priest, who felt a trickle of piss run down his leg.

"I didn't do anything to that boy. I would never do such a thing. It wasn't me, I... I would never."

"That's what you all say. 'I would never, could never, the Lord as my witness, yada yada.' Well, Father, it's me, John Deegan. I've come to give you a bit of the unholy terror that you left with me since 1958, when I was a first grader. I'm going to do it slowly so that I can enjoy it and you'll remember it for eternity." Deegan used his own voice this time, punching the words slowly. "I've been watching your comings and goings for weeks, waiting for the right moment when you were all alone." Deegan paused for a long 10 seconds.

"Now say the prayer after me! Father. You know, the one you taught me over and over and over, but let's say the revised, politically correct, Vatican-approved version, Father... C'mon...here we go...

"O, my God,

I am heartily sorry for having offended Thee, and I detest all my sins,

because I dread the loss of heaven

and the pains of hell but most of all, because

they offend Thee, my God, Who art all good and deserving of all my love.

I firmly resolve,

with the help of Thy grace, to confess my sins,

to do penance,

and to amend my life.

Amen."

O'Gorman mumbled the prayer, but his heart rate had risen to the point where he was light headed and confused.

Deegan slowly opened the compartment where he was kneeling just inches away from the pedophile priest.

"Help... someone, help! For the love of God, please, someone help me." The priest was screaming, but of course, no one could hear him.

Deegan slowly removed the block that he had wedged into the wooden confessional door then turned the knob. The priest was now sobbing and begging for both help and forgiveness.

Deegan laughed in the voice of a small boy as he opened the door.

"Father Edward, remember you used to tell me... 'This is what God's love feels like.' Well... feel this, Father."

Chapter 2

The ancestors of the Deegan family had first set foot in the States so long ago the date had been forgotten. What was left of the family lore were words that were familiar to nearly every Irish family, the potato blight, wet rot, the *drochshaol*, or bad times, coffin ships, and the great hunger.

The present day Deegans knew they had lost relatives in the famine. This was not surprising as one in five of the Irish population died from malnutrition, disease, or violence. They heard from their grandparents that the Irish were punished for "the sins of the people," a superstitious, more than religious saying that caught on like the airborne fungus itself. The Roman Catholic Church did little to allay the fears of the faithful. The great, unwashed masses were never told that they were not being punished by the one, true, and benevolent God in heaven, that the blight was actually a phenomenon of nature, and that there was plenty of food the English kept from them. The stranglehold the Church had around the necks of the Irish people came with them on the coffin ships and has lingered and flourished since 1845.

John Joseph Deegan was the second born of six children to Jack Joseph Deegan and Maureen Duffy. He was the shining apple of his parents' eyes. In his mother's heart, soul, and mind, Johnny Boy was destined to be a priest from the day he was born. With John as a priest and by the grace of God, one of her daughters perhaps would join the convent. Maureen Deegan would have been happy to have closed her eyes and gone to heaven that very day. Her work on earth would have been complete as her children would work on saving souls and doing God's will to alleviate the sins of the people.

When John was three, his older sister, Margaret, would dress in white sheets and towels like the Dominican nuns and wear a rosary around her tiny waist, pretending to be teaching John his catechism lessons with a ruler in her hand to whack him on his knuckles or knees. Maureen and her friends would laugh at the sayings "Sister" Margaret would pass on to her baby brother, who remembered his lessons with uncanny recall.

By the time John got to first grade at St. Martin of Tours School, he could read, print his name and address, tie his shoes, and accomplish the one thing the nuns absolutely loved: he could recite the answers to the Baltimore Catechism questions verbatim.

Question: Who is God?

Answer: God is the Creator of heaven and earth and of all things. Question: What is man?

Answer: Man is a creature composed of body and

soul and made to the image and likeness of God.

Question: Why did God make you?

Answer: God made me to know Him, to love Him, to serve Him in this world, and to be happy with Him forever in the next.

Question: Does God see us?

Answer: God sees us and watches over us.
Question: What is Confession?

Answer: Confession is the telling of our sins to a duly authorized priest for the purpose of obtaining forgiveness.

From the day he started school in September 1958, John was destined to be a priest and climb the ladder of the archdiocese all the way to receiving his red hat from the pope. When his mother spoke to him alone, she referred to him as John Cardinal Deegan with a smile that the angels themselves would envy.

A photographic memory and ridiculously good looks were gifts John was given to do the Lord's work here on earth. His blond hair and piercing, blue eyes made him the Mickey Mantlesque, all-American poster boy, who would win the hearts of millions all in due time. His mother knew it, his siblings accepted it as fact, and the nuns believed it. Throughout his first year of school, there was never a mark less than an A or a 100%. His papers and report cards had more red and gold stars than the rest of the entire first grade put together. He was brilliant, perfect, and gorgeous, and he was a genius. He would also wet the bed until he was almost fourteen years old.

Chapter 3

Father Vincent Ortiz returned from watching the St. Raymond Ravens beat Rice High School in the basketball tournament at around midnight. The young priest enjoyed the crowd and liked seeing familiar faces and of course, rubbing elbows with the powerful Monsignor Joseph Barry, who ran the richest parish in the Bronx along with the largest Catholic cemetery in the country. St. Raymond Elementary and High School had been a powerhouse not only in sports but also in the political world of the archdiocese for decades. From the late 1800s, the twin domes of St. Raymond's Church had stood sentinel on East Tremont and Castle Hill Avenues as a beacon for the predominantly Irish, Italian, and German immigrants. The elite, financial status was a monument to the hard work and religious dedication of these people. Father Vincent was in awe of this church and its history. It was where he wanted to wind up working one day. Unlike O'Gorman, Vincent was a career climber.

The exposure this particular evening could garner would be beneficial to his career, especially if the new archbishop decided to close St. Martin's Church down completely. The rumors were already flying around that the archdiocese planned to close the underperforming schools and churches. St. Martin's school was first, so the church could not be too far behind. The logic fueled the gossip mill, and the likelihood that Father Vincent would soon be a free agent was real.

After the basketball game, Father Vincent took the two former St. Martin student ball players out for a celebratory pizza at Ronnie's Pizza on East Tremont Avenue. When they'd had their fill of the great pizza and Coca Cola, Father Vincent drove them back to the neighborhood. He said a silent prayer that they would go directly home as he advised rather than remain out too late and in harm's way. He felt badly about not inviting Father Edward to join in the festivities, but the boys were not overly enthusiastic about the older priest's presence. Ortiz didn't press the issue. He noticed the boys became quiet and almost sullen when he mentioned the old priest's name but didn't pursue the awkward moment. After all, it was their night and just as well as the game ended in overtime after 10 o'clock. Father O'Gorman was usually in bed by 10 anyway.

When the young priest entered the rectory, the place was dark except for the dim light that was barely visible from under the closed door of Father O'Gorman's bedroom. Father Vincent knew that the elder priest usually fell asleep while reading and so he made his way quietly to his own bedroom. He had an early mass to say the next morning and fell fast asleep.

***

Mrs. Nelly Santiago arrived every day at the rectory at 6:30 in the morning. She always prepared breakfast and lunch for the two priests. Their personal wash, ironing, vestment preparation, and house cleaning were all her responsibilities, and she worked for minimum wage, tithing 20% of her wages back to the Church. For Nelly, this was a labor of love for her Church and for her devotion to the Blessed Virgin Mary. By 2 o'clock in the afternoon, Nelly would be walking back to her small but immaculately clean apartment, where she had lived since 1968. That year, she had arrived in New York from *Bayamon*, located in the mountains of central Puerto Rico. Nelly worked at St. Martin of Tours from that day forward and at 64, had no plans to retire. The Church was her life. Her English was practically nonexistent for a person who had lived in New York City for 44 years, but her lovely and caring manner made the language barrier part of her charm rather than an impediment.

When she opened the door of the rectory the morning after John Deegan made his visit to Father O'Gorman, Nelly felt a chill go down her spine. The only other time in her life she had felt that haunting sensation was when her sister had called from Puerto Rico many years ago to tell her that their mother had died suddenly in her sleep.

At the entrance to the rectory, Nelly blessed herself, shrugged off the odd feeling, and headed for the kitchen to begin her day's work. As she recited her morning rosary, Nelly busied herself preparing hot oatmeal, toast, and coffee for the two priests. Generally, Father O'Gorman would be roaming around the small living quarters, sitting in the study watching the morning news, or reading from one of his leather bound scripture books. Nelly found it odd that he was nowhere in sight, even though it was a Saturday. She went about her chores, awaiting the priests.

"*Buenos Dias*, Nelly, and how are you this beautiful day?" Father Vincent said as he entered the kitchen and made a beeline for the coffee pot. Nelly's *Cafe Bustello* was strong and aromatic just like the coffee Father Ortiz's dear mother made when he was at home.

"*Buenos Dias, Padre, el señor nos ha dado un día hermoso.*"

"Yes, indeed. He has given us a beautiful day and wonderful coffee. I hope one day you will be able to greet me in English, my dear Nelly. I will answer you in English as I know you can understand."

"Jes, I can unnerstand ju, Farrrthur." Nelly pronounced her words slowly.

"Wonderful, Nelly, that is very good," Father Vincent said through a beaming smile.

"Nelly, where are the keys to the church? They are not hanging on the hook. Has Father O'Gorman gone over?"

"I no see hin this day," Nelly said as she stirred the bubbling oatmeal.

"Yes, and the door to his bedroom is closed, that's strange," Father Vincent said almost to himself.

Nelly suddenly remembered the chill when she entered the rectory that morning and walked past Father Vincent quickly to check on the old priest.

Her heart skipped a beat. Had the old priest been called to the Lord in his sleep? 'A good death,' she thought. Curious about her rapid movement and odd behavior, Father Vincent followed her down the dark hallway to the bedroom. Nelly tapped lightly on the door.

"Padre? Padre Edward?" Silence.

She looked at Father Vincent and began biting her quivering lower lip. Nelly slowly turned the knob clockwise and opened the creaking door slowly. She peered into the room and sighed with relief, blessing herself and thanking Jesus. Father Vincent exhaled.

"Nelly, you are going to be the death of me yet," Father Vincent said under his breath as he looked around the room. Strangely, the bed was made, and the light was still on. Nelly insisted that she make the priest's beds and change the bed linens on Saturdays and Tuesdays. Something just didn't seem right. Nelly began to breathe heavily again.

"Relax, Nelly; he's in the church. That's why the key isn't in its spot. C'mon, let's go see him. I have mass soon anyway. You can help with the altar server and with my vestments." Father Vincent spoke soothingly in Spanish.

They walked over to the side door of the church and found it ajar. Nothing strange. Father Edward was always careless about leaving windows and doors open. Nelly walked briskly into the sacristy and toward the altar, calling Father Edward's name in a hushed tone. After all, she was in the house of the Lord, and decorum was always required. When she had left the kitchen, she had grabbed a lace doily from the table and placed it on top of her head. She was a very old-fashioned woman, and old habits die hard.

Father Vincent also looked around the sacristy quickly. No one. He checked in the small priests' toilet behind the dressing area. It was empty except for a rogue winter water bug that was trying to crawl out of the porcelain sink. The young prelate walked to the front of the church and opened the doors from inside so that any parishioners for his early mass would not have to wait out in the street. As he walked back into the church from the vestibule, something caught his eye.

In the darkened corner of the church, there seemed to be a water leak coming from the confessionals. As Father Vincent slowly walked over to the large puddle of liquid, his eyes fell on what looked like blood flowing from Father O'Gorman's compartment to the back of the last pew in the church. His heart pounded in his chest. The taste of his morning coffee, mixed with bile, caused instant acid reflux in his throat.

"Father, he is not here." Nelly's hushed voice from behind startled him. He felt himself jump at least an inch off the ground. Father Vincent quickly gathered his thoughts.

"Nelly... please, go to the rectory, and call 911. Right now, Nelly," he said softly. Nelly ignored his request.

Father Vincent put his right arm against the confessional door while being careful not to step into the wet area. When he pulled the door open, he was confronted with the nightmare that was once Father Edward O'Gorman.

"*Aye, dios mio. El diablo estaba aquí, él mató al Padre Edward. Aye, dios mio en cielo nos ayud,*" Nelly screamed at the top of her lungs before she fainted onto the cold, marble floor, hitting her head, causing a loud thud.

The priest stood frozen and stared at his butchered colleague, his brain not registering the carnage.

Chapter 4

September 1958

The day that John Deegan entered the first grade at St. Martin of Tours, the air was electric with anticipation. The Dominican sisters were well aware of this gifted boy, and only one of the first grade teachers could be selected to be his teacher. The honor of initiating John into the Catholic family fell upon the senior member of the teaching staff, the former Catherine Sheehan. A mild-mannered and caring woman of 60 years old, Sister Catherine truly loved children. She didn't believe in corporal punishment as many of the other sisters did. Those who approved of hitting children did so often and hard, especially the boys.

There were three first grade classes at St. Martin's, each with over 45 boys and girls. This was the mid-fifties, the heyday of Catholic education in which the nuns ruled with an iron hand and the parents were happy just to have a seat in the school for their child. Discipline was the order of the day and was meted out without the possibility of objection or appeal. If a student or family did not fall in line and obey every command the nuns set forth, the Mother Superior was quick to expel and exile to the public school with the non-Catholics. This meant banishment from not only the church but also from a happy and religious parochial school community. The Jews and Protestants, who were still plentiful in the neighborhood, did not share that particular view.

John's mother arrived at the school that morning with several other moms and their scrubbed and trembling children in tow. The four block walk from their tenement apartment on the brisk, clear, September morning was peppered with instructions about how to look both ways when crossing the street and understanding what the red and green lights were all about. Maureen Deegan imagined a greeting fit for royalty for

both herself and her Johnny Boy. After all, in her mind, her 6-year-old was to begin his education toward the priesthood. She might have expected the nuns to welcome them with palms like Jesus himself was as he entered Jerusalem. There would be no palms laid down on East 182nd St. and Crotona Avenue this day or any day for that matter.

Mother Superior, Sister Ann, was waiting in the figurative tall grass for the moms. With her hands together and her fingers interlocked and held just under her heart as if she were praying, the stern-looking nun leered at the women over her eyeglasses. The stiff, white coif that framed her face hid her hair as well as her femininity. The mothers would now be initiated into her world and would know who was boss from the get-go.

"Good morning, mothers," Sister Ann said with a stern face, when the Deegan contingent arrived at the boys' entrance of the school just as the acceptance letter had required.

"Good morning, Sister," the mothers said in unison.

One of the young moms, an Irish immigrant, actually curtsied. "Mothers, it is highly inappropriate for you to come to the school in

slacks. Our Blessed Mother Mary never wore slacks, and I expect when you present yourselves at the school in the future, you will be wearing an appropriate skirt." There was not a trace of emotion on Sister Ann's face.

"Yes, Sister Ann." The mothers all hung their heads.

With that, the children were sent to their respective class lines. A few did not want to leave their mommies and refused to follow instructions. They were met with an attitude and approach they had likely not experienced so far in their young lives. Boot camp was in session, and the drill sergeants were dressed in long, black gowns with white and black, starched head covers. Some of the kids were scared senseless, and the butterflies in their stomachs felt more like bats. John's cousin, David, threw up his breakfast on the pavement of 182nd Street.

John Deegan was beaming. He had heard about the first day of school, the nuns, and the church so often that he actually thought the experience was part of a dream. This was to be his life, school, church,

God the Father, Jesus, the Holy Ghost, and becoming a priest. This was his mission and the very reason God had made him.

John wore a crisp, white, Dacron shirt, blue pants, black belt, socks, proper, black shoes, and a blue tie with an embroidered SMT logo. He couldn't wait for school to begin.

He could have started in the 2nd or 3rd grade, at least, for all the home preparation he had received. He was far and away the most advanced first grader Sister Catherine had seen in all the years since she became a Sister of Complete Consecration 35 years ago. She would marvel at John's knowledge and ability to recall everything he read, saw, or heard. John Deegan was a boy wonder. One would think the other kids would resent his perfection and the attention he drew from the nuns, but he was so affable and his smile, so infectious that everyone was crazy for him. The boys all wanted to be his friend, and the girls all had their first crushes on him.

The first days of school were mostly made up of getting to know each other, explanation of the rules and regulations, and continuous religious instructions. Every aspect of the Catholic education was interwoven with stories of Baby Jesus, God the Father, the Blessed Virgin Mary, the repetitious learning of prayers, religious pictures, and of course, the ever- present crucifix that hung in every classroom, hallway, and even the cafeteria. The only places the crucifixes were not prominent were in the bathrooms. That would have been a really shitty place to hang the martyred Christ.

John excelled right from the starting line just as good Sister Catherine had expected. She absolutely adored his fresh, well-groomed, good looks. He reminded her of her brothers and every cousin she had back in Ireland. John was going to be her star pupil and the major contribution of her career to her beloved Church. By the end of the first week of school, Sister Catherine would be doing the math in her head. "If I'm 60 now and John will be 26 or 27 when he is ordained. I will be 86 or 87. I will pray to the Lord to reward me with this fervent wish." A lot of people were relying on John to fulfill their dreams. That's a lot of pressure for a 6- year-old boy even with a genius level I.Q.

John was no stranger to the Church and its priests. Maureen Deegan saw to it that he prayed every day since he was 4 and attended mass with her every Sunday and holy day of obligation along with pop visits to light some candles for the dearly departed, even saying a quick prayer on the way to the grocery store. When the priest spoke from the pulpit, the look of adoration on his mother's face toward the man in the colorful robes was the same look he saw when she looked at him. A priest was the closest thing to God and holiness that he could imagine. John knew this was the way he wanted people to look at him. Every priest was God's messenger and the savior of souls. Why would he ever consider doing anything else in his life?

Every Friday, the new, young priest, Father Edward, would go around to each class to remind them how important it was to attend mass on Sunday and most importantly, to remind their parents to send them with the color-coded envelope they received on the 1st day of school. The envelopes were to contain a generous contribution, paper money preferred, to the Church. They came in a nice, neat box and were printed with beautiful pictures of the Christ, Baby Jesus, the Blessed Mother, and .....

Follow Louis Romano on:

Facebook
Instagram
or
Youtube

www.louisromanoauthor.com